INDIAN SUMMER

INDIAN SUMMER

Elizabeth Darrell

severn House

This first world edition published 2010
in Great Britain and in the USA by
SEVERN HOUSE PUBLISHERS LTD of
9–15 High Street, Sutton, Surrey, England, SM1 1DF.
Trade paperback edition first published
in Great Britain and the USA 2011 by
SEVERN HOUSE PUBLISHERS LTD.

British Library Cataloguing in Publication Data

Darrell, Elizabeth.
   Indian summer. – (A Max Rydal military mystery)
   1. Rydal, Max (Fictitious character)–Fiction. 2. Military
   bases, British–Germany–Fiction. 3. Great Britain. Army.
   Corps of Royal Military Police–Fiction. 4. Murder–
   Investigation–Germany–Fiction. 5. Detective and mystery
   stories.
   I. Title II. Series
   823.9'14-dc22

ISBN-13: 978-0-7278-6918-0   (cased)
ISBN-13: 978-1-84751-258-1   (trade paper)

All Severn House titles are printed on acid-free paper.

Severn House Publishers support The Forest Stewardship Council [FSC],
the leading international forest certification organisation. All our titles that
are printed on Greenpeace-approved FSC-certified paper carry the FSC logo.

Mixed Sources
Product group from well-managed
forests and other controlled sources
www.fsc.org Cert no. SA-COC-1565
© 1996 Forest Stewardship Council
FSC

Typeset by Palimpsest Book Production Ltd.,
Falkirk, Stirlingshire, Scotland.
Printed and bound in Great Britain by
MPG Books Ltd., Bodmin, Cornwall.

ACKNOWLEDGEMENTS

My thanks, as ever, to Lieutenant Colonel (Retd) John Nelson, Royal Military Police, who patiently deals with my queries, no matter how bizarre. Also to WO1 Pamela Reid, Special Investigation Branch, who, I suspect, must have an iron fist beneath that velvet glove.

I feel it is time I also publicly thanked Dr Robert Youngson, late of the Royal Army Medical Corps, who is a walking encyclopaedia of medical knowledge which he has willingly shared with me throughout this series.

ONE

The British called a warm, balmy period in October an Indian Summer, although temperatures never reached the heights of that continent. Personnel on the British military base in Germany who were enjoying the pleasant, sunny days said it was more reminiscent of an English spring. Birds were mistakenly building nests, animals who normally hibernated remained full of energy and flowers continued to provide colour in gardens and parks. After the debilitating heatwave in August bees were appearing in unprecedented numbers, causing a nuisance to the unwary. Global warming, warned the environmentalists. Local Germans said it was nothing unusual after an exceptionally hot summer. After the last heatwave they had been pestered by hordes of ladybirds, and the one before that had bred millions of caterpillars.

The Army had more to think about than global warming. The 2nd Battalion West Wiltshire Regiment had departed to Afghanistan to replace troops of the Royal Cumberland Rifles, who had arrived back on base three days ago. It was the practice of the ruling Garrison Commander, Colonel Trelawney, to provide the returning men and women with some fun and entertainment whilst also fulfilling his obligation to maintain easy relations with the local populace. To this end there would be an Open Day on Saturday, three days hence.

For several weeks the non-transient soldiers had been working on the project with enthusiasm, which had raised spirits usually restless during the six-monthly change-over periods. There were the tears and fears of women as resolute, keyed-up troops in desert combat gear loaded their cumbersome equipment in trucks ready for the off. A few days later, there were the radiant faces of families welcoming home loved ones with tense, drawn expressions and staring eyes.

It was good for everyone on the base to have a period of relaxation before resuming their normal routine.

Saturday dawned bright and warm; perfect weather for the military to open the doors to all-comers. Aside from swings, roundabouts, a coconut-shy, a fortune teller and a test-your-strength machine, there were to be jousting contests by eight stalwarts dressed as knights on horses draped with their noble colours. Two were women, but the suits of armour would disguise the fact. There were also hijinks on a trampoline performed by NCOs of the Physical Training Corps made up as clowns; heart-stopping displays by a Royal Artillery motorcycle team; mock helicopter rescues by the Army Air Corps; a daredevil free-fall descent by Paras; precision marching without commands by Cumberland Riflemen; Military Police sending sniffer dogs out to find hidden drugs or explosives, and lavish refreshments provided by the caterers of the Logistics Corps.

In the face of all this regimental representation, men of the small Royal Engineers unit determined to make their own mark. One of their number was a highly experienced sub-aqua diver; another was a talented model maker. This combination produced an entertainment mainly for children, whereby the diver entered a huge glass-fronted tank filled with exotic ocean creatures in an attempt to reach a pirates' treasure chest. The modeller was a genius. The great white shark looked terrifyingly real, as did the purple jelly-fish with long trailing tentacles, the deadly sea snakes, the sinister conger eels and the spiny stone fish.

The opinion of more than a few that children would be frightened by the diver's simulated tussle with these monsters was refuted by the crowds drawn to the tank. The cynics had forgotten that children love to be visually scared. Demons, witches, Daleks, cybermen with ray guns, and evil creatures that lurk in the sea all provided a delicious thrill while they clung to a parent's hand.

All in all, the event proved to be a success. German visitors departed well satisfied, and the general mood on the base lightened. Litter strewn over the area, along with much of the equipment, was cleared by the end of the day. Sunday volunteers would remove the rest to prepare for resumption of normal routine on Monday.

That night was clear and moonlit, with a touch of chill to remind one that it was autumn despite the daytime temperatures. Privates Dennis James and Jock Johnston slowly patrolled their allocated stretch of perimeter wire. They, along with the rest of the guard squad, had ensured the departure of all civilians by 18:00 and were now mounting regular patrols. On reaching the limit of their sector, they headed for the guard post for a mug of tea and a pasty (if the greedy sods had left any) before setting out again.

As they approached the water tank, Jock began to chuckle. 'I saw a right little bruiser damn near peeing his pants watching that guy fight off the shark, yet the kid who looked to be his sister was smiling with vicious satisfaction.'

'Girls!' Dennis exclaimed. 'When I were a lad there was one in our street who led a reign of terror. Tough as nails and swore like a trooper. Never happy unless she had everyone dancing on her strings. Liar? They rolled off her tongue like . . .'

'Christ!'

Jock's vehemence halted the reminiscence. 'What?' Dennis demanded, instantly alert.

'There's a bloke in that tank.'

Dennis stared through the moonwashed darkness and saw a long vague shape in the water. 'It's not a bloke, you wanker, it's that bloody shark.'

'It's a *bloke*, I tell you, and he's not moving,' muttered Jock, starting towards the tank at a run.

Dennis followed, activating his torch so that its beam merged with Jock's. Now fairly well illuminated, the shape was revealed as a man clad just in underpants who was drifting among the synthetic creatures. Wrapped tightly around his neck were the tentacles of the life-sized replica of the purple-tinted jellyfish.

Tom Black had barely reached the depths of sleep when the shrill call of the bedside telephone brought him awake.

'Sar'nt Major Black,' he mumbled automatically, aware of Nora stirring beside him.

'Sorry to disturb you, sir,' said Military Police Sergeant Maddox in his ear. 'Perimeter patrol just found a body.'

'Where, George?'

'In that water tank. The death looks fishy, if you'll pardon the pun.'

Tom slid from beneath the duvet. 'Have you called Captain Goodey? It'll take her around thirty-five to drive in to the base, unless she's sleeping in the Mess tonight.'

'I checked. They signed her out through the main gate four hours ago. She's on her way.'

Grabbing the clothes he had recently shed, Tom headed for the bathroom. 'Who found the body?'

'James and Johnston, Cumberland Rifles.'

'Just back from Afghanistan?'

'No, they only joined four months ago. I've switched patrols to split them up; warned them you'll want to question them. I've got Meacher keeping watch on the tank.'

'I'll be there asap.'

Disconnecting, Tom dashed cold water over his face, combed his hair and dressed with practised speed before letting himself as quietly as possible from the rented house. On the drive back to the base he and his family had left as the last visitors had filed through the manned gate, Tom mentally reviewed the mock drama enacted in that tank. Nora and the girls had enjoyed it immensely; Beth and Gina for the clever reproductions of oceanic scarers, Maggie and Nora more probably for the hunky diver in brief swimwear. Was his the body in the tank?

George's comment that the death looked fishy meant apparent murder, which was why Tom had been called. Max Rydal, Officer Commanding 26 Section, Special Investigation Branch, Royal Military Police, was in the UK attending his father's wedding, so Tom was presently heading 26 Section. Most fatalities they dealt with were traffic accidents or the occasional outcome of punch-ups that progressed to broken bottles or knives wielded with alcohol-fuelled loss of control. This case promised to be more complex. More interesting.

When Tom arrived on the scene there was a powerful arc lamp illuminating the water tank, and an ambulance was parked near it. George Maddox and Corporal Meacher had roped off the immediate vicinity to preserve any forensic evidence, although they and the two guards had already trodden there. The body had been brought from the water to lie on the small platform from where the RE diver had entered for his performance. Squatting up there was Clare Goodey, Medical Officer for the base. Standing beside her were two men in swimming trunks, who must have rescued the body from its watery grave.

George Maddox crossed to him as Tom left his car. 'It's not the guy who did that act for the kids, and it's not Sar'nt Cruz who made that thing wrapped around his neck.'

Tom gave a grim smile. 'You're saying you don't recognize the victim?'

'Well, the features are bloated and wearing an expression more often seen in a field hospital, but the face doesn't ring a bell.'

'So we'll have to get identification from records.'

George glanced up to where Clare Goodey was on her feet instructing the pair who had pulled the body from the water to carry it down to where two orderlies waited with a stretcher. 'We'll get a match on the computer once we've taken a shot of him and checked for any identifying marks on the body. If the features are too distorted we'll have to go with dental records, which'll take longer. The *real* problem will be discovering who did it, and why.' George gave a sly grin. 'SIB's responsibility, not ours.'

Tom grunted. 'So where are the lads who found him?'

'Out on patrol. I've split them up so's we can call them in one at a time.'

'Good. We'll talk to them after we've had a word with Captain Goodey.' Tom moved swiftly to where it seemed the orderlies were about to push the stretcher into the ambulance. He wanted to see the dead man in the hope of recognition before he was taken from the scene.

Catching sight of the two policemen who looked set to bring a halt to proceedings, the Doctor confronted them with an air of irritation. 'He'll probably be in the Medical Centre until at least tomorrow afternoon. You'll have full access to him there until he's removed for the post-mortem.'

Tom wondered if she would have been as brusque with Max, who had suddenly rented the apartment next to hers a month ago, causing speculation in the Officers' Mess.

'We need to identify him asap so that we can notify next of kin.'

'And can you?' she demanded.

He studied the distorted features, the protruding eyes and the gaping mouth. This man had died desperately fighting to hold on to life as it was choked out of him. He glanced up at the woman dressed in casual grey trousers and a thick Aran sweater.

'We'll know who he is by morning. Can you give me your initial assessment of the time of death; how long he'd been in the water? Cause of death isn't in doubt, of course.'

'Isn't it?' she said crisply. 'All I'm prepared to say at this moment is that life is extinct. I'll have more for you when I've had a proper look at him, but the cause of death could remain uncertain until the pathologist opens him up.'

Tom and George Maddox were left watching her departure alongside the wheeled stretcher, as Tom murmured, 'We *knew* life was extinct, ma'am.' He turned to George. 'Call in James and Johnston. Let's hear their evidence. What's your impression of them? Did they do it?'

'They seemed genuinely shaken. Could have been an act, but I don't think so. They're average young guys still flushed with the excitement of achieving their ambition to join the Army. Only got their Cumberland Rifles badges four months ago. Everything's still shiny new.' He gave a caustic laugh. '*This* wasn't on their agenda. It's not a glorious death in battle, and all that bravado nonsense.'

'They'll learn,' commented Tom, still musing on Clare Goodey's remark. Those latex tentacles were tightly wrapped around the victim's throat, his death mask was typical of asphyxiation, there was no sign of blood darkening the water, no cartridge cases on the bottom of the tank. How the hell else did she imagine the poor bastard had breathed his last?

Jock Johnston bore out Maddox's description. Tom saw a squaddie whose uniform was new and proudly worn; a young man of around eighteen with bright eyes and downy cheeks that would need a razor only every other day, if then. If he had been initially shaken, excitement had replaced the sense of shock. He described the discovery of the body in upbeat manner which convinced Tom of his lack of complicity.

Dennis James was much the same type of youngster, albeit a little more streetwise. He told a similar version of the discovery, reiterating Johnston's denial of seeing anyone in the vicinity or hearing voices in argument, cries for help or sounds of frenzied splashing.

An hour passed before Tom drove to the Medical Centre leaving the uniformed men to search the area, and check the whereabouts of the RE diver and the model maker who had both been involved with the tank and its contents. Did they have solid proof of their movements at the end of the day?

Captain Goodey was in her consulting room writing when Tom entered shivering slightly in the early hours' chill. A small electric fire gave welcome warmth and flushed her cheeks attractively. A very attractive woman altogether, Tom thought, yet in this predominantly male environment she knew exactly how to hold her own. She had taken up her post on the base just six weeks ago, but no one was left in doubt that the new doctor was not in the least intimidated by the macho majority she worked with.

Without glancing up, she said, 'If you want to examine the body, Mr Black, you'll find him in the small room at the end of the corridor. I'll join you when I finish this report.'

He turned about without a word. The room was normally used for examinations. Aside from the couch on which the body lay there were shelves bearing packets of rubber gloves, lubricating jelly, syringes and swabs in sterile packs and a pile of folded drawsheets behind a concertina screen. Dimmed lighting gave an impression of a hallowed glow over the covered corpse. On a chair beside the couch lay the purple jellyfish in a sealed plastic bag.

Someone had removed the sinister-looking tentacles from the dead man's throat, closed the horrified eyes and the mouth that had appeared to be crying for help, giving the face a more peaceful expression. Efforts were always made to render the job of confirming identity less upsetting for loved ones or close friends, and a photograph taken now would be suitable for a computer match.

Tom had just uncovered the body fully to look for blemishes, scars or tattoos when Captain Goodey walked in the room.

'Two moles on the right forearm, a small scar behind the left ear,' she said. 'There's also a magenta butterfly with the name Brenda beneath it on the right buttock and an indigo one with the name Flip on the left one. Quite ingenious. They're positioned so that when he clenched his buttocks the butterflies would appear to kiss.' Seeing Tom's expression, she gave a faint smile. 'No accounting for taste, but it must have been bloody painful while it was being done.'

'Even more so to have it changed when the affair with Brenda ended on the scrapheap.'

'If it didn't, the poor woman's in for a shock tomorrow.' She pulled the sheet back over the sturdy body leaving the face uncovered. 'I'd say his first name is Philip, wouldn't you? Flip?'

'Possibly, but the lads take on all manner of names with no obvious origin.' He looked her in the eye. 'What have you put in your report, ma'am?'

'That's confidential.'

Holding on to his temper – it was three a.m, he had had no more than a brief shallow sleep, and he was cold – Tom said carefully, 'Kissing butterflies aren't much help in a murder investigation. Time of death is.'

Her voice softened. 'Yes, of course. I estimate that he died around ten to twelve hours ago.'

Tom stared at her. 'But there were hundreds of people milling around that tank at that time.'

She returned his steady gaze. 'He didn't die in the tank.'

'You're saying he wasn't strangled with that synthetic jellyfish?'

'All I can say is that he *probably* died from asphyxiation. The jellyfish was pure window dressing. It's up to you to discover why.'

Ninety minutes later an identity match was found. The victim was Corporal Philip Keane, Royal Cumberland Rifles, who had returned from Afghanistan six days ago.

'Survived the Taliban to end up dead in a water tank,' mused Tom. 'Give it another couple of hours, then round up the appropriate officer and the Padre to break the news to Mrs Keane and get a positive ID from her.'

Max Rydal stood alone holding an untouched glass of champagne, brooding as he watched his father and the bride greet their guests. After twenty-six years as a widower, Brigadier Andrew Rydal had just married a chic, vivacious French Cultural Envoy fourteen years his junior. Helene Dupres appeared to hold him in thrall because he had apparently acquiesced in the elaborate wedding arrangements Max considered more suited to the betrothal of young lovers embarking on their first experience of wedlock.

This reception at the Saint Germaine Cultural Institute promised to be as extravagant as everything else about this marital union. Designer frocks, huge hats, immaculate morning suits and colourful uniforms had progressed from the church to the elegant salon in the building where the bride held a semi-diplomatic post. She was elegant in cream lace; the groom was handsomely distinguished in full dress uniform. Both looked to be overflowing with happiness.

Max had been in two minds about flying over from Germany to attend. From the age of six, when his mother had died, Andrew Rydal's military career had led to Max attending boarding school before moving on to university and the Army. It was the lengthy separations rather than any quarrel between them that had caused father and son to become little more than polite strangers on the few occasions that they met.

The receipt of the wedding invitation had been a bolt

from the blue. Max had had no inkling that Andrew had formed such a close bond with a woman after all these years, yet it was not that which had hurt him so deeply. It was the fact that Livya Cordwell, Andrew's ADC and the woman Max loved, had not warned him of the impending marriage; had worked on the arrangements, written all the invitations, yet had said nothing of it even when lying in his arms a few weeks ago.

Her defence was that it had not been her place to jump the gun; that Andrew was the right person to break such news to his son. Max had been unable to accept that from someone who had already agreed to become his wife, if they could sort their careers so that marriage worked for them. They had quarrelled bitterly over where her loyalties primarily lay, and they had not been in contact since then.

Facing evidence that Livya's military career meant more to her than he did, Max had impetuously discarded all hopes of a future with her and rented an apartment adjoining Clare Goodey's with the intention of embarking on a bachelor life with women galore. Now here he was, watching Livya doing her duty among the many influential guests, knowing his feelings for her were still to be reckoned with.

As if conscious of Max's scrutiny she glanced across to where he stood, expertly excused herself to two high-ranking French military officers and their ladies, then approached. 'Hallo, Max.'

The familiar scent of her washed over him, reviving memories. 'Quite a shindig, isn't it? As a member of the Joint Intelligence Committee I thought my father would prefer to keep a low profile.'

She ignored that. 'You didn't write acceptance of the invitation so I was surprised to see you there in the church.'

'As the groom's son I didn't feel a reply was necessary. That gold embossed card was surely a mere formality. As it happens, I haven't a big case on at the moment, and they're holding an Open Day at the base.' He gave a faint smile. 'I might have been roped in to do conjuring tricks or put on a Mickey Mouse outfit. It's a good time to be away from there.'

Her dark eyes studied him appreciatively. 'Amazing, but this is the first time I've seen you in uniform.'

'Can't stand penguin suits and top hats, that's why.'

Although, like him, she was an army captain, Livya today wore an ivory silk cocktail suit with a tiny feathery confection on her dark hair. Very feminine. Very deceptive! He longed to tell her how lovely she looked, but resisted the urge. He nodded towards the doorway where guests had finally stopped filing past the newlyweds.

'They look appropriately blissful. *Hello!* magazine isn't covering this, by any chance? Or some French glossy equivalent? Has the MoD approved this exposure?'

'Don't be beastly, Max! Helene was widowed at nineteen after six months of marriage to a TV cameraman. He drowned filming submerged wrecks. She adores Andrew and this is her big day.'

'And his, presumably.'

'You know it is.'

'No, I don't,' he said swiftly. 'Until that invitation arrived I knew nothing about this connection. He wouldn't think of confiding in his stranger son, and *you* decided . . .'

'*Don't* Max! Wrong time and place.' After a short hesitation, she said, 'We have to talk. Tonight, at my place?'

'I'm booked on the late flight back,' he lied, uncertain how to play this.

'You're not working on a big case . . . and tomorrow's Sunday. Change the flight booking.'

'What is there to talk about?' he challenged.

'*Us.* You proposed to me over the phone last month. Have you forgotten?' She began edging away. 'I have to go. Time to ease the top table guests in to the restaurant, or it'll be dinner rather than lunch by the time four hundred are seated.' Still edging away, she added persuasively, 'Don't let's behave like sulky children over things said on impulse. Kiss and make up? Please come tonight, Steve.'

He watched her walk away all brisk efficiency again. Her use of that pet name prompted by his confession that he had always wanted to emulate Steve McQueen's motorbike escapade in *The Great Escape* had shaken his defences. She was not the type of woman to go all dewy-eyed at weddings and she would certainly not want an extravaganza like this, so he was reasonably sure her olive branch had not been offered on a surge of romantic fervour.

He strolled across to join the great and the good filing through to a restaurant bedecked with masses of flowers. He had at least three hours in which to decide whether or not to take up Livya's invitation. He hoped to God when the meal ended that some fool would not give a speech full of risqué honeymoon jokes that would make him want to crawl under the table.

When Nora appeared in the kitchen, dressing-gowned and yawning, Tom was just finishing off a couple of fried egg sandwiches. Glancing at his empty cereal bowl and the dregs in the tall cafetière, she said, 'Lucky for you I'm not one of those wives who expect breakfast brought to them in bed on Sunday morning.'

He grinned. 'I'm no sucker. Start that and I'd be expected to do it for the girls, too.'

'No, you wouldn't. They don't emerge from their duvets until half the morning's gone.' She filled and switched on the kettle, then took a pot of yoghurt from the fridge. 'So what was the emergency that wrenched you from my loving embrace this time?'

'Loving embrace? You were snoring fit to drive a pork butcher wild with delight.'

Surprisingly, she did not cuff him playfully for that teasing comment, simply asked what had happened in the early hours. So he told her of the discovery in the water tank and the curious time gap between the murder and the immersion with the jellyfish wrapped around the corpse's neck. Nora frowned as she sliced bread for the toaster and considered the facts.

'You need Max here. He's good at working out why a killer needs to make a statement, and this is surely another example of that.'

'I don't think Max would have any more idea of the

symbolism behind this than any of us, at present. What statement can a jellyfish make?'

'They're deadly. At least, they can be.'

'Anything that kills is deadly, and the guy had been a corpse for hours before being dropped in the water with that thing twisted around his throat. No, we have to concentrate on the actual killing. Mustn't get sidetracked by what we found last night. Priority is to get the widow to confirm identity.'

'What a shock to wake up to, just six days after she gets her man safely back from rockets and roadside bombs. You won't give her the gruesome details, will you?'

'Love, you should know by now they'll be all round the base by sundown. Better to hear the truth from us than the more gruesome version from the neighbours.'

'Any kids involved?'

'Two. Both under school age.'

'Poor little devils having to grow up with that knowledge.' She set about making fresh coffee. 'A dead man who is symbolically killed again in a tank filled with oceanic illusion. Can't wait to hear what you make of it before Max returns.'

Tom wanted to have solved the case by then, but he was not rash enough to say so. Clare Goodey's estimate of when the murder occurred widened the range of suspects to include German civilians. However, they all left the base in the early evening so, unless someone other than the killer had put the body in the tank, they could be discounted.

Gazing blindly at the cafetière Nora was refilling, Tom considered that premise. It seemed highly unlikely that Keane had been strangled and left lying around for someone else to discover and throw in the water wrapped around with the jellyfish. No, it was surely a non-starter, which then made it almost certain the perpetrator was military. Not only would that lessen the number of suspects it would mean the *Polizei* would not have to become a partner in the investigation. Through determined tact and openness 26 Section maintained a cordial relationship with Klaus Krenkel, the commander of the local German police unit, but when the victim was a British soldier **SIB** preferred to work solo.

Automatically stretching out his hand for the full mug Nora pushed towards him, Tom concentrated on the slender evidence they had so far. Keane was big and muscular. While it was possible for a normally fit man to transport the body, carry it up to the small diving platform, hook the jellyfish out and tie it tightly before tipping the corpse in the water, it would have taken two women. Or a man and a woman.

Could Brenda of the buttocks still be in the picture? Mrs Keane's first name was Starr – where did parents get these names? – so she had had to live with the kissing butterflies. What kind of woman would be willing to do that? Ah, maybe her real name was Brenda, but she had chosen to be called Starr after a celebrity she admired. He was just deciding to ask his daughters about 'celebrities' he had never heard of when the phone rang. It was George Maddox with further unsettling news.

'No one at the Keanes' married quarter, sir. Neighbour heard them rowing on Friday night. Said it sounded so violent she considered calling us. Then it went quiet and she went to bed. I'm concerned about the safety of Starr and the kids. Have they been attacked, too?'

Tom got to his feet. 'Until they're traced we have to consider that possibility. Set up the usual checks, George. Finding them is top priority now.'

Tom knew they had a task and a half on their hands. Since the abolition of border checks people could pass from one country to another with ease, and Starr Keane could have mingled unnoticed with her children amid the visitors to the Open Day. The *Polizei* would have to be brought in on their disappearance in case they had left yesterday by this means, but a full search within the base must be undertaken in view of Keane's murder. Tom fervently hoped the small family would be found alive and well.

George Maddox and his uniformed staff would organize the combing of those acres within the perimeter fence, while **SIB** tracked down witnesses who might lead them to the truth of what had happened during a day of fun and relaxed military routine, when a man had been murdered and a woman with two small children had vanished.

Driving back to base Tom faced the fact that he could well have *four* deaths on his hands. Maybe he needed Max here after all.

TWO

Tom called in as many members of 26 Section as were contactable on that Sunday morning. Apart from Staff Sergeant Melly on UK leave in hopes of a reunion with his ex, and Sergeant Prentiss, whose wife had gone into labour last night, the entire team had soon assembled at Section Headquarters. They were all keen and widely experienced. Tom knew he and Max were fortunate to have such people under their command.

He issued the known facts, adding, 'We have to pull out all the stops on this. First we have to establish whether we're dealing with two stand-alone cases, or whether they're linked. At first glance they could be, but until we discover whether Starr and her kids left the base after the row with Keane or whether they're still here we can't be certain of that.

'The uniformed boys are out searching for bodies. Our job is to trace the movements of Starr and Philip Keane following their violent row overheard by the neighbour. Keane got back from Afghanistan six days ago. After deployment in a warzone it's not unusual for troops to be tense, aggressive and quick to react to confrontation. We're all aware of the tricky few weeks couples have to get through while one partner finds it difficult to shrug off those months of intense combat with only their mates around.

'In the past few years we've dealt with one or two cases of injury due to loss of control in those circs, but I sense we have something different here. We need to unravel the Keanes' marriage and what makes them both tick.'

Sergeant Derek Beeny, a quiet, thoughtful team member, said, 'If Keane had been shot, poisoned or bled to death from slashed wrists, the first premise would be that he did for his family then committed suicide, but no way could he then have got in the tank with that thing tied round his neck ten hours later.'

'Which leaves the premise that Starr Keane killed him and scarpered with the kids,' reasoned his friend Phil Piercey.

'Then she wouldn't have been here to put him in the tank at midnight,' Heather Johnson pointed out. 'Almost impossible for a woman to deal with such a dead weight.'

'And where would the kids have been while she was "killing" him a second time?' added Connie Bush.

'And why would she want to make that bizarre gesture,' said Beeny reflectively. 'Strangulation isn't a favoured method for women, and to do it twice is highly unlikely.'

'And it's *men* who tend to make symbolic gestures after killing,' agreed Piercey.

Tom nodded with satisfaction. 'So we're left with several options. One: a third party killed off the entire family, hid the bodies of Starr and her children but needed to make some kind of statement with Keane's. Two: as before but someone other than the killer put Keane's body in the tank. Three: Starr killed her husband and scarpered, then someone else decided to metaphorically kill him in the tank.'

'There's another scenario,' said Piercey.

'So let's have it,' invited Tom. Although this sergeant often irritated him with his wild notions, the man did sometimes come up with sharp ideas.

'Keane returned from Afghanistan to learn his wife had been having it off while he'd been away, hence the violent row overheard by the neighbour. So he tops her and the kids. Lover boy finds them, then does for Keane.'

'So where are the other bodies?' demanded Heather, who always delighted in deflating Piercey.

'When the uniforms find them, you'll know.'

'So what's with the jellyfish?' she returned.

Tom looked towards Olly Simpson, who was engaged in his usual doodling. Dedicated to mental puzzles of a cryptic nature, next to Max's this sergeant's mind was sharpest at reading the meaning of symbolic gestures.

Aware of the sudden silence, Simpson glanced up. 'We can't even make a guess at that until we know more about the Keanes.'

'That's what we have to start doing,' ruled Tom. 'For now, I intend to assume we have two separate cases; the murder of Keane and the disappearance of his family.' He indicated Connie Bush, Piercey and Beeny. 'I want you to concentrate on the latter. Talk to Starr's neighbours, friends and the gate guards who might have noticed her leaving the base sometime on Saturday. She could have German friends in town who she's gone to because Keane threatened her during that heated row.'

He turned to Heather Johnson and Olly Simpson. 'We three will focus on Keane's murder. Find out how he spent the six days following his return. Interview everyone who saw or spoke to him during that time. One fact: the body wore only underpants, yet Captain Goodey reckons he died around midday. So, was he killed in bed? If not, what happened to the rest of his clothes, and why?'

He spoke generally in winding up. 'We'll meet here at eighteen hundred to collate our findings. As usual, if you get anything of vital significance, call it in to Jakes who'll stay here to take any info that should be shared to save valuable time. Go to it!'

Sergeant Jakes was happy to stay on duty. He and his Swedish fiancée were planning their wedding and he had been tasked to produce a seating plan for the reception. He had a note from Ingrid stating which of her guests were on no account to be placed anywhere near each other, and another from his mother with similar instructions. He welcomed the chance to get to grips with this almost impossible task.

They all departed, Tom debating whether or not to update Max, who would relish working on this, maybe *these*, cases. However, he had taken fourteen days' overdue leave which Tom guessed would be spent with Livya Cordwell if Max could get the affair back on track. Wait a while, he told himself. There could be a simple solution to the tragedy that had overtaken the Keanes. The case could be wrapped up in a matter of a few days.

Tom drove across the base to the married quarters where he hoped to speak to Sergeant Major Priest of the Royal Cumberland Rifles. He knew Frank Priest only slightly through meeting at several social events in the Sergeants' Mess, and trusted him to give an honest assessment of Philip Keane's personality. Official records gave bald facts; senior NCO's were a source of more expansive information.

Drawing up before a house where several small children were having fun with a yellow plastic barrel, Tom approached the neat front garden with a smile. His own girls had had something similar years ago.

'Hallo,' he said cheerfully. 'If I wasn't so big I'd ask if I could join in.'

A dark-haired boy of around five years said, 'You can, if you want to.'

Tom laughed. 'I don't think I'd better. I might get stuck in it.'

Two little girls fell into giggles, while the other boy in the group demanded to know who he was. Tom gave his name and explained that he was there to see Sergeant Major Priest.

'Daddy's out the back mending my bike,' said the first boy. 'You can go down *there*,' he added, pointing to a side path. Then he turned on the giggling girls. 'If you can't play properly you can go home.'

Another sergeant major in the making, thought Tom as he made his way around the house to where Frank Priest had a child's bicycle upside down with a wheel off and was squatting beside it.

'Sorry to disturb your Sunday, Frank, but I'd like a word.'

The sinewy man in cut-off jeans and a grubby T-shirt appeared to take several moments to register the identity of his visitor, then he rose and nodded. 'That grotty business with Flip Keane.'

'News travels fast.'

The deeply tanned features twisted in disgust. 'Poor bastard gets topped on his own doorstep after six months out there. Where's the justice in that? You've come to ask who did it? If I knew I'd've sorted the bugger out good and proper by now.'

'Leave that to us. We'll do it legally. I didn't know Keane so I'd like your input on the kind of guy he was, how he was regarded by B Company, some slant on his private life.'

Priest wiped his brow with a grimy hand then indicated a garden bench. 'Let's have a beer.' So saying, he went into the kitchen from where Tom heard a short altercation with a woman, ending with Priest saying, 'Sod the bike!' before coming out with two cans. He handed one to Tom.

'Problems, Frank?'

Priest yanked back the ring-pull and gulped thirstily. 'You get back and all you want is to unwind. What d'you get? A long list: see to the leaky tap and the window that won't open, mend the gap in the fence, put up a shelf in the kitchen, get someone to replace the dodgy boiler, sort out the neighbour whose dog barks the whole bloody night. I tell you, Tom, I've had it up to here.' He rested the can against his throat. 'Now it's "we've got to have a holiday." Brochures piled up everywhere I go. The Maldives, the Bahamas, Florida – you name it. And it's "I've been stuck here alone for six months worried out of my mind, now I want to enjoy being together. We can leave the kids with Mum and have a second honeymoon." *A second honeymoon!* They've no idea, have they?'

Tom downed his beer and let the frustration pour from his companion. Army wives had a tough time when their men went to war, but they found it even tougher to understand why it took so long to resume a loving, harmonious relationship when they returned. Had that problem ended in the murder of Keane? And his family?

Gripping the can tightly and staring into the distance, Priest eventually said, 'Flip Keane was a bloody good soldier, but the poor sod couldn't handle women. I've not met a more selfish bitch than Starr, and you come across a few in this game. Flip and her were an item a few years back and she had a kid while he was in Iraq.'

'Keane's?'

'So she reckoned. He'd never wanted to set up home with her, so if it *was* his it wasn't meant to happen. Out in Iraq he took up with a nurse. Real serious, that was.'

'Was she called Brenda?'

Frank managed a dry chuckle. 'Tattoos on his arse? Should've been on his dick, he was that gone on her.'

'Yet he married Starr.'

'No, mate, *Starr* married *him*. Had the whole bloody family working on it. Two truckie brothers saw to him one night, and her mother . . . Christ, send her out there and she'd sort even Bin Laden! He didn't have a hope in hell.'

'I get the picture,' said Tom. 'In addition he was getting grief from his company commander, and his career was in danger of going down the drain.'

Priest's dark eyes bored into Tom's. 'It was in the bloody balance, mate. Your blokes almost did for him in Iraq.'

'Say again.'

'That "friendly fire" balls-up.'

'Tell me about it,' invited Tom, sensing an important revelation.

'Look up your records. It'll be in there, including the withdrawal of the charge the following day. The target *was* a bloody raghead. But something like that doesn't go away. Flip was real strung out over it for that last month of the tour. Had no ammo left to fight with when that woman waggled the kid at him outside his parents' house, and shouted obscenities while her brothers made threatening gestures. Modern day shotgun wedding, it was. Talk about kicking a man when he's down!'

'So Brenda was out of his life?'

Priest nodded. 'He reckoned he wasn't good enough for her. Shows how low he was over that period. Should've made sergeant by now, but that's all on his record.' He crushed the beer can with his hand. 'He'll never make sergeant now, thanks to some pervert.' He turned haunted eyes to Tom once more. 'What're you doing about getting who did for him?'

'We're talking to people like you who knew him, garnering evidence that'll eventually point us in the right direction,' Tom told him quietly. 'There's another kid – a girl of eight months – so the marriage was working out, was it?'

'They must have been having sex; doesn't mean the marriage was working. Just satisfying basic needs. Flip loved those kids. Always gassing about them.' He appeared lost in thought for a moment or two. 'Back at the start of the year Starr starts nagging him to quit the Army. In spite of what happened, it was Flip's whole life. Only thing he wanted to do. So that bitch set about getting what *she* wanted. You know the drill. Headache most nights, dried-up corned beef and limp lettuce day after day, dirty washing piling up. When it came to soiled nappies being dumped on his kit, he had a chat with Captain Steele, who called the Welfare people. We were on standby for Afghanistan and the Company Commander wanted the situation sorted.'

'Would that be *Ben* Steele? Guy who got involved in the abduction of Major Kington, Defence Liaison Officer, a coupla years ago?'

'The same. Know him?'

'Oh, *yes*,' said Tom, recalling the young subaltern Max had dubbed the military Miss Marple.

'He defended our action in Iraq. Backed Flip to the hilt. He's all right. The guys really rate him.'

'And Steele sorted Starr's attempts to get Keane out of khaki?'

'Welfare did. They arranged for the kids to go two days a week to a crèche in town run by several Brit women, giving Starr some time to herself, and Flip agreed she could take them to her mother's, all expenses paid, while he was in Afghanistan. He also said he would give some thought to leaving the Army when he got back.' Priest grimaced.

'Between you and me, I think he was uptight about going into action again, and if it turned out he couldn't hack it any more he'd be better off getting out.'

'And did he?'

'Did he what?'

'Hack it.'

'Yes, mate. When he got back here he had everything going for him.' He flung the crushed can at his son's bike. 'He's out of it with a vengeance now. That cow's got what she wanted.'

Connie Bush was talking with the wife of a corporal of the West Wiltshire Regiment, now in Afghanistan. A neat, voluble woman, Sarah Goodwin had insisted on making extra coffee and sandwiches before settling on the settee to tell her visitor all she knew about her neighbours. Childless, she was clearly lonely and seized the opportunity to share an early snack lunch with a young woman eager to hear her titillating account. SIB members were plain-clothes detectives. The absence of military uniform and the unwelcome red-topped cap made interviewees more relaxed and confiding. This particular woman certainly chatted as if Connie were a friend who had dropped in for a gossip.

'He was terribly henpecked, you know. Starr had a voice on her. These walls are too thin at the best of times – you can even hear sounds of an intimate nature, if you get my meaning – but when they had a barney we heard every word she said. Cutting him down to size. I started out feeling sorry for him, but then I had a think about it and changed my mind. I mean, any man who lets himself be treated like that deserves to be.' She took a large bite from her cheese and pickle sandwich, saying through it, 'Don't you agree?'

Connie just smiled and sipped her coffee, privately labelling her companion a probable doormat. 'You told Sergeant Maddox that you didn't hear Mrs Keane depart with the children either on Saturday or early this morning, but surely you noticed how quiet it had become. Presumably, she shouted at her kids, too.'

'I've been out a lot. I can't stand it here without Den.'

I couldn't stand it at any time, thought Connie. Little or no effort had been made to soften the austerity of standard army accommodation with colour or imagination. It was not a home, simply a basic living unit.

'Are you friendly with Mrs Keane?'

The plate was proffered. 'Have another sandwich.'

'I've had enough, thanks. Are you?' Connie persisted.

'Den said it wouldn't do.'

'Oh? Why?'

Sarah poured more coffee for them both. 'A woman like that would take advantage. Start gossiping over the fence, showing too much interest in our private affairs and blabbing about them to all and sundry.' She shook her head. 'Give her an inch and she'd take a mile, Den said. Before I knew it I'd be asked to babysit, and those kids would be forever in here.' She took another large bite of sandwich. 'Of course, I said hallo if we came face to face, but I always made an excuse not to stop and chat. Didn't want any unpleasantness. That's not in my nature.'

So you stayed in your little tight shell, thought Connie. 'How about the other wives? Did they get on with Starr?'

Sarah's plain face screwed into an expression of dislike. 'She was part of a clique, all of them loud-mouthed and hung around with babies. They had an unpleasant smell, somehow. Babies do that to people, don't they?'

Connie studied this tidy, colourless woman and tried to guess whether that statement indicated her reason for deciding not to have a family, or whether it was a kind of warped consolation for having tried and failed.

'Who are Starr's particular friends in this clique?'

The other woman got to her feet with a smile. 'I've something nice in the kitchen. I'll fetch them then we can go on with our chat.' A moment later she returned holding a fancy tin. 'I made these last night. Didn't know what else to do with myself knowing I wouldn't get to sleep if I went to bed. They're Den's favourites. Have a couple.'

Connie declined the chocolate-covered buns and repeated her question. She heard the reply through a mouthful of cake.

'They're all as thick as thieves. Do everything together.' She took a gulp of coffee. 'Starr's never lonely. I mean, she doesn't need anything from me. Not that I'd refuse to help her if she was in trouble. You mustn't think that. But she has plenty of friends who are her kind, who would see she was OK. Mind you, soon after Melody was born she was very unhappy. Wanted him to leave the Army. Den told me Flip was uptight about it, but that was before Welfare sorted out the crèche for the kids. Starr calmed down after that, especially when he agreed she could go to her Mum while he was away.' She gave a fey kind of smile. 'Lovely and quiet here for five months. No banging and clattering; no kids squalling.'

Connie picked up on that news. 'Mrs Keane went to the UK while her husband was in Afghanistan?'

Another bun began to be devoured. 'Den said it was the only way Flip could stop her persecution. I couldn't repeat to you what I was told she did to make him get out.' She shuddered. 'How any woman could behave like that I . . . *Apparently*,' she continued with relish, 'he said he'd consider leaving when he returned at the start of this week. Well, she arrived here ten days ago – I heard doors banging and the kids whining so I knew they were back – and she starts going at him the minute he walked in the door.' She appealed to Connie. 'Do you feel sorry for him, or not? I was feeling low with Den going off just a few days before, and I admit I did think she should have made a bit of a fuss of him after what he'd been through. But not *her*!'

'This quarrel you heard on Friday night,' prompted Connie.

Sarah Goodwin's eyes lit with excitement. 'Oh, *that*, I almost called the Redcaps. I mean, it was much worse than the usual mud-slinging and Starr's screeching. It sounded like furniture being thrown about, and Flip was shouting as much as her. I've never heard him yell like that at her before. Talk about *swearing*! He'd really lost it.'

Crumbs of chocolate bun dropped from her mouth as she warmed to her theme. 'After a whole lot of thudding and crashing, when I thought someone must be getting hurt, it suddenly went quiet. That frightened me more than the ding-dong. Alone here without Den I just huddled in the duvet and prayed it had stopped.'

'But you didn't call the RMP post on the base.'

'Den says it's always best not to get involved. We have to live next to them and Starr could make things very unpleasant for me without a husband here to sort it out. I didn't get any sleep, you know, worrying about it,' she offered as if by way of mitigation.

Connie lost her patience with this feeble woman. 'You have heard that Philip Keane has been murdered, haven't you?'

'It's all round the base,' she murmured, fiddling with the paper cases from three chocolate buns she had eaten. Then she had a thought and looked up swiftly. 'No, no, he wasn't killed *then*. I'd never forgive myself if . . . No, I heard them both talking at breakfast time.'

'Talking, or continuing the row?'

'Starr always shouts, but he sounded quiet. The kids were crying and I think he was trying to calm them.'

'Now, this is important, Mrs Goodwin. At what time did you grow aware that the Keanes had all left their house yesterday?'

'Oh, I can't tell you that. They were there when I was eating my usual bowl of banana and cornflakes.'

'That was when?' Connie demanded impatiently.

'Eight thirty. I washed the bowl and coffee-mug – that always brings it home that Den's not here; just *one* of everything – and I went out at nine to spend the day with a friend who was also not keen on all the noise and fuss of the Open Day. I came home after supper with her.' Her brow wrinkled. 'I *was* surprised that the place next door was in darkness. That small bedroom at the front is the nursery. There's a low light burning all night for the kids.'

'So the house looked empty?'

'Well, yes. I got used to it being dark for five months, but they're back now. There should've been lights.'

'Was their car in the drive?'

'No . . . no, so she must have taken the kids to friends,

mustn't she?' A moment later, 'Oh, my God, she won't
know Flip's been killed.'

Connie got to her feet. 'That's why we're trying to find
her. Thanks for your help. I'd like details of the friend you
were with on Saturday.'

Sarah Goodwin stood, cake crumbs dropping from her
lap to the carpet. 'Whatever for?'

'We need to know where people were between ten and
fourteen hundred . . . for elimination purposes.'

'Elimination from what?'

'Murder, Mrs Goodwin.'

Tom drove back to his office digesting a significant fact
Priest had revealed. He was now eager to check SIB records
for the report on a case involving Philip Keane during a
tour in Iraq two years ago. It might throw some light on
the man's murder. Had Frank Priest lied about Keane's
ability to cope with active service? Had the Corporal funked
it in Afghanistan, putting his men in danger's way? Would
the company sergeant major defend him so solidly if that
had been the case? It was essential to interview Keane's
platoon before some of them went to the UK or to a
European destination for their well-deserved rehab leave.

On a huge military base it was impossible for everyone
to know everyone else, even those within the same regiment. For a small unit like 26 Section, whose headquarters
were on a far boundary, the situation was worse. Because
of their general unpopularity Redcaps tended to stay within
their own ranks and territory. It was the best plan; a mistake
to make close friends they might have to arrest and report
to the Garrison Commander one day.

It so happened that Tom had encountered Ben Steele,
commander of B Company, the Royal Cumberland Rifles
– the RCR as they were frequently called – on a compli-
cated case of abduction and murder in the regiment.
Promoted to captain now, Steele would be the best man to
question about one of his NCOs who had been murdered
in this curious manner. According to Frank Priest, Steele
had been involved in the trouble in Iraq and with Starr's

bid to get her husband out of the Army before the Afghan
deployment, so he would know Philip Keane well enough
to provide some input.

Approaching the water tank Tom saw two Redcaps
dismantling the posts and crime scene tapes, so he pulled
over and crossed to have a word with them. He was not
surprised to learn that close examination had produced negative results. The area had been trampled and scattered with
litter by hundreds who had enjoyed the performances
throughout yesterday. The small platform had been more
rewarding. The fingerprints there could be checked with
those of people known to have been on it, which would
leave others from whoever had put the body in the tank.

They all knew that these alone would not lead them to
the killer. This forensic evidence would only become useful
when they had definite suspects for comparison. As things
stood, Keane would have been killed by one of thousands
on the base. Only by interviewing anyone intimately
concerned with the activity in the tank, and every person
who knew the victim and his absent wife, would they begin
to piece together the events leading to the disaster that had
overtaken this soldier and his family.

With that in mind Tom moved to where a small group
of men were emptying the tank, and addressed a muscular
man with three stripes on his sleeve, who was overseeing
the job.

'Sergeant Figgis?'

The man swung to face Tom. 'Who wants him?'

'Sar'nt Major Black, SIB.'

'Ah, guessed you'd be along soon, sir. I'm Cruz. That's
Roley Figgis by the pump. We're real upset about what
happened here last night. Should've been emptied right
away, but Lieutenant Sears said it was OK to do it today.
Would've had it completed by mid-morning 'cept the Redcaps
wouldn't let us near until half an hour ago.'

Tom nodded. 'So you're the guy who made the shark
and other fearsome creatures?'

He grinned. 'My old man used to fashion them for us
kids. I got four brothers and three sisters. When Mr Sears

said we had to put on some sort of show to keep level with the others, I got this up with Roley.' His grin widened. 'Better than blowing things to bits as a demo of what Sappers do, eh?'

'How well did you know Phil Keane?'

Cruz was unfazed by the sudden question. 'Never heard of him until the Redcaps woke me up middle of the night asking where I'd been after we finished here. Apart from our Field Section I don't know any regimental guys 'cept other athletes.' His grin broke out again. 'I'm a sprinter and hurdler. Inter-Services champion two years ago.'

'I'll need details of where you obtained the materials for creating those models, and the names of everyone who was in any way involved in their manufacture. While you get your brain around that, I'll talk to Sar'nt Figgis.'

The diver had moved up on to the platform where he was taking the shark, sea snakes, conger eels and other synthetic creatures from two men in swim trunks who had entered the quarter-filled tank to get them.

Tom climbed the metal steps to the platform. 'Roland Figgis?'

The Sergeant studied Tom's starched white shirt and grey trousers, but clearly did not identify the Corps tie for he asked somewhat harshly, 'Who the hell are you?'

Tom told him equally harshly and was gratified by the immediate change of manner. 'Sorry, sir, this business has shaken me up. Cruz and I were willing to clear this last night – we hadn't any plans – but Lieutenant Sears said to leave it. He was insistent. Said we'd need a rest after a heavy day. Well, I *was* pretty knackered. Been at it since mid-morning. Needed a feed, too. Best to operate in water with empty guts. Soon as we finished here, Cruz and I had some nosh, played a couple of games of darts, checked our emails then hit the sack.'

'So how well did you know Philip Keane?'

Same unfazed response. 'Never heard of him until now.' Figgis's tanned face registered curiosity tinged with concern. 'Why would someone choose to kill him with that bloody jellyfish? Points the finger at us, doesn't it? The Section's only been here two months and we've had blokes on staggered leave for most of that time, so what's the deal with using our gear for it?'

'You'll know when we find out,' said Tom, keeping quiet the fact that Keane had not been killed in the tank, just dumped there later. 'Where were you before coming here?'

'In the Stan,' he replied, using the abbreviation some troops favoured when speaking of Afghanistan.

'With the Cumberland Rifles who returned six days ago?'

'With whoever needed our help. You've no idea. Kandahar base stretches for eight miles in most directions. It's a bloody circus.'

'I know. I was out there a couple of years back when some of our guys were slaughtered,' Tom said tensely.

Figgis nodded. 'You have to take it on the chin as part of the job . . . but *this*.' He waved a hand at the almost empty tank. 'The work of some psycho, must be.'

Tom chose not to follow that direction. Instead, he asked for the names of people who were in any way involved in yesterday's performances, and those of any other service personnel who used the aqua club of which Figgis was a member. 'You and Sar'nt Cruz should bring that info to my office by noon tomorrow,' Tom instructed, eyeing the shark that was being lifted from the water. It looked all too real. 'Have you ever wrestled with a real one?'

Figgis laughed. 'Christ, no! They scare the shit out of me.'

Back in Headquarters and starting to access the report on Keane's action in Iraq, Tom was obliged to answer his mobile.

'Sar'nt Major Black,' he muttered, his attention on the computer.

'Clare Goodey here, Mr Black. Corporal Keane's body is to be collected from the Medical Centre at fifteen hundred. If you want to view it again you should come along before then.'

'Thanks, but I have all the info I need until the pathologist's report comes in. How long before we get it, d'you think?'

'Who knows? I'll do my best to get him to speed it up.'

'That'd be helpful, ma'am.' He made to disconnect then realized she was still speaking.

'. . . glad of his input.'

'Sorry, say again,' he murmured, his attention still on the facts rolling up the computer screen.

'I heard sounds in Max's apartment, so I went to investigate knowing he was supposed to be in the UK. He's back.'

THREE

I t was hardly a good start to what they had planned, but Max could not help relishing what had happened. A little competition often spiced up an uncertain relationship.

He and Clare Goodey rented self-contained, one-bedroomed apartments which had a spacious dining-cum-sitting-room between that they both were free to use if entertaining on a large scale. During the few weeks they had been in residence neither of them had had occasion to use the adjoining room which, in fact, also provided access to both apartments without going from one front door, down two flights of steps, along the pavement and up two flights to reach the other front entrance.

Max had given Clare the key to his door leading to the shared room so that she could gain access in an emergency. It had not occurred to him to email her about his change of plans, so Clare had walked in ready to do battle with whoever was taking advantage of his absence. She had come face to face with Livya in primrose bra and pants, and himself wearing just a small towel after showering. The initial silence could have been cut with a knife.

Max had performed introductions and both women had handled the situation with self-assurance as each studied the other in critical manner. Clare had swiftly withdrawn leaving another heavy silence soon broken by the sound of running water as Livya took her shower.

After the bride and groom had departed yesterday for a secret destination, Max and Livya had talked long into the night about the demands of their professions against the demands of their emotions. The problem still seemed insurmountable, which upset them both. Eventually, Max had suggested that as they both had fourteen days' leave they should take a carefree holiday. It would be the longest period they had yet spent together, and would surely bring

a resolution to the question of whether marriage would
work for them. Livya had been doubtful on that score,
maintaining that their professional lives would remain the
stumbling block. However, she had finally agreed that a
long holiday in Europe would be highly enjoyable provided
they did not discuss the pros and cons of marriage the
whole time.

She had been impressed by the apartment, where they
planned to spend the night before setting out in Max's car
across Germany, stopping whenever and wherever they
fancied. They had been too tense for lovemaking last night
so, taking an early morning flight from Heathrow, the intention had been to go to bed until late afternoon when they
would drive to Max's favourite riverside restaurant for
dinner. Guessing that programme was now a non-starter,
Max dressed in cotton slacks and a polo shirt for *lunch* at
the riverside inn. Nighttime sex was the better option,
anyway. They could have been at it when Clare walked in.

Livya made no comment when she came from the bathroom to find him fully dressed. The fact that she had on
fresh underwear confirmed what Max had suspected. Sex
had been put on hold for now. Livya took pale green trousers
and a cream shirt from her case and began to dress.

'You didn't explain that you'd moved into *shared* accommodation.'

'There's a large room for entertaining, which can be used
by the tenants of both apartments, that's all. Individually,
not at the same time.'

She raised her eyebrows in mock surprise. 'No joint
Christmas parties; drinks and hijinks to see in the new year?'

'Haven't been here long enough to find out,' he replied
calmly. 'Anyway, I was hoping to be with you at Christmas.
You know I'm not one for drinks and hijinks with a rowdy
group.'

'Mmm, bit of a spectre at the feast, you,' she said in
throwaway manner. 'Working for Andrew means I have to
attend a number of parties, which I actually enjoy as much
as he does.'

'Yes, well, my father ticks all the boxes whatever he

participates in.' Max wondered if she was doing a bit of
tit-for-tatting here, knowing his occasional suspicions of her
true feelings for her charismatic boss.

'He certainly ticks them all for Helene.' She buttoned
her shirt over her lacy bra and changed direction abruptly.
'Do you have a key to her apartment, too?'

Ah, so they were definitely flexing foils, were they?
'When she goes away, I'll doubtless hold one in case of
emergencies.' He pointed to the small table by the door to
the central room. 'She returned mine, as you see, but I'll
give it back to her when we leave tomorrow.'

'You know her well enough to trust her, do you?'

Thinking how lovely she looked in the casual but very
smart clothes, with her dark hair tumbled after confinement
in the shower cap, Max wanted an end to this senseless
episode. 'I work with Clare. She's the base Medical Officer,
and a damned good one. We're colleagues. And friends, I
guess. Of course I trust her. There's no cause for jealousy,
you know.'

He had said the wrong thing; he knew from the bright-
ness of her eyes. He could have kicked himself.

She sat heavily on the nearest twin bed and gave a light
laugh. 'Darling, I know you resent my close relationship
with Andrew; suspect my admiration for him swamps my
feelings for you, is a barrier to your need for a gold ring
and a marriage certificate as proof of my love. *I* don't need
reassurance, believe me. What is there about that woman
to cause jealousy? She's a typical doctor: cool, clinical,
unemotional. My only concern is whether she should be
allowed access to your living quarters in your absence. I'd
never give a key to my apartment to a neighbour.' She
paused significantly. 'The work I do for Andrew is highly
confidential. In the wrong hands . . .'

'The work I do is also highly confidential, don't forget,'
he returned, growing angry, 'But it's locked away at
Headquarters. You surely don't keep sensitive documents
at home. That would constitute criminal negligence.'

'Of course I don't! You should know me . . .'

Her hot denial was interrupted by the shrill of the landline telephone. Max was initially tempted to ignore it, then decided the call would provide a cooling down period. Without taking his glance from Livya's flushed face he took up the receiver.

'Captain Rydal.'

'Your famous guts surpassed themselves this time,' Tom's voice said cheerily. 'How the hell did they know there was a complex case under way which you wouldn't want to miss out on?' When Max made no immediate comment, Tom added more quietly, 'I guess things didn't work out in the UK. Sorry about that, but there's plenty for you to get your teeth into on this.'

Still studying the woman on his bed, Max murmured, 'We're overnighting here before heading off for two weeks by car.'

A brief silence from Tom. 'Your neighbour forgot to mention you had company. Drive carefully . . . and leave your mobile at home.'

'*Tom*,' Max said sharply before his friend could disconnect. 'Tell me what's under way.'

'Sure you want to hear?'

'Yes.'

As Max listened to all Tom related his interest grew sharper and sharper, and his sense of professional responsibility overrode the irritation of his spat with Livya. No longer watching her, he threw questions at Tom to clarify certain points.

'The wife and children haven't been sighted anywhere?'

'Not so far.'

'Every effort is being made to track them down?'

'Maddox has instigated a search for possible bodies on-base and the normal all-points notification has gone out. I have my doubts about Keane killing them, then being topped by his wife's lover. What I've heard so far suggests he would have dished out violence to her long ago, if he'd been that type.'

'Frank Priest told you Keane had been deeply affected by whatever happened in Iraq? We need to look into that asap.'

'I'm in the process of doing that. Then I plan to speak to our old friend Captain Ben Steele, who defended Keane.'

Max grinned. 'For God's sake don't let him mount a private investigation again. Have you considered the possibility that Keane had got into something dodgy prior to going to Afghanistan? Owed money, had double-crossed someone, and that someone made heavy demands that Keane refused to meet when he got back here?'

Tom sounded slightly irritable when he reminded Max that the body was discovered only twelve hours ago. 'I've called a meeting at eighteen hundred when there'll be more evidence to work on.'

Max persevered, however. 'I think that theory has strong possibilities. After waiting six months, the guy wants what he's due and gets nasty. What if it went too far; Keane wasn't meant to die?'

'Hence the decision to dunk the body in the tank ten hours later, shifting the focus?'

'Mmm,' mused Max. 'I can't wait to solve the significance of that jellyfish.'

A chuckle greeted that. 'By the time you return from your two week touring jaunt we'll have wrapped up the case and have the answer to that for you.'

Max became aware of his companion once more, so merely nodded. 'Yes. Well, keep me up to speed on it, Tom.'

When he replaced the receiver, Livya got to her feet. 'I don't know about you, but I'm ready for a substantial lunch.'

'Oh! Yes, a long time since breakfast at your place.'

'That wasn't breakfast, darling. Coffee and a pot of yoghurt isn't enough for a tough hunk like you.' She smiled as she reached up to kiss him, her eyes dark with the promise of passion.

Max recognized the olive branch despite his mind being busy with the intriguing facts Tom had just disclosed. He took up his wallet and car keys. 'The inn by the river suit you?'

'Sounds lovely.' She linked her arm through his. 'Feed the beast first and what comes later will be all the better.'

'Girly wisdom?' he teased.

'*Cordwell* wisdom. It never fails.'

He led the way down the steps, wondering who else she
might have used it on before he came along. Clare's sporty
car was not beside his, so he guessed she had driven to the
base to oversee the collection of Keane's body. Why would
his killer hide his victim for ten hours, then strangle the dead
body with a synthetic jellyfish and dump it in the water
tank? Max's agile mind was fascinated by the quirks of
human behaviour. He revelled in uncovering the legacy
behind them, which then made sense of what had initially
seemed bizarre. Keane would have been murdered for a
straightforward reason – revenge, resentment, betrayal,
greed – but behind that basic emotion a more aberrant one
had been simmering. That jellyfish was saying something.
He longed to know what.

When he pulled up in the inn's carpark Max realized he
had no memory of driving there. It had been one of those
'autopilot' occasions when his mind had been so occupied
he had taken the familiar route automatically. He glanced
apologetically at Livya.

'Sorry about the lack of tourist guide chatter.'

'I was busy looking at the scenery,' she said, 'but I'd like
you to be mentally as well as physically present while we eat
lunch. You'd better talk it out of your system before we find
a table. I gather Tom told you he has a murder case of some
complexity on his hands . . . and you don't feel he can handle
it without you.'

He twisted to face her. 'No, no, he's intelligent and
experienced enough to deal with anything that comes up.'

'So it's envy. You want to be in on the investigation?'

He smiled with contrition and took her hand. 'You know
what it is that I want . . . and I have two weeks with you
in which to work out how I can get it. Let's go and eat.'

'Just the two of us? No metaphorical third person?'

'Just us. Promise.' He kissed her and got out to lead her
to a garden table where gentle sunshine highlighted the
profusion of flowers and sparkled the gliding water beyond
the low bank, and immediately there was a third presence
with them.

Herr Blomfeld greeted Max as a friend, and so did Friedl the waitress – proof of how frequently he ate there. Blomfeld gave a small Germanic bow on being introduced to Livya, and instantly muddied the waters with his eager account of Max's rescue of a local girl who had almost drowned during a drunken student frolic in the river.

'Max went directly into the water and pulled her out. Captain Goodey did the life-saving for to rid the water. She is the very good doctor, eh Max?' He laughed gustily. 'You both had to have the drying of your clothes in the kitchens. I am honoured that you both continue to come to my establishment.'

Left in peace to study the menu, Livya asked what Max would recommend. 'What do you usually have when you come with the good doctor?'

He played it cool. 'On the first occasion during that terrible heatwave, the place was crowded and we were drawn into a middle-aged group celebrating a birthday and a wedding anniversary who plied us with slices of sausage and plates of salad as if we were also guests. Then some students jumped in the river and began larking about until a girl was accidentally knocked off her feet and went under. Her friends didn't notice, so I fished her out. Clare dispersed the water in her lungs and called an ambulance. It wasn't much of a meal.'

'And the other times?'

Still cool, he said, 'The one other time was to celebrate her acquisition of that apartment. She'd asked me to view it with her and offer my advice, so she bought me dinner by way of thanks. I really can't recall what I ate.'

He did recall walking afterwards along the riverbank softly lit by tree lights, and being beguiled into confessing the problems of his relationship with Livya. Something he had deeply regretted the next morning. He regretted it even more right now. It seemed to smack of betrayal.

The afternoon was not a success in spite of their efforts to adopt a holiday mood. The two week trial of personal and professional compatability had got off to a rocky start. Max cursed his idiocy in taking her to a place where he was well-known, not only because of that river incident but because he rowed on the river every Sunday morning and breakfasted at the inn afterwards. A faint sensation of guilt over having used Clare as a kind of agony aunt, and lingering interest in the case being handled by his team without him at its head, curbed his natural warmth towards this woman he loved. Livya sensed his distraction and acted on it when they arrived back at the apartment.

She held his arm as he made to get from behind the wheel. 'Let's write off today as a non-starter, Max. I'm tired after the run up to the wedding and the effort of ensuring everything ran smoothly yesterday. We didn't have much sleep last night and we set off at six this morning. I need a quiet period on my own, and you need to see Tom Black. Your mind's been on the job all through the meal. For God's sake go and put your oar in before we leave tomorrow or you'll be a very dull companion on our make-or-break fortnight.'

Max watched her walk to the steps with the key to his apartment, then he fired the engine and backed on to the road leading to the base. She was probably right. They were both tired, and keyed-up over the outcome of the next two weeks. Better to make a fresh start tomorrow. After an in-depth discussion with Tom he would be able to put aside all thoughts of a missing wife and children, a murder by strangulation and a dead body with a jellyfish fastened tightly around its neck. That really was intriguing.

Phil Piercey was conscious of a strange smell in the Keanes' house. He could not identify it, but felt instinctively that it should be telling him something significant. The downstairs area was surprisingly tidy. Toys were stacked in a cardboard box, cushions were plumped up and arranged on the large sofa, washed dishes were in the drainer, cereal boxes were neatly arranged on the worktop. No signs of a struggle or any kind of violence, no evidence of the row the neighbour reported overhearing.

He climbed the stairs. The smell grew stronger, so he approached each room cautiously. The small front bedroom contained a cot and a child's bed. Both had covers with cartoon characters splashed over them. Piercey opened the drawers of a small chest. Practically empty. On a hook at the back of the bedroom door hung a small blue dressing gown and an even smaller pink one. They bothered the tough, experience-hardened sergeant. What had befallen these children of a soldier bizarrely murdered yesterday?

In the larger bedroom he found the root of the smell. On one wall was a stain where liquid had splashed and run down to the carpet. Piercey squatted to examine a broken bottle lying there. Turning it over with a pencil in order to read the label he saw that it was some kind of herbal mixture guaranteed to remove blemishes. He thought it smelled like perfumed paint-stripper. The bottle must have been thrown at the wall during a row that had resulted in one of the wardrobe doors being yanked from its upper hinges to hang lopsided.

The yellow duvet also showed signs of being spattered with the stuff, and the base of the bedside lamp was chipped. He righted it but could not see the missing fragment. Perhaps it was long-standing damage. The clothes in the wardrobe were mostly Starr's, with a couple of posh frocks at one end. There were two pairs of jeans, some cheap T-shirts and a couple of fancy blouses, all rather large. Starr was apparently a big woman. A glance in the chest of drawers confirmed that. Two outsized bras and large knickers, but surely not enough to suggest she was still in residence.

On the short wall a wooden rail had been fixed to take Keane's clothes. The usual mix of uniform and leisure garments was there in abundance. No way of telling if anything was missing, so Piercey looked for the obvious in vain.

Hearing Beeny, who had been knocking on doors, enter the house, Piercey called to him. 'What d'you make of this?'

Beeny studied the room. 'A real ding-dong. *She* threw the bottle – women throw, men slap. One of them slammed the wardrobe door hard enough to break it, or they had a fight over removing clothes from it. She says she's leaving,

he says she's not, and in the struggle they pull it off its
hinges.'

'Conclusion?' asked Piercey.

'She walked out with the kids after he left the house
yesterday morning.'

'But she tidied the place first and left some of their
clothes.'

'Toys, too.'

'So she intended to come back.'

'Exactly,' Beeny agreed. 'There's no evidence here of
killing.'

'Which leads to the near certainty that Keane went from
here alive and fully-dressed. I've not found a wallet, loose
change, keys or a mobile phone. I checked his kit items,
and I'd lay a bet he didn't go in uniform.'

'Mmm, let's rate that as just a possibility. One of them
took the car. Soon as George, or Krenkel's lot, find it we'll
have the answer to that one, but we need to find Keane's
clothes.'

'Difficult, difficult,' tutted Piercey. 'Whoever stripped
him will have disposed of them. There must be some significance there. If you had a clothed dead body would you
bother stripping him down to his pants before dropping him
in a tank of water? I mean, it wouldn't matter if his shirt
and trousers got wet, would it?'

Beeny stared at the broken wardrobe. 'Maybe he was
wearing only pants when he was killed.'

'Caught *in flagrante* with some other guy's woman?'

'After the row with his missus he might've needed some.
He'd been in a combat zone for six months. A long time
without!'

They inspected the bathroom. Apart from the usual items
there were a number of bottles and pots bearing labels
similar to the one on the smashed container. Starr Keane
apparently needed an entire shelfful of herbal remedies for
every female problem. Was there a clue there? Piercey
asked.

'Not unless one of them contains jellyfish ink, or
whatever the creatures squirt at their prey,' said Beeny,

'but the bees seem to fancy the stuff. Look at all these dead ones.'

'Maybe Keane used some of it, with the same result,' joked Piercey.

On hearing Connie Bush arrive from the house next door they started down the stairs. 'Get anything from your door-to-door?' Piercey asked his friend as they descended.

'Guess.'

'Nobody saw or heard anything suspicious.'

'Right on the button, which proves that the best time to commit murder here is when there's an Open Day.'

After thirty minutes of intense computer searching, Tom called Frank Priest's number only to be invited to leave a message. Frustrated, he decided to pursue another avenue in his bid to get on top of this case from the outset. Having delegated himself, Simpson and Heather Johnson to concentrate on the actual murder he went out to his car to chase up a fact Sergeant Figgis had told him about the water tank.

Lieutenant Sears RE was in his garden pushing a chubby toddler on a swing when his wife led Tom through the house to the patio. The grass was scattered with several brightly coloured balls, some soft toys and a baby-walker spilling alphabet blocks. Mrs Sears laughed.

'Julie has not only taken over the house but also my lovely garden, as you can see. We've had to drain and cover the lily pond, and put protective barriers everywhere. When you start a family you have no idea it will make such an impact on your whole life. Do you have children?'

'Three girls.' He grinned as he indicated the changes she had mentioned. 'This is nothing. Wait until she's the age of any of mine.'

She laughed again, then called to her husband. 'John, Mr Black's here to talk to you about what happened last night.'

The young officer steadied the swing, lifted the child from it and walked across to hand her to his wife. 'Get her interested in those building blocks. It'll take her mind from the swing and there'll be no tears.'

Prue Sears glanced up at Tom. 'I don't know how he

thinks I coped with her while he played desert games for six months.'

Sears gently patted the head of the daughter he clearly adored, and led Tom indoors to a room he used as an office. 'SIB, I take it?' He waved an arm at a chair, then sat at the desk and swivelled to face Tom.

'Sorry to disturb your Sunday afternoon, sir, but there's an urgency to this case in respect of the safety of the dead man's missing wife and children.'

Sears frowned. 'Sounds serious. Can't help you there, I'm afraid. I've never met Keane or his family. Had no reason to. You've come to ask me about my section, I guess. All I can say is that they're a very professional, close-knit group of men and women I'd trust with my life. Cruz and Figgis are naturally concerned because someone chose to kill Keane in the tank with something Gabbi Cruz created for the amusement of spectators. I spoke to them this morning and they know nothing of what happened after they packed up and left the tank, around nineteen thirty. I've no reason to disbelieve them.'

Tom nodded in agreement. 'They've just told me they would have drained the tank last night, but you insisted that they wait until this morning. Why was that?'

John Sears' dark eyes narrowed. 'Not so that I could commit murder. It takes ninety minutes to pump that tank dry, and another ninety to fill it with chlorinated water, to say nothing of the business between the two operations. My men had been on the go all day, and tired men make mistakes. Colonel Trelawney gave permission for us to leave the task until this morning. In addition, I like to oversee any activity with that tank, and I didn't fancy doing it at the end of a day I'd spent on horseback dressed in armour.'

'You took part in the jousting?'

'Unfortunately, yes. I'm presently black and blue.'

Tom greeted that with a faint smile before saying, 'You're not overseeing the activity right now, sir.'

Taking exception to what he regarded as criticism, Sears said coldly, 'Our eight o'clock start was delayed for three and a half hours by your men. The draining process was

well under way when I took this lunch break. I'll be spending
the rest of the afternoon and evening on the job.' He got
to his feet. 'You'll be wanting to get on with yours, Sar'nt
Major.'

Tom followed the subaltern to the front door. 'I will, of
course, be questioning any of your men who were involved
with the Corps enterprise for the Open Day. Thank you for
your time, sir.'

On the point of driving away, Tom's mobile rang. A
glance told him the caller was Max. He grinned. Having
given his lady lunch, had he claimed an urgent need to call
for an up-to-date sitrep? He had known Max would be
unable to dismiss what he had been told of the case. The
jellyfish was almost certainly the lure. There was nothing
Max liked more than puzzling out how a killer's mind
worked.

'You're supposed to be romancing your ladyfriend for
two weeks,' he said lightly.

'Where are you, Tom? I'm coming in for a full report.
Should be at HQ in forty-five, possibly less if the traffic
has thinned by now. Are you able to r.v. around then?'

'On way,' Tom said, still smiling as he disconnected and
turned on the ignition. That love affair was on the road to
nowhere.

FOUR

Heather Johnson was combing accommodation blocks to track down RCR soldiers, all of whom were presently officially on several weeks' leave as part of the wind-down from Afghanistan. They had spent the first few days back at base in surrendering equipment, kit and desert combat uniforms, having medical checks and being debriefed by Intelligence staff. This had led up to the fun and relaxation of the Open Day, which many of them had enjoyed.

On this, the day after it, those troops planning to spend time in the UK were packing, consulting ferry timetables, preparing for the long drive, making steamy calls to wives or girlfriends and cheery ones to parents and mates. The men with families on the base were more likely to be starting a holiday in Europe when they had recovered from the inevitable rehabilitation period.

The stay-at-homes could not fully grasp what it was like to come from a day-to-day existence in a vast camp filled with mainly male personnel, living in a small unit with four bunk beds, or spending four days and nights with just a handful of mates way out in the desert, potentially vulnerable, where you sweltered and sweated by day and often awoke to find frost coating your sleeping bag. At the base there was the constant thunder of aero engines, the thwak-thwak of helicopter rotors and the rumble of the eternal passage of trucks. Alcohol was forbidden; so was sex with any of the women serving there, military or civilian. And, all the while, there was the risk of any day being your last on earth. It took time to slough off the warzone skin and resume the former one.

Heather was mainly seeking men of B Company, of which Keane had been a corporal. Olly Simpson was visiting married quarters and the Sergeants' Mess. Heather had

drawn the short straw which obliged her to traipse through
these accommodation blocks in the hope of finding squaddies who might have seen Keane on Saturday morning just
before he was killed. It was a thankless task for a young
woman dressed in a fitted grey skirt and a starched white
shirt. Often found on their beds wearing just underpants,
the soldiers jeered, cheered or wolf-whistled when she
appeared. Even when she revealed her identity they pushed
their cheeky masculinity as far as they could during the
interview.

She had taken a break for lunch and now, late in the
afternoon, she was confronting two riflemen of B Company
who had plenty to say. Heather had discovered them playing
darts in the recreation area, and they now sat in leather
chairs facing her. This pair were close friends, clearly NCO
material, if not higher. It was a relief to get intelligent replies
from men of relatively serious vein. They revealed that they
planned to fly to Canada the following day to trek through
the Rockies.

'We miss the wide open spaces,' explained one with a
smile.

'You're both in Corporal Keane's platoon?' They nodded.
'What's your opinion of him?'

Rob Kelly, a serious twenty-year-old with brown hair and
eyes, spoke without hesitation. 'He made a good job of it
out there. I never questioned what he told us to do. Seemed
OK to me.'

'And you?' Heather asked Rick Beavis, another dark-
haired man.

'I trusted him. He was a born soldier. His problem was
his missus, so far as I heard. Tried to stop him being
deployed out there.'

'Wanted him to come out altogether,' added Kelly. 'Stupid
cow! What else could he do that would give her a place to
live in and all this base offers? He loved the Army.'

'He talked to you about his private affairs?' asked Heather
dryly.

'Look, it's different out there. You're in it together; living,
sleeping, fighting in close proximity for six months. You can't

have a can or two, you can't have a session with a girl. So you get very close, help each other, get your probs out in the open around a camp fire when there's nothing but miles and miles of dark desert in every direction. You become a family out there.'

Heather had heard this before. 'So Flip Keane was in an aggressive mood over his wife's demand?'

Beavis smiled. 'He was in an aggressive mood over the Taliban, who disturbed our peace.'

Kelly replied more seriously. 'He was real choked-up when we left here. A lot were. Saying goodbye to weeping wives and girlfriends. You know. The Corp had kids. He probably cared more about leaving them than getting away from Starr.' He frowned and glanced at his friend. 'Most guys are OK once they're on their way, but he . . . we both thought he took a little longer to settle in than the others.'

'That's right,' agreed Beavis. 'He was morose, edgy for several weeks. Did his job, but seemed to be fretting about something back here. Spent a lot of time calling home.'

'He was very nervy, at first.'

'That all changed when we ran into an ambush. The setting sun was in our eyes; couldn't see the buggers moving around,' Beavis explained. 'It was a tricky one, Sergeant, but he got us out with whole skins. After that he always pulled out all the stops. Got us through anything, cool as you like.'

Heather finished writing a note, then looked up. 'You've described a man with courage, expertise and assurance, someone you liked and trusted, yet somebody killed him yesterday in a most specific way. Can you guess why, or who might do that to him? Had he enemies in the platoon, in B Company, or even in the battalion that you know of?'

'No,' they said together.

'Can you think of any link Corporal Keane had with jellyfish or ocean creatures?'

Kelly put forward an opinion. 'Wasn't it just a case of being convenient?'

'Unpremeditated murder is usually committed with the weapon nearest to hand in a sudden loss of control. That synthetic thing in a tank of deep water wouldn't be the most convenient means of strangling a victim.' She held up her hands. 'These would be.'

'You're saying someone planned it?' asked Beavis. 'It's *weird*. He'd been in the desert for six months, nowhere near the ocean.'

Realizing she was allowing the interview to run away from her with these pleasant young men, Heather fired a more pertinent question at them.

'What did you do yesterday from mid-morning until midnight?'

They both looked startled. 'You can't think *we* killed him,' cried Kelly.

'I need to know your movements during the Open Day. We're checking out anyone who knew Keane in case they noticed anything that'll lead us to the killer. Did either of you see him yesterday?'

'No,' said Beavis. 'We slept in late, then spent the morning running over the details and timetable of our trip, checking our gear, emailing Rob's sister who we'll be staying with for the first three days.'

'Then we had a late lunch and took a look at what was going on around the base, until the whole shebang packed up after the locals were shooed out. No sign of the Corp,' said Kelly. 'It doesn't mean he wasn't there in that mass of people.'

'What did you do after that, until midnight?'

They were starting to resent her approach, and reacted. 'D'you want every detail, including the number of times we visted the pisser?' demanded Beavis.

Heather had been questioning soldiers long enough to be able to handle anything they might say. 'If it's relevant to the murder case, yes.' She added, straightfaced, 'You might have to give it as evidence in court.'

Kelly then said quietly, 'We went for fish and chips and a jar or two, chatted up a couple of girls who'd been running the lost kids corner all day. Must've been around twenty-three hundred when we turned in.'

'Did you get the girls' names?'

'Fanny and Annie,' offered Beavis belligerently.

Heather gave him a glare. 'Don't get smart, sonny!'

'But that's right, Sarge,' insisted Kelly. 'You can check.'

'I will. So you didn't sight Corporal Keane at any time yesterday, or see anything you thought suspicious or odd?'

'I wish we had,' murmured Beavis, suddenly serious. 'To come through six months out there safely only to . . . which bastard would do that to him?'

Heather prepared to leave. 'We'll get him, don't fret. Have a good time in the Rockies.'

'We did see one of those guys who'd been jousting, as we came back to our rooms,' ventured Kelly suddenly. 'He was still kitted out in armour, with the visor down. We reckoned he was having it off with someone he shouldn't and didn't want to be recognized. Why else would he be riding around dressed that way after dark?'

When Max arrived Tom was in his office drinking coffee. He got to his feet and held up the mug. 'Kettle's only just boiled.'

Max diverted to the counter where drinks were made by members of 26 Section. Above it was a cupboard containing a tin of biscuits, another filled with small cakes and tarts, and a wide selection of crisps and chocolate bars, all of which frequently had to substitute for a meal. Unhealthy, but very satisfying. Although he had enjoyed a large lunch just over two hours ago, Max helped himself to two chocolate digestives and returned to Tom's office with them and a full mug.

'What have we got so far?' he asked, pulling a chair round to sit facing his 2IC.

Tom leaned back and outlined what he knew for certain. 'Piercey phoned in a report on his search of the Keanes' home. No signs of foul play or abduction. Half-empty drawers and wardrobe, tidy house and absence of nappies, feeding bottle, pushchair and handbag suggests willing, organized departure of Mrs Keane and her children. Piercey says there's visual evidence of marital violence in their bedroom, which supports the neighbour's report of hearing them rowing on Friday night.'

Max munched a biscuit. 'Points to a classic case of aggrieved wife deciding to put some distance between herself and a violent partner until things cool down, Tom.'

'She could have killed him before leaving the scene.'

'*I'm* the one who chases wild geese, not you, and that's so wild I'll pretend I didn't hear it.'

Tom grinned. 'You're supposed to be planning a romantic tour of Germany, not finding fault with my ideas.'

'OK, let's probe the implications of an organized departure. We must assume she didn't go directly after the row on Friday night, because fear of further violence from her husband would've meant taking the kids from their beds and snatching up the minimum necessities to make a rapid exit. That would apply also if she had lost it during the row and killed Keane, either accidentally or in self-defence. Keane's body would then still be in the house.'

'All right, you've made your point,' agreed Tom. 'So we can probably rule her out as the killer.'

'And as a victim, I suspect. Although,' Max continued thoughtfully, 'she could have gone off in good faith with someone she knew and trusted, only to discover her mistake. It happens. The same could apply to Keane himself.'

'Piercey says Keane's clothes and shaving gear are there, which suggests he had every intention of returning. He almost certainly left the house fully dressed. There's no sign of wallet, cash, keys or mobile.'

'Mmm, first thing tomorrow we'll get a list of recent calls to and from their landline. There's a strong possibility both of them were lured from the house by telephone contact. Once Keane's mobile – and his wife's – turn up we can vet all the calls on and before yesterday which will surely give us a lead.'

Max finished his biscuit and washed it down with a gulp of coffee. 'We really need to move on this, Tom. The Cumberland Rifles guys will be dispersing all over Europe on leave before we can question them. After the briefing at eighteen hundred we need to get out there and follow the info the team brings in. I particularly want to pursue my theory that Keane was involved in something over which he either reneged or double-crossed.'

Seeing the scepticism written across Tom's face, he said, 'It makes sense, man. Keane's away for six months. Soon as he returns he has to face the consequences from whoever he cheated or ratted on before he departed. Clear as daylight.' He pondered further. 'I'm sure that jellyfish is a strong indicator.'

'Keane had a thing going with a fishmonger?'

'Yes, very, very funny, Tom.'

'I'll apologize if you're right, but I'm certain there's something classically military behind this killing.'

'Why, for Pete's sake?' he questioned in surprise. 'The dumping of a man you've already killed into a tank of deep water that represents an ocean surely has no military overtones.'

Tom's face puckered up. '*Naval* links?'

'No. Ocean depths link with deep sea divers. We need to grill the guy who performed in that tank. He's the most likely person to put his victim in it.'

'I've already talked to him. He's never heard of Keane, and the RE detachment has only been here two months. There's no chance he and Keane could have been in cahoots.'

Max was reluctant to abandon his theory. 'So it needn't be a recent connection. We should check both their records; find out where they might have served together before.' He saw Tom's expression. 'Hit a button, have I?'

'The REs were in Afghanistan before this.'

'Ha!' cried Max. 'You can bet the solution lies with that diver. Who is he?'

'Sergeant Figgis, known as Roly. Not because his name is Roland, I've discovered, but it's short for roly-poly.'

Max considered that for a moment, then got it. 'Figgy pudding, also known as roly-poly. Hmm, and Keane is Flip. More understandable. He probably called himself that when he first began to say his name, and it stuck. I congratulate your mother on her sensible choice. Not much anyone can do to Tom.'

He grinned. 'As a squaddie I was known as Blackie.'

Max grinned back. 'Pursuing that line, must we look for someone nicknamed Polyp?'

The situation was too serious for extended levity, and Max returned to the need to contact Starr Keane. 'We have a duty to inform her of her husband's death, in addition to satisfying ourselves of her safety along with the children.'

As if on cue, George Maddox entered Section Headquarters, coming directly to Tom's office. He stopped dead on seeing Max. 'Hallo, sir. I thought you were on leave.'

'So I am, George,' said Max, guiltily aware of the fact. 'What news?'

'Negative, I'm glad to report. We've checked all likely dumping areas and found nothing. No bodies, no evidence of trampling or digging; no baby shoes, dummies, scraps of fabric or strands of hair lying around. We haven't searched accommodation blocks, looked in wardrobes and cupboards, and so on. Before I start the lads on that I thought I should check that you want it.'

As Maddox had addressed Tom, Max let him reply. It was his case, after all.

'Call a halt for now. Evidence at the house strongly indicates the woman made a normal departure with the kids. Until we have cause to think otherwise it's pointless to search the base. We do, of course, need to discover where Keane was actually killed. There's no certainty that it was on the base; but I'd say it's most likely. Soon as we get confirmation on that I'll let you know. The *Polizei* are watching out for the car, or a woman with two small kids getting on a bus or train. Meanwhile, I think you should contact Starr's mother in the UK for some idea where or whom she might have gone to in an emergency. You know the drill.'

Maddox had been gone a mere five minutes when the team members began returning. Each one expressed surprise on seeing Max. 'I thought you were on leave, sir,' was the common cry that began to irritate him because he knew he should return to Livya and leave them to it. However, so greatly was he intrigued by this case, he wanted to hear their reports before heading for his apartment and the planned holiday tour.

Connie Bush teed off. 'Sarah Goodwin is a meek, unfulfilled young woman compensating for the absence of her husband, who surely pulls her strings, by comfort eating. Her description of Starr Keane as loud-mouthed and overbearing to the point of keeping her man under her thumb became extreme when she said women who produce babies are cliquey and have an unpleasant smell. I then recognized her unwilling envy of a woman totally her opposite, which she can only handle by hating Starr.

'Focal points: before Keane deployed to Afghanistan Starr did her utmost to make him leave the Army. Made life grotty at home. He eased that by fixing for the kids to attend a crêche a couple of days a week, and by agreeing to fund the family's holiday with her mother while he was away. He apparently promised to consider giving up his career when he got home. Possible root of violent row on Friday night heard by Mrs Goodwin? The other significant point is that she heard both Keanes talking normally while she ate breakfast on Saturday morning. She said the kids were playing up and it sounded as if he was trying to pacify them. Time, eight thirty. The witness left home at nine. Couldn't say whether or not the car was in the Keanes' drive. Said she didn't think either of them departed before she did because they always slammed the door so hard it made her ornaments rattle on the shelf along the shared wall.'

She glanced around. 'My conclusion is that the Keane family was alive, well and reasonably stable at the start of the Open Day.'

Piercey said, 'I can strengthen that assumption. Breakfast dishes had been washed and left in the drainer, cereal packets were closed and neatly stacked. Whatever the cause of the row, there was a ceasefire in the morning.'

Beeny came in on that. 'Although other neighbours disclaimed seeing anyone leave the house that morning, they all reckoned it was an uneven marriage. Starr had the upper hand. When she was worked up her voice could be heard several houses away, but Keane usually calmed her down. It's general knowledge that he went to the altar with one of Starr's truckie brothers each side of him, and it's no secret that she was determined to make him leave the Army.'

He flipped through his notes. 'Corporal Major's wife beat Starr's drum – she's one of her close chums – and gave a different slant. According to her, Keane always had a bit on the side and put Starr down at every opportunity. She wants another kid – two more, actually – but he's slept on the sofa since he got back here last week.'

'Another point of contention between them,' murmured Connie.

'It's not unheard of for guys to get back from a warzone and find they can't hack it,' said Max, trying to form a true picture of this couple's relationship. 'It sometimes takes a week or more, and it's less stressful to keep out of the marriage bed until he relaxes enough to do the business.'

'There could've been another reason,' mused Piercey. 'The bathroom was full of bottles and jars of herbal gunge guaranteed to remove blemishes, unwanted hair, surplus fat – you name it. Maybe she *did* smell unpleasant.'

'Oh, come on!' protested Connie. 'I saw how tidy and clean the ground floor was. No woman who keeps a house looking so good with two infants in it would surely ignore personal hygiene.'

'As to that,' put in Tom, 'Frank Priest told me she went so far as to drape dirty nappies over Keane's kit during her bid to drive him into quitting the service. She doesn't sound too hygienic to me.' He glanced at Max, who just gave him the nod to continue. 'I asked him for a character ref. According to the Sar'nt Major, Keane was an excellent soldier who could handle the enemy but was putty in the hands of women. With an overbearing wife like Starr, if he had bits on the side who can blame him? Which bids the question, was he with another woman when he was killed? Did she kill him, or another lover who caught Keane with her? This is a definite line to follow.'

'It's also a strong motive, whichever way you look at it,' put in Max, relishing all this input and being unable to stay on the sidelines. 'He was down to his underpants with this woman when someone turns up. Her husband, another lover, or Starr Keane? He's been sleeping on the sofa for six nights instead of coupling with her and making her pregnant, yet he's ready to shag another woman . . .'

'Who doesn't need herbal remedies for improvement,' inserted Piercey unwilling to drop his theory.

'Yes, a real looker,' agreed Max. 'Starr's a large, domineering woman. She grabs him around the neck and shakes him in her fury until he suddenly grows limp. Substitute the other woman's husband or lover, and where's the snag in all three hypotheses?'

'The killer then has to get rid of the witness,' said Connie.

'Precisely. Now, Starr Keane has taken the car and could drive the second body away fairly easily – we'll put aside where her kids were during this slaughter. However, Keane ends up in the tank ten to twelve hours later. In my view that puts Starr at the bottom of the list. A husband or second lover is more likely to carry out the second part of Keane's murder, and he has no need to dispose of the witness.'

'We assume the woman can be trusted not to reveal what she witnessed?' asked Connie. 'So she's either a prossie who has no feelings for the men who use her, or she's been rescued from rape by Keane and is a willing accomplice to his murder.'

'So she keeps the body at her place until *he* comes after dark to collect it,' mused Beeny. 'It works.'

Heather Johnson spoke up at that point. 'I had a long talk with two riflemen called Kelly and Beavis. Lots of interesting stuff concerning Keane, but they gave almost as an afterthought the fact that as they returned to their beds at twenty-three hundred on Saturday they spotted a knight in armour riding across the Sports Ground. They thought someone was up to naughties with a woman he should not be seeing, but it seems to me that a horse would come in very handy if you wanted to move a large dead body from one place to another in the dark.'

'And so it would,' crowed Tom with delight. 'We've maybe cracked that angle. First thing tomorrow we'll get a list of who did the jousting yesterday – Lieutenant Sears was one, he admitted it – and we'll grill them all.' He smiled at Heather. 'Let's have the rest of the interesting stuff you mentioned.'

'These guys are sharp. Noticed a lot. Keane was palpably nervous at the start of their stint in Afghanistan. They were concerned that he wasn't on top of the job. He kept phoning home, and was very definitely worried and uptight about something back here. Eventually, they heard about Starr's determination to get Keane out of the Army, and accepted that as the explanation. Seems they were out with Keane on night patrol when they ran into a Taliban ambush. He proved his courage and ability to lead by getting them all away safely. He was tops with them after that.'

She glanced at her notes. 'Neither this pair nor any others I spoke to had seen Keane on Saturday, but the general opinion of him was favourable. They were all disturbed by his murder.'

Olly Simpson still had to give his report. Tom noted the time and asked him to be brief, unless he had information he considered to be highly revealing.

'Nothing of that nature, sir, but I did track down Keane's best mate, Corporal Ryan Moore. He answered my questions without telling me anything. He needs further attention. No suggestion that he could be the killer,' Simpson added swiftly, 'but I'm pretty damn sure he could tell us a lot more about the victim. His best friend has been murdered after six months of exposure to the enemy, yet he's so controlled you'd think it hasn't touched him. It has, believe me, and it's my opinion he's afraid to let go for fear of betraying his friend.'

'Is he off on leave?' asked Tom.

'No. Both sets of parents are arriving here on Wednesday. The plan is to visit local sights for a few days, then head off for a Rhine cruise at the weekend.'

'I'll have him in in the morning,' Tom promised. 'Connie, you can have the chance to break through the barrier, soften him up.'

'One more thing,' said Simpson with a furtive grin.

'Apropos knights riding around after dark yesterday, I have a reported sighting of a clown wending a somewhat unsteady way between the accommodation blocks just before midnight.'

'Anyone could have got hold of that gear, but we'll start with the PT guys who did the comic act on the trampolines,' said Tom heavily. 'Jesus, they hold an Open Day, military discipline goes to hell and the garrison runs amok! OK, let's get back out there and clear some of the smoke-screen so we can see a way forward. Priority is still to find Starr Keane. Next in line is to trace where Keane was actually killed. Once we have that we can concentrate on how the body was shifted to the tank, and why.'

'My money's on the knight,' put in Piercey. 'Ever see that film where the inspirational hero gets it, so they stick the dead man on a horse with a pole up his back and send him in at the head of the troops to demoralize the enemy?'

Tom glared at him. 'You can question the clowns. You'll be at home with them.'

As they all began to disperse Max knew it was time he also departed. Tom could not *tell* him to bugger off, but it was clear he wanted shot of him. Tom was one of the old school who believed in discipline and respect of rank so, despite their long-standing friendship, he would be feeling hamstrung by Max's interference in a case he was perfectly capable of handling. Yet that jellyfish was so intriguing.

Tom was standing, car keys in his hand, ready to lock up and set off on further investigations. Max took the hint and walked with him to the car park.

'Good luck with the clowns and jousting knights,' he said.

Tom waved an acknowledgement. 'We'll have it wrapped up by the time you get back from your trip, clowns and knights notwithstanding. Enjoy your leave. Hope it works out for you both.' He drove off into the autumn darkness.

As Max followed the perimeter road he thought deeply about Tom's last remark. The two years he had spent here had been interesting and fulfilling. 26 Section was comprised of individuals who made the ideal team. They had been very successful, on the whole. Max thrived on puzzles, and there had been one or two intriguing cases interspersed between the more usual aspects of military life.

Before he had gone to the UK for his father's wedding the Section was involved in claims of sexual harassment, bullying in the swimming pool which led to near drowning, and evidence of drugs being circulated to young squaddies. Those cases were still ongoing, but the murder took precedence, of course. Max caught himself cursing that it should have taken place at a time when he was aiming to sort out his private life.

Driving through streets that grew busier with traffic as he neared the town, the difficulties facing him on that score were piled high. Livya had made no secret of her refusal to leave her position as his father's ADC, which meant Max would have to make the change. Loath though he was to leave 26 Section, would it even work if he did? Livya was dedicated to her career and, when the subject of babies came up, she had said perhaps later.

Max wanted children. His wife Susan had been pregnant when she was killed in a car smash. They had chosen a name for the boy, and Max sometimes fantasized about his son when he saw little ones together with their fathers. Alexander would have been four now. How good it would have been to play with him, teach him to catch a ball, ride a tricycle, build things. Max would have given him swimming lessons and taken him on the river in his skiff; let him wield a scull once he was strong enough to handle it.

He would be just as delighted with a daughter. Tom had three. Although he claimed to feel severely outnumbered by females in his home, Tom loved them all dearly. He was a lucky and happily fulfilled man. Max wanted to be like that. Loneliness was getting to him. He wanted someone to go home to; someone to hold close in the night. And he wanted small images of himself or their mother to raise and be proud of. If the strength of his feelings for Livya made him settle for less would he be like Philip Keane; an excellent soldier but a fool with women? Had that been Keane's undoing?

His hands-free phone rang to bring him from introspection. Drawing up behind a queue at the three-way junction, he answered it.

'Good evening, Max. Here is Klaus Krenkel.'

'Evening, Klaus. What can I do for you?' he asked, knowing he would have to pass the request to Tom.

'It is what I do for you. I think I must tell this immediate to you; there is urgent in this. You have ask for where to find Mrs Stakeen, and also car belonging to her man. I have just now read a report from the traffic section. This car was smash this late morning. Very bad. It burn. Only now is possible to see the number. It is the one you ask for.'

The vehicle queue began to move forward, but the lights changed again before Max could cross. He braked, asking, 'Who was in the car?'

'One woman. Because there is fire there is no identity found. She had been taken to the hospital.'

Max's concern grew. 'Any children in the vehicle?'

'Moment!' Max heard the rustle of paper before the German policeman said, 'There is no mention. Just one woman. This car comes out without enough looking to cross the autobahn at the junction of Mühlebachstrasse. One is dead. Seven badly hurt. There will be a charge taken against the woman.'

'Right. Keep us up to date with that. Thanks, Klaus. I'll go to the hospital now. Wiedersehen.'

Only after he had turned right at the junction instead of crossing it did Max remember he was not supposed to be dealing with this case. He called Tom's mobile and explained that he was just five minutes from the hospital and would get whatever he could from the injured woman regarding the safety of her children.

'They don't have proof of identification so she's probably out of it, at the moment. I'll get back to you on that, Tom. Krenkel said she drove straight out across the autobahn, so you can dismiss any notion of her being another victim of Keane's killer. Everything points to a normal RTA. Good thing is the kids weren't with her. I guess whoever's looking after them is anxious to know where Starr is by now.'

'Unless she dumped them for the whole weekend,' said Tom. 'George called the family in the UK. He says they couldn't suggest anyone Starr might be staying with, although she had called her mother yesterday morning saying she wouldn't stand any more of Keane's other women and was going to split with him because he still refused to leave the Army. The mother threatened to send her sons over to sort Keane out. You can imagine George's response to that.'

Max had arrived at the hospital and turned in between pillars leading to the car parking area. 'Time to inform them that he's dead once we've told the wife. Keane's parents have been given only the basic fact, I take it?'

'Until we've got to the root of what happened, yes.'

'That's all I'll give Starr. My main object is to discover where she's left the children. A bientot, Tom.'

Max never entered a hospital without recalling the day he had had to identify his wife's damaged body. There was something daunting about those long corridors and the unique blend of antiseptic and the reek of sickness. Today was no exception. His enquiries at the desk regarding the car crash casualties confirmed his guess that Starr would be in Intensive Care.

Arriving at the hushed ward Max gave his identity and asked to speak to the unidentified woman who had been in the traffic accident.

The nurse eyed him sharply. 'She is soldier?'

'Married to a soldier. I believe she is Mrs Starr Keane. Is she able to confirm that for me?'

'No, Captain. She has died since two hours ago.'

FIVE

Max called Tom's mobile from the car park. It was tuned to voice mail, so he simply said, 'The woman who was in the Keanes' car died without regaining consciousness. No certainty she's Starr. Call me soonest.'

He drove home and entered his apartment to find lights on and the door leading to the central connecting room open. He cautiously approached the sound of voices; Livya's and Clare's. They were seated in two of the deep armchairs, drinking white wine and apparently on amicable terms with each other. Max was momentarily speechless.

'Hi!' said Livya, holding up the bottle. 'We've left you some.'

'Good of you,' he murmured, unsure whether to join them or to stand his ground until she got the message that the feminine twosome should now split up.

She gurgled with laughter. 'Oh, this is the second bottle. I grew tired of waiting, so I suggested Clare and I should get together and christen this room. We both know a lot more about you than before.' Her intoxicated merriment slowly faded. 'Only joking, darling.'

Well, he would show her he could take a joke. He fetched a glass from the cabinet well-stocked with them, and sank into a third chair. 'I guess you know a lot more about each other, too. Amazing how alcohol banishes inhibitions.'

Clare took up her half-filled glass. 'I'll finish this while I'm getting my supper.'

'Don't go,' said Max as she made to rise. 'You'll want to hear what detained me for so long.'

His mobile then rang and he deliberately remained where he was to take the call. 'We've a hell of a situation here, Tom. They dragged her from the burning car, but any means of identification went up in flames. I took a look, but I don't know Starr Keane. Someone will have to formally identify her. As the husband's also dead, it'll have to be a close friend. Soon as possible. It won't be harrowing. She looks OK; damage was mostly internal. She could very well be someone who borrowed the car and was unfamiliar with the controls. The kids weren't with her and, bearing in mind Piercey's report of so many remedies for blemishes etcetera, the woman I saw had a clear skin and would have been chubbily attractive.'

'I'll have Connie or Heather take someone there now,' said Tom. 'If it *is* Starr we'll have no way of knowing where she left the kids, unless one of her friends can come up with something. I'll follow that up right away.'

'Keep me informed.'

'Will do.'

Max disconnected and focussed on Clare. 'You heard that? There are two youngsters out there who lost their father yesterday and probably their mother today. We know Keane was murdered. Until we receive the full accident report from the *Polizei* we have to wonder if the car could have been tampered with. One of my team is going to drive someone to the hospital pronto. If the woman is Starr Keane I'd like you to contact the doctors for full details of her injuries. Chat to the pathologist. She apparently drove straight across the autobahn. Is there anything to suggest she was actually incapable of controlling the vehicle at the time? That's important.'

He glanced at the clock. 'Too late to get anything from them tonight. As soon as I have confirmation of identity, I'll call you. You can start on it first thing tomorrow. We're responsible for her and we'll get medical data quicker through you.' He frowned. 'Our main hope is that whoever is babysitting for Starr gets in touch with us before long.'

'They'll have been put to bed by now,' Clare pointed out. 'If the arrangement was to keep them overnight the minder won't start to worry until well into tomorrow.' She got to her feet. 'In view of this I'll lean on the pathologist to work on Keane. His body was taken away this afternoon and would normally join the end of a waiting queue, but there could be something significant about his murder that would connect with his wife's death. I'll do whatever I can and give you the results asap.'

Max stood and, for some inexplicable reason, offered his hand. 'Thanks, Clare.'

She did not grip it, merely brushed his palm with her fingers. 'It's my job. Goodnight.' She glanced down at the woman watching them. 'Thanks for Max's wine . . . and the chat.' The door leading to her apartment closed behind her and was locked very audibly.

After slight hesitation Max resumed his seat, began on the full glass of wine, then cast a glance around the large room he had only crossed once when he had accompanied Clare to view with the prospect of renting her apartment.

'Neutral territory,' he commented caustically. 'Checking up on me?'

'You'd do the same if the position was reversed.'

He neither agreed nor denied that. 'Satisfied that we're no more than professional colleagues?'

She smiled sexily across the top of her glass. 'I rest my case, Steve.'

That secret little endearment failed to work its magic. 'Did you get some rest before the girly get-together?'

'Mmm. A welcome couple of hours on your bed. Then I had a long luxurious bath.' She got to her feet. 'Why don't you have one while I rustle up some supper? You look tired and it'll help you to unwind.' Putting out both hands, she said teasingly, 'Upsy-daisy.'

He ignored her hands. 'You've imbibed too much of my Chablis.'

'Quite probably, but it's the start of a long holiday and we're going to be touring wine-producing areas, so it's only courteous to enjoy the juice of the grape.' She closed with him and kissed his mouth with wine-wet lips. 'We've delayed it too long. I'd like you nicely relaxed and up for anything when we get to bed.'

This was what he had wanted. She was promising him a joyous start to his bid to persuade her they should be together permanently, so why wasn't he elated? She looked lovely in close-fitting oatmeal trousers and a white cotton shirt with faint gold threads running through it; there was the familiar inviting glow in her eyes. Yet his mood was wrong. He should not have gone to Headquarters and become involved in this complex case. It was not fair on Livya.

Max would have taken a long shower, but she insisted on running a bath laced with some of her scented oil designed to soothe and relax the body at the end of a hectic day. She had wasted her money, he thought, for he felt no different after the ten-minute soak. If it should turn out that the brakes on the Keanes' car had been disabled, focus on the case would shift dramatically to suggest Tom was quite wrong to believe there was something classically military about it. Killing Starr too suggested a more normal crime. Extortion, revenge, sex? Had Keane's partiality for a 'bit on the side' taken him into adulterous territory? Had he – Max's pet theory – been involved in some wheeler-dealing and fallen foul of his co-conspirators? In either case, why kill Starr *after* killing him? Murdering her as punishment for stealing another man's wife/woman, or as a threat to force his compliance in some deal would make sense, but once Keane himself was dead what was the object in making two small children orphans?

Livya appeared at the bathroom door. 'Supper's almost ready. It's only scrambled eggs, that lime mousse we picked up on our way from the airport, and cheese and biscuits. There's plenty of fruit if you're still hungry later.'

'Sounds fine,' he said, rising from the bath.

She held out a towel, studying his dripping body with appreciation. 'All that rowing you do certainly builds up muscles.' She ran a finger from his throat to his groin and let it linger in that area. 'The rest isn't bad, either . . . and it's all mine for the next two weeks.'

He stepped out on to the bath mat. 'For far longer than that, if you want it.'

She reached up to kiss him. 'Let's see how things are after the two weeks.'

They had more wine with their light supper, by which time Livya was more intoxicated than Max had ever seen her. She was also amazingly sexy over the normal business of eating and drinking. That it was alcohol-fuelled he did not doubt, but he had been starved of sexual release for too long to resist what was on offer. Perhaps it was that very abstinence that turned their lovemaking into fierce grappling which brought a climax far too soon. Max was annoyed with himself but, as he lay waiting to recover his impetus, Livya demonstrated her enormous hunger with amazing energy, her hands and mouth all over him.

Max met her demands with delight tinged with a sense of not being in control. She had never dominated him like this before; never been so desperate for gratification. Had jealousy of Clare prompted this drive for possession?

Later, when Livya appeared to be sleeping, Max gently withdrew his arm from beneath her and padded to the kitchen. The men in the black and white films he collected and loved to watch always lay smoking a cigarette after sex. He drank ice cold milk. Replacing energy? He glanced at the clock. An hour before midnight. There should be word from Tom by now. He had left his mobile on the kitchen worktop after their meal, and now picked it up. The text confirmed that Starr Keane had been in the crashed car.

Tom had done as asked, with nothing added. Fair enough. Tomorrow morning he and Livya would leave the base and not return for fourteen days. By then, Tom and the team would hopefully have the case neatly tied up and presented to Colonel Trelawney for further action.

Rinsing his glass beneath the hot tap, Max returned quietly to the room which, in fact, was fitted out as a bedsitter with a table and chairs, a couple of armchairs and a computer desk along with the usual bedroom furniture. Ideal for one, or a busy couple away all day and sometimes for longer. For Max, used to living in a basic room in an Officers' Mess, it was real luxury. It flitted through his mind that he might have to leave the apartment if they decided marriage was the way forward for them. Livya's response tonight suggested that she was finally thinking along those lines.

The glow from the fire and security alarm panel on the far wall provided enough light for him to see his way to the bed. It also enabled him to see the tears on Livya's cheeks as she lay wide-eyed facing that wall. He halted as the truth hit him with a crushing awareness as painful as if he had been physically struck across the chest. What a fool he had been not to recognize her insistence on in-depth discussions of the difficulties surrounding marriage last night, for her subtle evasion of lovemaking before lunch, for the generous intake of wine before her desperate lust just now, for that was what it had been. *What a fool!* Jealousy of Clare? No, unbearable jealousy of the woman she had watched marry his father yesterday.

Had she pretended it was *Andrew* Rydal in this bed with her, fantasized throughout her wild coupling with his son? He shrugged on his bathrobe and moved to the window, gazing at the lights of speeding traffic along the distant autobahn. He had always suspected it; now he knew for certain. He tried to believe she had only realized the true nature of her feelings for her boss when she saw him pledge the rest of his life to Helene Dupres, but that small inner voice of honesty told him otherwise.

He stood for a long while facing the truth, then he said tonelessly, 'How do you imagine you can go on working with him?' She lay silent, facing the wall. 'Did he ever give you an indication that he returned your feelings?'

Still no reaction from her, so he turned to study her averted face and the tangle of dark hair on her pillow. 'My days of acting as substitute for the lover you can't have are over.'

That brought a response. She sat up clutching the duvet as if it was a shield. '*No*, Max. I love you for the person you are.'

'The only problem being that I'm not him.'

In the faint light her eyes looked like dark bruises in her pale face. 'We've had some wonderful times together, but I did my best to persuade you that it could never go beyond that, you *know* I did.'

'Oh yes, I'll accept that in your defence, but you're guilty as charged over what happened here tonight. I'll be leaving early to start work on this murder case. I'd like you to be gone by the time I get back.' Taking up the key to the central room he left her sitting in his bed.

After an uncomfortable, tormented five hours in an armchair Max walked in to his kitchen to find a note propped against the toaster. The bedroom door was open. Livya's suitcase and cabin bag had gone, although her perfume lingered. He opened the folded sheet and read her words.

Dearest Max, I've loved you as fully as I could and I've valued those times we spent together. That will never change. Please accept my word that I've never used you as a substitute for him – until last night. For that I'm deeply, deeply sorry. I don't expect you to forgive, but please try to understand that we've *both* loved and lost.

Tom had had a disturbed night after an in-depth session with Cheryl Major, Starr's close friend who had gone with him and Connie to identify the crash victim. She had been very upset, crying the whole way back to the base where another of Starr's friends had been baby-sitting the Major children. Both women had mounted a case for Starr, claiming she had been forced to become the dominant partner because Flip was such a wimp.

Tom had pointed out that Keane had achieved rank and was an excellent soldier, which was hardly indicative of wimpishness. They had both sneered and maintained his refusal to leave the Army was because he knew he would be totally pathetic as a civilian. They rounded off their tirade of contempt by revealing that he had been sleeping on the sofa because Starr had wanted another baby and he could no longer get it up.

Neither of them knew where their friend had left her children. The best they could come up with was the fact that Starr had an old friend who had married a German bookseller, and now lived with him outside the base. They could offer no more on the subject, and echoed Tom's belief that whoever had the youngsters would call in once they realized Starr was long overdue to collect them.

About to go to bed, Tom had then taken a call from George Maddox which added a further slant to the case and prevented sleep for more than an hour. Starr's family had been informed of her death, and of Keane's. Her mother had lost control and said a number of wild things: Starr had called saying she had something important to do before coming home for good; *she was leaving the bastard and suing for divorce; she was going to take him for every penny he earned and get a court order to prevent him from seeing the kids. That would punish him for what he'd done.* Now her poor girl would be unable to get her revenge on him.

Gloria Walpole stated that she was coming immediately to Germany with her two sons to collect Prince and Melody. She had been deaf to warnings that the children would be put into foster care by the British Forces Welfare Services until their future was decided in court. The woman had then let fly invective, stating that if anyone tried to keep her grandchildren from her they would be very sorry. When it had been pointed out to her that there was another pair who might be eager to claim their grandchildren, Gloria had demonstrated surprising shrewdness. Flip had died first, therefore the kids had belonged solely to Starr when she was killed. That surely gave *her* full rights to them. The Keanes were nowhere in the picture.

Tom had lain awake knowing they could not prevent the woman and her two truckie sons arriving to further complicate the case, and he wished the hours away until whoever Starr had left her little ones with contacted the base. As a policeman he was concerned for their safety; as a father he felt pity for the young orphans.

Weekday breakfasts during term time were noisy and busy. Tom always descended first to the kitchen leaving, as he had once said to Max, four females of varying sizes and in varying states of undress to wander back and forth to the bathroom moaning, groaning and generally being feminine.

As usual, Nora sensed his mood, but there was no opportunity for discussion between them and Tom was keen to reach his office. There was a lot to cover today, and the returning members of the Royal Cumberland Rifles could well be heading off to the UK or to a European destination before they could be interviewed.

Driving to Section Headquarters, Tom reminded himself that the problem of Starr and her children must not obscure the fact that they had a murder investigation on their hands. He needed to read through the reports submitted so far, familiarize himself with the salient points.

Only when he started on this did it come home to him with a jolt that no more than thirty-six hours had passed since George had woken him to report the discovery of Keane's body. 26 Section had been bloody busy during that short time!

He had set noon today for a meeting to collate his team's reports, before deciding on further action this afternoon. Connie was set to bring in Ryan Moore for more intense questioning about his friend Keane's private life, although Tom did not support Max's belief in some kind of criminal link to the killing.

Heather was tasked to seek out and interview four of those officers who had acted as jousting knights: he planned to tackle the remaining four, among whom was Lieutenant Sears who had insisted on keeping the tank full overnight. A knight in armour riding around after dark would have been up to mischief of some kind. The team needed to know the identity of that knight, and the nature of his mischief.

Hearing someone enter the building and approach along the corridor, Tom glanced up to see Max enter the office. Swallowing the comment he meant to make, after seeing the expression on the other's face, Tom got to his feet in silence instead.

'The two-week tour has been cancelled, by mutual consent, so I'll defer my leave for a while and get stuck into this murder case.'

Knowing enough about his friend not to probe a relationship which had clearly come to an end, Tom said, 'Glad to have you aboard. Let's have coffee while I fill you in on what's come in overnight.'

Now Max was officially in command Tom privately admitted that it was good to have his sharp brain working alongside his own. He knew he could have sorted the tangled facts and produced a satisfactory resolution, as he had done on several occasions during his career, but working in harness with Max was more energizing because he frequently pursued what the team referred to as WGs. Once or twice these had borne fruit. More often they had proved to be no more than wild geese.

After updating him, Tom was surprised by Max's dismissal of his own earlier theory that Keane had been involved in criminal activity and had paid the price of duplicity. Munching a chocolate digestive he instead gave his opinion based on what he knew so far.

'Sex is behind this, Tom. Stands out a mile ... if you'll pardon the gross exaggeration. Keane liked his bits on the side and the itinerant army life gave him plenty of opportunities for unfaithfulness. No way would he sacrifice that for a settled civilian job, living in a small semi with a weighty mortgage and the wife's eagle eye recording his every coming and going.'

'To say nothing of her aggressive family on his doorstep.'

'Precisely. Looking at that scenario in reverse, it would be Starr's ideal solution to a wandering husband. She wanted more children, and it's easy to guess her aspirations. A house they could call their own and do what they liked with; a man whose regular working hours he'd be unable to change without a solid alibi. There'd be no furtive shagging on the way home, no overnight sessions with the boss's secretary. He'd be well and truly shackled to a domineering wife and a clutch of noisy kids. Poor bastard! No wonder he refused to leave a profession that provided a gratifying escape from his personal life.'

Taken aback by the ferocity with which this had been said, Tom was forced to protest. 'She apparently kept the house very clean, and the kids were well looked after. We've known situations where the wife was a slag, the house had to be gone over by the sanitary guys, and the kids were filthy and neglected. Keane had it good, by comparison.'

'I wonder if any of his friends tried to point that out to him.'

'Connie's bringing in Corporal Moore, Keane's main buddy. Simpson reckoned he knows more than he gave out to him yesterday. I've called a meeting at noon. She'll have more to report on that.'

Max got to his feet, holding his empty mug. 'Then there's this business of pots of herbal remedies in the Keanes' bathroom. The woman I saw at the hospital would have been quite a decent looker. Outsize, but attractive. She was either a nutter about her image, or those potions, ointment – whatever – were his, not hers.'

Tom grinned as he followed Max to the bench where they made more coffee. This sounded like a wild gosling. 'I've never seen Starr, but Keane's body was firm and muscular; nothing to suggest he'd need a shelf full of enhancers. They were hers, all right. You know what women are like. They'll buy anything that claims to turn them into a replica of Cheryl Cole.'

'Who's she?' asked Max, pouring hot water into their mugs.

'No idea, but my girls all want to be her.'

'Not Nora?'

Tom took up his full mug. 'She has more sense. Besides, she's hooked me so she's no need to fish around for a better catch.'

Even as he said it, Tom realized it was not the most tactful joking comment to make on this particular morning. That was confirmed when Max failed to reply in kind and walked back to his chair, his shoulders rigid with tension.

'Then there's the fact that Keane was wearing only underpants. I don't believe the killer removed his corpse's outer clothes before putting him in the tank, so we have to work on the assumption that he was with one of his ladyfriends when he died. Sex, you see, is linked to everything in this case.'

'Even the jellyfish?'

Max nodded. 'Near strangulation is used by the sexual

dilettanti as an orgasmic enhancer, as you know, and sometimes it accidentally kills a participant. That's what we have to look for here.'

'Not the straightforward choking to death in a momentary loss of control?'

'Of course, and the straightforward choking to death with cold deliberation.' He got to his feet. 'I'm going to seek out our old friend Ben Steele and get his views on Keane, who was in his company. Back at noon.'

Tom watched Max walk from the building and sighed. The split might well have been mutual, but it was certainly not amicable or he would not be so tightly wound he could easily snap. What had brought such a sudden, drastic end to a relationship any sane person could see was certain to result in disaster? Sadly, Max appeared to have been deeply committed for the first time since the death of his wife Susan, so it was a second heavy blow for him to sustain. He gathered up the spread case reports and locked them in his desk drawer, then left the office to go and talk to four pseudo knights about possible nocturnal wandering.

Lieutenant John Sears was in his office frowning at a computer when Tom knocked on the open door and asked permission to enter. The frown remained as the officer registered the identity of his visitor.

'Still worrying about that tank, Mr Black?'

Taking several steps into the office, he said, 'No, sir, we have a witness sighting of a knight riding a horse around the base late on Saturday night. I'm checking on the movements of all eight riders who participated in the jousting. Would you tell me what you did at the end of the Open Day?'

The frown deepened. 'I told you that yesterday.'

'Concerning the tank, but not your routine regarding the horses and accoutrements. Who procured them?'

'Horses or *accoutrements*?'

He was going out of his way to be obstructive and Tom wondered how soon he would get the chance to puncture this man's inflated sense of importance. 'I know about the horses; some are privately owned and the rest are on the strength and used mainly for ceremonial events. I haven't before had cause to investigate suits of armour,' Tom said crisply. 'That's why I'm after enlightenment on the subject. Were they hired from a fancy dress supplier?'

Sears took exception to that. 'It's clear you know very little about our "Court".'

'Your *court*?'

'On this base there's a shifting nucleus of "knights" who regularly joust. We're all accomplished riders who enjoy the skill required for this medieval style of combat. We use blunt lances, of course, and because we do this purely as a sport – much like those cavalry regiments who still enjoy tent-pegging and splitting melons at the gallop – we wear padding to prevent injury when falling.

'Whenever we give a display, as we did on Saturday, we each wear a tabard bearing our personal emblem of chivalry over a hauberk – that's chain mail, Sar'nt Major, not a suit of armour – and our horses are fully comparisoned with our colours.'

Tom was starting to be amused by this man's fulsome description of mounted gallantry, feeling certain he would make light of, or not even mention, his highly dangerous work during his recent deployment in Afghanistan.

'Where's all the fancy dress kept, sir?'

Sears looked irritated. 'The heraldic vestments are hung in a cupboard at the QM Stores. When there's a top-flight do held at any of the Messes we're asked to provide two knights to flank the main doors. It impresses civilians. So all our equipment is listed as military supplies.'

Deciding he had heard enough about medieval pomp, Tom asked, 'What happened to it at the end of the afternoon?'

The subaltern lay back in his chair. 'We left it in the pavilion where we dressed and rested between each contest.'

'So it would have been possible for someone to get hold of it for their own purposes that evening?'

'If they did so before it was collected and returned to Stores.' His eyes narrowed. 'What are you getting at, Mr Black?'

'We have a witness who saw a knight riding through the base at twenty-three thirty. Would you tell me what you did between the end of the jousting and midnight, sir?'

Sears regarded Tom with a return of disparagement. 'I took a long shower, dressed in jeans to stable my horse, checked the guys at the water tank, drove home, played with my little girl, ate a meal, sat in the garden while my wife weeded, linked up with my sister in Oz on Skype, phoned my parents, read two chapters of *Churchill's War Years*, went to bed. At no time did I ride around the base dressed as Sir Bloody Lancelot.' He sat upright again. 'If that's all, I have two promotion assessments to write before fourteen hundred.' He turned his attention back to the computer, effectively dismissing Tom.

Corporal Ryan Moore strongly resisted Connie's demand that he should go with her to Section Headquarters for questioning. She found him at home cradling the son who was born while he was in Afghanistan, expertly feeding the baby while reading a fairy story to twin toddlers seated on the floor by his chair. Very much a family man delighted to be back with them after six months in the desert.

'I already told Sar'nt Simpson all I know about Flip Keane,' he protested. 'We came home, handed in our kit, had the usual debrief, celebrated with a booze-up and went our separate ways. I never saw him after that. On Saturday these two charmers at my feet wanted to see what was going on and have some fun. So my missus took them out and had some fun herself while I looked after this little chap.' He appealed to her. 'First time I saw him just a few days ago. Thought Jean was going to lose him at one stage, but he wasn't going to miss out on something good and here he is, fully fit and raring to go.'

This obvious delight in his new son swayed Connie into dropping her insistence on interviewing him at Headquarters, but she used his tender mood to her advantage. Deprived of the fairy story, the curly-haired girls got up and ran out to the garden where their mother was pegging out her washing.

Once they had gone, Moore said, 'Flip was my best

mate. No way would I have done for him.'

Connie smiled. 'You're not being accused of anything.'

'Then why're you nagging me like this?'

'Because you *were* his best mate. You know more about Flip Keane than anyone. He would have told you things only mates tell each other about their wives or girlfriends, about their problems with sex, about fears of a medical condition, about mounting debts. Even about a dread of going into action. Isn't that true?' she prompted gently.

Moore's relaxed attitude vanished. His square freckled features tightened, his greenish eyes darkened with anger. 'Flip was no coward. Whoever said he was is a bloody liar.'

Retaining her gentle tone, Connie reassured him. 'We've been told about how he brought his men safely from an ambush. That's not the action of a coward. There was simply a reference to Flip's very real edginess during the first few weeks of your deployment, which could have been construed as reluctance to face possible danger.'

'They're bloody liars,' he repeated, pulling the teat of the empty bottle from the sleeping baby's mouth.

'He *wasn't* worried or anxious out there?'

'No! He was . . . look, it had nothing to do with . . .' In some agitation, Moore got to his feet and walked through to the kitchen where his wife was being bombarded with demands for milk and biscuits by her daughters. Handing the baby to her with a few quiet words, he then returned to the room where Connie had settled in a chair, and shut the connecting door. Minus a suckling baby he looked tough and aggressive in patched jeans and a new T-shirt across which was emblazoned in bright blue HERE'S LOOKING AT YOU, KID.

Connie addressed his back as he gazed from the patio doors, his entire body tense. 'You were saying that Flip's anxiety had nothing to do with being in a warzone.'

It was a while before he spoke, anger in every word. 'You're right about mates telling each other things they wouldn't want made public. The same applies when they're dead. In fact, that's worse because they're not here to speak up for themselves. What right have you to question me about him?'

She knew she was getting to him emotionally and continued to use a calm, friendly tone. 'As an infantryman you know precisely what your job entails; as a corporal you have a responsibility to your platoon. As a military policewoman I know precisely what my job entails; as a *detective* I have a responsibility to get justice for a brave man whose life has just been taken by a vicious killer.' She paused to let that sink in. 'If you know something that would help me do that for your best mate, refusing to tell me is a bigger betrayal than revealing it.' After another pause, she asked, 'Why was Flip worried and forever phoning home during those first weeks?'

'It's not relevant.'

'*Why*, Ryan?' she repeated with gentle insistence.

She sat through his silence, hearing children's voices and a short burst of an infant's fretful grizzling in the adjacent kitchen. Maybe it was these sounds that weakened him, caused the tenseness to leave his body, soften his voice.

'He met Brenda in Iraq. She was *the one*! I thought it was because she helped him through that blue on blue fiasco, but he swore she was everything he had ever wanted . . . and he'd played around a lot. They were all set to get married when she finished her stint over there two months after we came back.'

He turned into the room and perched on the arm of a chair, looking at the carpet and speaking as he would to just a sympathetic woman. 'Once he was back here, he got stressed out again about what had happened. Couldn't get it out of his mind, even though it had been sorted. He went on leave to the UK and the Walpoles descended on him. The whole family! There was Starr waving the baby at him, her mother shouting rape, and the brothers inviting him to come out and get sorted.

'His parents are churchgoers – had Flip late in life – so they put pressure on him to make Starr an honest woman and accept his responsibilities to his child. Between them they piled stress on stress which, along with his bloody stupid guilt trip, tipped the balance. He believed he was not good enough for Brenda, ended the relationship and allowed the Walpoles to march him down the aisle.'

At that point he slid from the arm into the chair and glanced at Connie, suppressed grief for his lost friend now released. 'After a coupla years Starr had had enough and wanted him out. Gave him hell when we were on standby for Afghanistan.' He stared at his linked hands between his knees. 'That's when he told me he'd been seeing Brenda again and she was pregnant. He was going to tell Starr when we got back after the six months; get a divorce.

'For those first weeks he was strung out about having to fire to kill; kept calling Brenda for reassurance like she gave him before. Then he pulled them out of that ambush and he was fine. Those last four months he was strutting around like the cock of the farmyard, so full of himself his platoon wondered if he'd been taking something on the quiet.' He gave a strained smile. 'Brenda had told him the kid was a boy, due about the time we'd get back here. He was that wound up on the flight home, wondering if she'd had the baby and everything was fine. At the airport he gets a text saying she'd gone into labour, then he jumps down from the bus to find that fat bitch waiting for him with her two kids, whingeing about leaving the Army like he promised.'

He suddenly lost the fight for control. Doubling up, shoulders heaving, he said with difficulty, 'Daft bugger sees to the Taliban, then goes out like that before he can sort everything the way he wants, at last.'

SIX

Heather Johnson had to drive to the other extremity of the base to interview the third of her four mounted suspects. Lieutenant Melanie Dunstan, one of the two female knights, served with the Intelligence Corps, which operated from a small block of offices similar to SIB's. Half expecting her to be the product of a county set who all lived in large houses with stables attached, people as much at home on a horse as in a 4x4, Heather was surprised to meet an unpretentious daughter of a market gardener, who spoke with an attractive Cornish burr.

Tall and bony, with a cap of smooth tawny hair she greeted Heather with some puzzlement. 'Something you think I can help with, Sergeant?'

'I'm just checking out a witness statement, ma'am,' she replied, envious of this young woman's colouring. The one time she had dyed her hair a rich red it had caused so many tiresome comments from colleagues and interviewees she had felt her authority was being undermined. It was now back to its natural shade akin to that of peanut butter.

The subaltern waved at a chair. 'Have a seat. How does this witness statement concern me? Oh, one of my staff, I guess.'

Heather shook her head. 'A knight in armour was seen riding in the vicinity of the Sports Ground around twenty-three hundred on Saturday. We're checking with the eight people who participated in the jousting displays so that we can eliminate them from our investigation into the murder of Corporal Philip Keane.' She held her pencil poised above her notebook. 'Would you tell me your movements after the displays ended?'

With a slight frown Mel Dunstan said, 'I took a shower in the pavilion, then rode Jetset, my own horse, to the stables where I rubbed him down and gave him his feed. Then

I had my own feed in the Mess. Jousting takes a lot of energy. The shields are bloody heavy, and when your lance hits the opponent's at the gallop it sends a jolt up your arm.'

Studying the woman's slender build and very evident weariness, Heather could not help asking why she had volunteered for something so strenuous. 'I thought jousting was a male thing.'

'As a rule it is, but Staff Fuller is a champion eventer and a truly awesome rider who persuaded me to join the "Court" when she saw my ability in the saddle. There were three women members, so I was talked into joining to even the number. Of course, membership is constantly fluctuating – the men mostly because of re-deployment – but there are enough to keep it going. We don't tilt at the men, and our weapons are less weighty, but we get satisfaction and as much enjoyment as they do from the ancient art. I love the histrionic aspect of it; the chivalry.'

Her face had become flushed with zeal. 'It was open combat with set rules. Knights knew their enemy and fought him with honour.' After a short silence, she said heavily, 'Warfare is now sneaky and *dishonourable*.'

Heather was curious. 'Why become part of it, then?'

'I'm not. Not in the way you mean, Sergeant. My job is to discover who our enemies are, and to interpret their intentions. In short, I work to provide an even playing field for our soldiers. Track down what they're up against.'

This woman must be well able to hold her own among male colleagues. Brainy, too, Heather reasoned. A personality to be reckoned with.

'So you packed up at eighteen hundred?'

'About an hour earlier. We'd all had enough, and people were starting to drift away.'

'According to the programme, the jousting was to take place during three sessions. What did you do during the breaks between those sessions?'

The other woman leaned back, folding her arms. 'Sergeant Johnson, are you regarding me as a murder suspect?'

'As I said earlier, ma'am, we're questioning everyone

involved in the jousting to discover who might have been riding around in that guise just before midnight.'

'Some joker, obviously. Have you yet spoken to Staff Collyns? That sounds about his level.'

'He's next on my list.'

'Then you'll see what I mean.'

Heather merely nodded a response to that. 'So would you tell me what you did between the jousting sessions, particularly during the break from noon to fourteen hundred?'

The hardness in those large brown eyes became shrewd speculation. 'The time when Keane was killed? I discarded the heraldic gear, took a shower, ate some sandwiches and fruit, read a book.'

'Where was this, ma'am?'

'In my room, and no one can confirm that. Even if I was the type to have a swift shag in lieu of lunch, I was too exhausted to do more than lie on my bed and relax. Alone. Sorry, Sergeant!'

It was a commonly held belief by many regiments that I Corps personnel were too clever for their own good, and Heather began to feel that way about this self-assured officer who owned a horse called Jetset and was not the type to have a swift shag when the opportunity arose. It would be worth studying Mel Dunstan's service record before the noon briefing, not that it would mention that she had a low opinion of men and might, perhaps, be into more than friendship with Staff Sergeant Fuller, the champion persuader.

'And after your dinner in the Mess, ma'am?'

'Ah, this'll look good in that notebook of yours. I went to check on Jetset in the stables; stayed there talking to Staff Fuller about the race meeting next month when she should carry off the trophy from beneath the nose of John Sears, who's boasting of his success on the track. It'll be interesting. His Section arrived here from Afghanistan just two months ago, so we've had no chance to see him in action.' She gave a grim smile. 'But neither has he had advance proof of Sheila Fuller's superb horsemanship.'

'How long have you both been on the base?'

'Fuller's been here more than a year. I joined the Section five months ago.'

Heather returned to the subject Mel Dunstan seemed to be adroitly avoiding. 'What time did you leave the stables following your discussion on the races?'

'Mmmm,' she pondered, 'must have been around twenty-two thirty. I had no reason to record the exact time.'

'And then?'

'And *then*,' she repeated with mock drama. 'And then I caught up on my emails, made a couple of phone calls, had a long, luxurious bath to ease my aching limbs, went to bed with a book. You can check the phone calls etcetera, but nobody can confirm my bath and bedtime reading, I'm afraid.'

Heather closed her notebook. 'You'll be surprised. We manage to get verification of most things. Someone could have found your room empty and, seeing a light beneath the bathroom door, guessed who was in there. Someone passing might have identified the scent of your usual talc or shampoo. We'll possibly find someone who spotted your backview as you entered the bathroom.'

The shrewd speculative quality returned to the woman's eyes. 'You mean to interview all the residents of the Mess?'

'If we have to. One more question. When you checked out Jetset were any of the horses missing from the stables?'

'Sorry, Sergeant, I don't have your investigative drive. Can't help you there.'

Heather prepared to leave. 'Sar'nt Major Black will be talking to Staff Fuller this morning. Let's hope she noticed an equine absentee during your evening meeting at the stables. There are a set number of horses on the base and somebody was seen riding one across the Sports Ground at twenty-three hundred, which means there would have been an empty stall at around the time you were there.'

'Identify the horse, identify the rider?'

'Not necessarily, ma'am. My investigative drive will have to discover who was wearing the disguise. If it was to carry

out a joke, a lark, all well and good. If not, it's unlikely
the rider would have been careless enough to take his, or
her, own horse.'

Having been told that Captain Steele was running at the
Sports Ground, Max drove to it via the longest way around
the perimeter road hoping to psych himself up into
conducting a professional interview. Anger, a deep sense
of humiliation, ruled him. It was intensified by the unpalat-
able fact that Susan had also lusted after another man, and
had died in a car with him at the wheel.

His mouth twisted with painful cynicism. Livya had
rejected him for a brigadier rather than a corporal, at least
aiming higher than Susan. Should that soften the blow of
betrayal? No, it bloody well did not! The only difference
was that the corporal had given Susan what she wanted,
whereas Livya lusted in vain. Andrew Rydal was charming
and charismatic, but Max was certain he had never given
his ADC the least sign that he returned her adoration. So
she had tried to make do with the younger Rydal . . . but
he had not reached an acceptable replacement standard.

Realizing he had just driven past his destination Max
made a three-point turn, parked the car, counted to ten, then
headed for the stand overlooking the running track in the
centre of which were a long jump sandpit and other equipment for field events regularly held there. There were half
a dozen runners presently on the track, three of them women.

Spotting Ben Steele on the far side of it, Max walked to
where the white enclosing rails left a wide gap allowing
access from the changing rooms. A selection of towels and
coloured sweatshirts hung there, deposited by the runners
after their initial warm-up exercises.

Keeping his eye on Ben, Max reflected that this kind of
running had never appealed to him. Constantly circling a
prepared track would surely be utterly boring. When he ran,
which was fairly often, Max drove to the upper reaches of
the river and jogged over meadows, through a copse and
along the overgrown towpath now used solely by ramblers
and runners.

Clare Goodey had once pointed out that he appeared to indulge only in sports he could enjoy on his own – rowing, trekking and cross-country running. It had been said on the evening when he had impulsively spoken of the problems surrounding his relationship with Livya, and later regretted. He had also confessed his reason for shunning team sports. Andrew Rydal was a superb all-round sportsman, so his son had been expected to emulate his prowess. After a series of slightly less than perfect performances the youthful Max had decided to concentrate on activities that he could enjoy without spectators urging him to match his father's excellence. No, entering races on a track like this one would be certain to have him invariably coming second instead of the expected first.

Ben Steele recognized Max as he neared, and he slowed to a halt with a smile of greeting. 'Hallo. Guessed I'd be seeing you sooner or later.'

'Sorry to interrupt your dedicated pounding, but it is rather urgent.'

Snatching a towel from the rail, Ben mopped his face and neck. 'Interrupt away! No dedication involved. Just finding it difficult to ease down into normal life after six months of pretty high tension.' He pulled on a red sweatshirt, saying, 'Give me ten and I'll join you in the canteen for coffee.'

Max was soon facing a refreshed, casually dressed younger man with damp dark hair struggling to spring into curl in spite of ruthless combing. He liked Ben, had actually been instrumental in saving him from an official reprimand for involving himself in a serious case SIB had been investigating.

'You've been promoted since we last met up, Ben.'

He grinned. 'A week before we flew out there. Typical military timing! Make a man commander of a company just as it's going into action.'

'Better that than taking it over because the other guy's been killed.'

Ben's grin faded. 'You want to talk about Flip Keane, of course.' He made hand signals to the girl behind the bar for two coffees, then turned back to Max. 'When I first joined B Company he was a lance corporal, and I knew right away he was likely to go fast up the ladder. Good team guy with sound common sense and bags of courage. Only minus was his weakness for women. He never let it interfere with duty, but I'm wary of soldiers who habitually play around. Sooner or later they land themselves in a messy situation which affects their efficiency, and that can put lives at risk.'

'Keane was guilty of that?'

The girl brought their coffees, smiled warmly at Ben and told him in German that the biscuits in the saucers were a gift from her. Ben's colour rose slightly as he thanked her.

'What was that you were saying about weakness for women?' asked Max dryly.

Ben gave a self-conscious laugh. 'I lifted some heavy crates for her once, that's all. To get back to your question, Keane never put lives at risk over his amours but he did become serious over a nurse when we were in Iraq. She was in the Territorials and came out for four months with reinforcements for the field hospitals. He haunted the place. I mean, he was really deeply committed to her.'

'Brenda?'

'Oh, you know all this already.'

'No. All we have is a name beneath a butterfly tattoo on his buttocks.'

Ben grimaced. 'We all express our feelings in different ways, I guess. If she knew about it she clearly didn't take offence, because she was as serious as he. She certainly supplied the support he needed after the blue on blue fiasco.'

Max remained silent, sensing that his companion was mentally elsewhere as he gazed into the past.

'We were on a night patrol. My first experience of real warfare as a platoon commander. We were all keyed-up; imagined dark figures moving wherever we looked. Suddenly, it was no longer imagination. Four men wearing Arab dress were moving stealthily on a parallel route a hundred yards away. They were sitting ducks. We outnumbered them four to one. I told the guys to seek cover before opening fire and, as soon as we dropped behind a rise in the ground, Keane let fly. The leading hostile went down, a perfect target. We all began firing seconds later.'

Ben's forehead creased with unhappy recollection. 'The remaining three targets dropped flat and I was appalled to see that day's identification signal pierce the darkness. It suggested we had ambushed some of our own guys, yet we'd been given no intelligence of friendly forces operating in the area we were tasked to cover. I swiftly ordered a ceasefire and waited for a response to my own signal. None came, and I realized that in that confused moment the dark figures on the sand had slipped away. I contacted base with a sitrep. Five minutes later my patrol was called in.'

Max was intrigued by this revelation. 'You were ordered to abandon the patrol?'

'That's right. The men were held in a room while I was questioned by Major Quail, who was in command of operations that night. He agreed there had been no info on other forces moving in that area, but he said there had been a request for a casevac helo to collect a body.

'My men and I were then grilled for two hours by SIB before Keane was hauled off under suspicion of manslaughter by friendly fire. I was forced to confess, along with the majority of the guys, that Keane had fired before I gave the order, which put me in a bad light for not having full control over my men. All the same, I insisted that the four we saw appeared to be hostiles and we had attacked in good faith until the identification signal was given. I demanded a full inquiry to ascertain why we had not been alerted to friendlies in the same area, but I was told by your colleagues to keep my tongue between my teeth. We were all forbidden to speak about the incident to anyone, and sleeping bags were brought for us to the room in which we had been interrogated. Breakfast was also brought there.'

'How long were you kept incommunicado?' Max asked briskly.

Ben leaned back in his chair and surveyed Max candidly. 'Your colleagues out there had to eat humble pie. Around mid-morning they brought Keane back, cleared of any charge. Turned out we *had* attacked ragheads, who had somehow got their hands on some of our equipment and knew the identification code for that day. SIB had shifted their attention to discovering who among the locals we employed there was in league with the enemy.'

Max returned the candid look. 'We get things wrong occasionally, like everyone else. How was Keane after that?'

'He took it badly.' Ben glanced up at the waitress who had come to rebuke him for letting his coffee grow cold and to offer to bring fresh supplies. '*Ja, bitte.*'

She took up the two large cups and walked away with waggling hips. The lure was wasted. Ben was looking at Max. 'Yes, I have to admit Keane was badly shaken having for nine hours believed he'd killed one of ours. Well, we were all somewhat subdued.' He flushed slightly. 'I felt responsible; should have prevented it somehow. Keane's close friend Ryan Moore did his best to get him back on track, but it was Brenda who succeeded by assuring him that no casualties had been brought in that night, dead or wounded. Her nursing training would have taught her how to deal with people under stress.' He gave a faint smile. 'Her understanding at that time sealed his devotion to her. Male patient falling in love with his nurse? I guess so.'

'Yet he married another woman.'

Ben sighed. 'Ye-es. Brenda was still in Iraq when we left. I'm sure it wasn't a case of out of sight out of mind, but he was unsettled without her and when he was faced with the child he'd fathered before he met her he turned all noble, would you believe? Said he wasn't worthy of Brenda, didn't deserve such a wonderful woman – that kind of nonsense. It's my personal opinion that he was still so unsettled by that night patrol fiasco he didn't have the strength of character to defy Starr. Phew, a real steamroller of a woman, Max.'

'She's dead. Killed in a pile-up on the autobahn yesterday.'

Ben was genuinely shocked. 'Oh, God, *both* of them?'

'We don't yet know the exact circumstances of the accident. There could be no connection between the two deaths.'

Fresh coffee was brought, along with fresh biscuits, and they drank in silence until the girl wandered disconsolately back to the bar. Max then broached the subject he had initially wanted to discuss with Ben.

'Any ideas of who might have wanted Keane out of the way? Had Keane become involved in a personal conflict serious enough to result in murder? Had he possibly lost his nerve and put a colleague in harm's way?'

Ben was shaking his head before Max finished speaking. 'I'll admit he was clearly on edge for the first three or four weeks of our recent deployment in Afghanistan, but once he had been in action and had successfully brought his team safely from an ambush he was, if anything, an even better soldier. For the major part of the stint he was on top form. Certainly not a man about to satisfy his wife's demand that he leave the Army. His murder is an undeniable blow.' He raised both hands, palms upturned. 'You sign on knowing you could be putting your life on the line, but *that*! What a tragic end for a bloody good soldier.'

The briefing at noon was fruitful. A deal of valuable information had been gleaned and needed to be sifted. Each member of the team either added or discarded a piece of the jigsaw to leave an accurate partial picture. Piercey had interviewed the clowns and been told that one of the fancy outfits had been borrowed to surprise a wife at her birthday supper.

'Seems this woman follows her daily horoscope, and Saturday's prediction mentioned admiration from a tall stranger at a romantic gathering.' Piercey grinned. 'So the guy puts on the outfit, walks in with a big box of chocs and starts kissing her like nobody's business in front of the guests. When she recovered from the shock and discovered it was hubby, she ignored him for the rest of the evening. She's still not speaking; didn't appreciate his sense of humour, poor bastard.'

Derek Beeny had reinterviewed Sergeant Figgis, the diver. He had no substantial alibi for Saturday after twenty-three hundred. He had been occupied with his performance at the time of the actual murder, but he could have wound the jellyfish tentacles around the dead body and dumped it in the tank shortly before it was discovered.

'I spoke to all the personnel immediately available and I'd say it's highly unlikely that Figgis is involved. I couldn't see the slightest connection between him and Keane. Yes, the RE Section had been in Afghanistan at the same time as the RCR, but there had been little contact between them. Most of the time the Sappers were out clearing mines. Everyone I interviewed had never met or heard of Corporal Keane. In my opinion that's a blind alley, despite Lieutenant Sears's insistence on keeping the tank filled overnight. He's popular with them all. Saved a couple of guys who wandered on to a minefield and froze, until he cleared a safe path out of it. Takes guts to do that.'

Connie Bush then outlined the conversation she had had with Ryan Moore. 'I soon realized I'd get more from him by questioning him at home when I found him feeding the boy born in his absence, and reading a fairy story to cute twins. He was initially resistant to my probing out of loyalty to his best mate – they had been really close – but once he accepted that telling what he knew would help us get Keane's killer, he cracked.'

She spoke eagerly as she revealed her surprising fact. 'Flip had been seeing Brenda again and had made her pregnant. I think we'll find that it was she he kept calling when he arrived in Afghanistan. He told Ryan he was going to divorce Starr when he got back, then marry Brenda asap. He had a text on the flight home saying Brenda had gone into labour. Ryan knows nothing more. He was too taken up with his girls and the new baby, to say nothing of the wife he hadn't seen for six months.

'We now have a good idea why Flip slept on the sofa, and he could have told Starr about Brenda on Friday evening which caused the row overheard by the neighbour.' Her brow furrowed. 'My only reservation is that all we've been told about larger-than-life Starr suggests the row wasn't violent enough for such a confession, for it would surely have resulted in one of them walking out that night. According to the neighbour it went quiet after the sound of furniture being pushed around, and they were apparently communicating normally at breakfast on Saturday. So what else could have caused the row?'

'If he'd told her about fathering Brenda's child, when Starr so much wanted more kids, she would have half killed him on Friday night,' reasoned Piercey. 'But if he confessed at some time on Saturday it would give her a motive for seeing him off then. We know he was putty in women's hands. What if guilt led him to give Starr one last thrill before telling her he wanted a divorce? Cuddled up to her, he breaks the news. She grabs him round the throat and chokes the words out of him, then realizes he's dead. Panic rules. She sticks a pair of underpants on him because she can no longer stand the sight of his goolies, while she thinks what to do next.

'First she puts the kids in the car and takes them to her friend outside the base, leaving the body at home in bed. Late afternoon, when the locals are drifting out through the main gate, and crowds are still milling around, she drives back and parks the car in a quiet spot until it's dark. She then goes to the house, puts Keane's body in the pushchair and wheels it down the stairs – she's a big woman, don't forget – and out to the car where she tips it on the rear seat. Then she dumps him in the tank.'

'How?' demanded Heather.

Piercey grinned. 'I've done the groundwork. It's up to you to fill in the details.'

With obvious reluctance Tom said, 'The first part is actually a workable scenario. We're told Keane loved his kids, so he could have tried to make the break less painful by softening Starr up for what he meant to tell her before the day ended. It's happened. I knew of a woman who cooked her husband his favourite meal, then had wild sex with him before leaving while he slept off his exhaustion and went abroad with her lover.'

'But *surely* . . .' Heather began.

'I said the *first* part,' said Tom. 'It would explain the death

occurring at lunchtime, and the fact that the corpse wore
only underpants. We've been unable to get evidence of
when either of the Keanes left their house on Saturday, and
I think we've probably ruled out the idea of the body lying
around for another person to find and decide to drop in the
tank – for reasons as yet unknown. The actual murder and
the jellyfish business *have* to be linked.'

'The jellyfish has something to do with Brenda,' observed
Beeny, always quietly thoughtful during discussions. 'I'd
guess because of the butterfly tattoos on Keane, she has a
jellyfish somewhere on her body.'

'How would Starr know about it?' said Heather, making
useful input by questioning every supposition.

'We need to find Brenda,' stated Connie. 'Ryan Moore
only knows her first name. I contacted the maternity unit
at the hospital and several private homes, but no woman
named Brenda had given birth there in the past week. She's
a nurse, so she could have a friend who did the necessary
in her own home. I also contacted the registry, but the birth
hasn't yet been documented.'

'The whole of B Company seems to have known about
the woman, so one of them must be aware of her full name,'
said Tom. 'Failing that we can contact the TA and get the
details of nurses who were in Iraq with the Cumberland
Rifles. There'll be a Brenda among them.'

As that subject appeared to be shelved for the moment,
Heather related her results with the knights. 'The four I
interviewed all denied riding around the base after dark,
but I'd like to check out the I Corps Lieutenant, Melanie
Dunstan. Very sharp, very on the ball. She admits to being
in the stables for an hour shortly before midnight with Staff
Fuller – another knight and on excellent terms with her
boss. How excellent I couldn't decipher, but a reference to
'the sisterhood' could be translated that way. Dunstan can't
prove she left the stables and took a bath before reading in
bed for an hour.

'When I asked for her movements during the lunch break,
she said, "The time when Keane was killed?" How did she
know that? The general belief is that he died in the tank.'

Tom gave a faint smile. 'We've been asking so many people where they were at that time, they've jumped to the correct conclusion. Besides, the orderlies at the Medical Centre know the truth, and info gets leaked and travels round the base like wildfire.'

'I still think she's worthy of further attention, sir. Although she was in the stables at the vital time she didn't notice an empty stall, which I find curious because a horse would have been missing by then. You questioned Staff Fuller. Did she mention that late meeting?'

Tom nodded. 'I asked about an empty stall. She didn't recall seeing one, and justified that by explaining that she had entered by the door nearest to her horse in the adjacent stall to Jetset, owned by Lieutenant Dunstan. The far end of the stables was unlit so she couldn't have noticed there was an animal missing.' He grinned. 'Although she's rather butch, I'd say she's more likely to be in love with her horse than with her boss.

'On the subject of missing horses, there are an established number on the base, and two witnesses saw one of them being ridden across the Sports Ground. Either one of the jousting knights is lying, or some other person laid hands on their gear and then sneaked a horse from its stall without being noticed.'

'And had to return it the same way,' put in Heather.

'Yes. Don't tell me there's another buffoon who wanted to give his wife a birthday surprise by entering on horseback and riding off with her beneath the eyes of bewildered guests.' He nodded at Heather. 'Keep on with that. Check who each of the animals belongs to, then ask the owners some pertinent questions. Also check with the QM when the armour was collected and stored on Saturday evening, and ask if any member of his staff can ride a horse. We might find he's harbouring a joker in his bosom.'

Max had listened to this evidence, waiting for a session with Tom on their own. It was not exactly a wild goose, but it was curious and he wanted Tom's thoughts on it. As Olly Simpson began describing his tussle with the local German telephone authority to get a list of calls made on the Keanes' landline, Max's mobile rang. He walked to his office to take the call from Clare Goodey.

'I've been harassing the hospital authorities on your behalf, and I'm afraid I'm now going to add to the complications of your case, Max.'

'Go ahead.'

'Starr Keane was a user. There was enough cocaine in her system to make her driving erratic to the point of having greatly reduced command of the vehicle.'

'Dear God, she's been transporting her children around.'

'Criminal, isn't it? Any info on where they are?'

'Still waiting for whoever's minding them to call in.'

'Shouldn't be too long now. I'm about to tackle the pathologist about Philip Keane. Let you know soonest.'

'Thanks, Clare.'

A slight pause. 'You can give me dinner beside the river when the case is sewn up.' She disconnected.

Max returned to the Incident Room to find Tom taking a call on the internal line. 'Thanks, George. We'll be on it pronto.'

All eyes were on Tom as he replaced the receiver and said, 'The Keane children are with Starr's friend in Rathausstrasse. George has just taken a call from a worried lady who was expecting them to be picked up this morning. He's informed Families Welfare, who are on the way to collect them.' He indicated Connie and Olly Simpson. 'You two get over there and question Mrs Reiter about Starr's state of mind, her plans for the kids, what she revealed about the situation between her and her husband – anything she can tell you about the last days of Starr Keane's life.'

Before the pair went out Max revealed what Clare had just told him, adding, 'Find out how much this friend knew about the drug taking. Was she the supplier?'

Tom looked fierce. He disliked cases concerning children, and he hated drug addicts. Put the two together and he became almost incandescent in his desire to make the punishment fit the crime. He set Piercey and Beeny to questioning Starr's friends and their husbands for the source of the cocaine. Was it linked to the case they were already pursuing? Follow all leads.

While the team dispersed Max went to make two mugs of coffee. He offered one to Tom, who muttered, 'The evidence is piling up against Starr Keane. She had motive and opportunity, and drug-fuelled rage would easily lead her to choke him to death with her bare hands.' He gulped coffee, eyeing Max over the mug as he drank. 'I'll wager she discovered where Brenda lived and was on her way to give her a taste of the same, when she drove across the autobahn without looking.'

'We should trace Brenda as a matter of urgency. She won't be aware that the father of her new baby is dead,' Max pointed out. 'You told me Starr's mother and duo of beefy brothers are on their way here. If they hear about Brenda, I wouldn't put it beyond possibility for them to have a go at her. She might need protection.'

'I'll get on to the TA Headquarters asap. Once we have her full name we'll contact hospitals, nursing homes and health centres. She must be working locally now.'

Max nodded. 'I'll be in touch with the hospital for a full report on Starr Keane's condition – a document we can use as evidence – and I'll chase up the Veterinary Officer to talk about the horses on base. He might know who else rides them aside from the people taking part in the jousting. We need to know who was on that horse just before midnight. I hope it was not to commit another crime not yet discovered. We've enough on our plate.' He sipped his coffee thoughtfully. 'I've stumbled on something puzzling, Tom. Ben Steele told me his platoon, of which Philip Keane was a member, was involved in a suspected friendly fire incident in Iraq two years ago.'

Tom hit his forehead with the flat of his hand. 'Jeez, Frank Priest mentioned that and I began to follow it up when something developed and it went from my mind because it doesn't connect with this case. What did Ben say about it?'

'Quite a lot. Enough to make me decide to check it out. There's no mention of it on Keane's record.'

Tom frowned. 'Well, Frank said it was a legit attack. SIB withdrew the charge.'

'Ben echoed that, but SIB would have documented the case.'

'And?'

'I went on line, entered the date and details and . . . blank! According to SIB records it never happened.'

Tom stared at him. 'You mean it's been *wiped*?'

'Yes, I think that's what I do mean, Tom.'

SEVEN

As Connie drove to Rathausstrasse she had to listen to a long account of the rise and fall of Spartan power. Olly Simpson's passionate interest in ancient kingdoms found expression during car journeys whether he was driver or passenger. Connie turned down the sound in her right ear and concentrated on the jigsaw of roads that would take her to the apartment where Starr had left her children. George Maddox had alerted the Welfare people, so Connie was not surprised to see a car bearing military registration outside the block of flats.

'They beat us to it,' she commented.

'Who?' asked Olly, returning from the exotic and bloody past.

'Not the Spartans.' She brought the Land Rover to a halt behind the parked car. 'Julia Reiter has climbed several rungs up the property ladder by divorcing her squaddie husband and marrying a local businessman. Sizeable place, by the look of it.'

He grunted. 'Starr should have done the same. Better option than badgering the poor bastard to leave a job he loved.'

The front door was an inch ajar, so Connie rang the bell then walked in. The sound of women's voices and of children crying came from a room at the end of a corridor. Despite the elegance of thick cream carpet, crystal chandelier and gilt-framed oil paintings along the walls, the odour of babies' vomit and urine hung in the air. Connie turned to wrinkle her nose at her companion who appeared not to be affected by it. Maybe Spartan homes smelled worse!

A petite, dark-haired woman clutching two small boys was seated on a pale leather settee to the left of the large square room. She looked deeply distressed; her eyes showed the blankness that comes with a state of shock, and the narrow hands holding the two boys close to her body were shaking. The children looked terrified, too scared to utter a sound. It was the chubby baby sitting unwillingly on the lap of a plain-looking woman in her early thirties who was crying ferociously, holding out her arms towards Julia Reiter while she kicked her fat legs against the woman's knees in her fury. A tall, younger woman standing by the settee turned sharply on growing aware that people had entered the room.

Connie spoke quickly, showing her identity document. 'Sergeants Bush and Simpson, SIB. Who are you?'

The woman made introductions, and the Keane boy, Prince, was identified. 'Our task is to take him and Melody into care, but we only arrived five minutes ago and Mrs Reiter is, of course, very shaken by what we had to tell her about her friend.'

'My colleague and I need to talk to Mrs Reiter about that,' said Olly. 'Perhaps the children could be taken into another room.'

Knowing that would solve nothing in the short term, Connie suggested a cup of tea for Mrs Reiter, with milk and biscuits for the children, might calm things down enough to embark on vital questioning. Addressing the Reiter child, she asked if he could show her where the biscuit or cake tin was in the kitchen. After a few wary moments he edged away from his mother and went across to Connie, followed by Prince who clearly believed safety lay in sticking close to his small friend. The same thought must have been in Olly's mind, for he also went to the kitchen where he kept the boys occupied selecting iced biscuits to arrange on a plate while Connie made tea.

'We can't do our stuff until they've settled everything with Mrs Reiter and taken the kids away,' she murmured to Olly. 'She'll be more receptive with these two out of earshot for a bit.'

It was almost forty-five minutes later before the orphaned pair, Melody thankfully asleep and Prince clutching a toy hippopotamus and a currant bun, were installed in a large saloon car along with two bags containing their clothes and

supplies then driven away. Starr's clothes and toilet arti-
cles remained in the bedroom she had taken over, awaiting
scrutiny for any evidence of relevance to the murder of
Philip Keane.

Julia Reiter was more controlled once her friend's children had left, although she still looked stricken as Connie
sat facing her to ask questions certain to be painful.

'I feel terrible allowing them to be taken away by
strangers,' she confessed, her eyes filling with tears.
'Starr would never forgive me. Or poor Flip.' Her voice
thickened. 'I can't take it in. *Both* of them gone, just
like that!'

'It's the best solution for their children right now,' Connie
said soothingly. 'The Welfare people are trained in how to
handle youngsters who've lost their parents, and you aren't
equipped to keep them indefinitely. Fortunately, they're
both very young. At that age they usually adapt quite
quickly.' She indicated Olly in the far corner. 'See how
trustingly your Bernard is playing games with Sergeant
Simpson so soon after Prince left.'

The woman nodded as she dabbed her eyes with a tissue
from a box beside her, and Connie then asked how long
she had known Starr Keane.

'She was Flip's steady when he and my Harry were at
Tidworth, way back. We'd been married just a few
months and often made a foursome with them at week-
ends. When Flip broke with her – she was Starr Walpole
then – she and I still met for coffee or a matinee at the
local flicks.' A wobbly smile appeared. 'We used to fanta-
size about the male hunks on the screen. It was just a bit
of a giggle.'

'Your husband was happy enough about that? Continuing
to see Starr, I mean.'

'You know what men are like. Anything that keeps their
wives happy so long as it doesn't affect *them*.'

Connie nodded agreement. 'But the foursomes were at
an end?'

'Yes. The lads were in serious training for imminent
deployment to Iraq. Harry simply wanted to crash out on

the sofa with a couple of cans after a hefty meal each evening. Wasn't much fun, I can tell you.'

'You maintained the friendship after the men left for Iraq?'

She nodded. 'I suppose we need companionship much more at those times, although I did go off her a bit when she told me she was pregnant. She was over the moon; said she'd stopped taking the pill so he'd give her a baby. I thought it was unfair on Flip. Trapping him like that. She reckoned the only reason he'd split up with her was because he thought they shouldn't take it any further just as he was going to a warzone.'

Her expression betrayed her cynicism. 'Flip was OK, but he certainly wasn't the *noble* type. Harry told me Flip had had enough of Starr and her pushy, gobby family and used Iraq as a get out. Well, *I* found Ma Walpole and the two bruisers Starr called her brothers more than I could take, to be honest. I usually arranged to meet her in town.' She grimaced. 'A Christmas party at her mum's was the last straw for me. Talk about a free-for-all!'

Connie had the picture well enough and turned to essentials. 'When did Starr tell Flip about the pregnancy?'

'She didn't. And she made me promise not to let on to Harry. Some rubbish about waiting until it was born because she might miscarry like her mum did twice.'

'And you said nothing to your husband?'

Slight colour tinted her pale face at the faint tone of surprise. 'Harry and I had been trying for a baby with no luck. He wouldn't have wanted that kind of news from me while he was out there under stress. Anyway, it was Starr's secret. Not mine to tell.'

'Of course. She didn't miscarry and produced Prince.'

Julia Reiter frowned. 'A lovely healthy baby. I agree Flip had to be told, and that he should take responsibility for his son, but they should never have done what they did when he was just ten days back from Iraq.'

'Oh?' said Connie, knowing what they had done.

'The whole family went round to the Keanes' house and created a scene. At least, that's what Flip told Harry. The neighbours all turned out to see what was going on, which was terrible for the Keanes who're very religious. Next thing, the Walpoles are planning a wedding. Right over the top, it was.'

There was a pause as Julia controlled her excessive emotion once more. Connie glanced at the corner to see Bernard was now asleep on the floor and Olly was on his feet. He inclined his head to signal to Connie that he would go to examine the things Starr had brought with her to the house. She nodded agreement.

'That wedding began the breakup of my marriage,' came the sad comment as Connie turned back to Julia. 'Harry was disgusted with Flip for letting himself be dragooned by that awful family. Apparently, he'd been on the verge of getting engaged to a nurse he met in Iraq. The lads fell out big time over it, and Harry refused to attend the wedding. We had a major wrangle over it and I went more to annoy Harry than anything.'

She sighed deeply. 'Everything went downhill from then on. Harry had lost a good mate, for which he blamed *me*. I was losing my husband because I was sure he was also blaming me for our failure to have a family. Harry was all wound up inside over feelings of inadequacy while his best friend had managed it without even trying. When the battalion was deployed out here I only came with him because I thought we could make a fresh start. Ha, what a hope!'

There was a longer pause, and Julia's box of tissues was raided again. 'I like living in Germany, so I moved to a bedsit and got a job in town. When the divorce was final I married my boss. Bernard is his son, but I think of him as mine.'

Connie smiled. 'He's a charming little boy. So polite over sorting a plate of biscuits. You've remained Starr's friend, Julia?'

'Didn't really have a choice. Don't get me wrong. She can be good fun, and she's marvellous with the kids . . . but . . .'

'You have a new life, fresh interests now?'

'Yes. You know, I'm not part of the Army any longer.'

She hesitated. 'Friedhelm finds her . . . he's a quiet, cultured man, you see.'

'There's a lack of rapport between them?'

Julia nodded.

'So how does your husband feel about this present visit?'

'He's away on business, thank goodness. Starr turned up here without warning in a real state. Said she was leaving Flip because he'd broken his promise to quit the Army when he got back from Afghanistan; said they'd had a serious row and he claimed she disgusted him so much he couldn't sleep with her any more. I thought she'd be upset over that, but she was just frighteningly vindictive. I've never seen her like that before. She said she'd come to me because I'd been through it and knew how men could be utter brutes.'

At that point emotion overwhelmed her. 'She said *that* . . . she . . . had no idea Flip had been *killed* . . . no idea he'd just been murdered, or she'd never have . . .' She peered through tears at Connie. 'It's a nightmare! Who could have done that? Who could have . . . ?'

'That's what we're endeavouring to find out, Julia,' Connie told her gently. 'You can take some comfort from knowing neither of them was ever aware of what had happened to the other.' Allowing a little time for Julia to recover somewhat, she said, 'There was no sign that Starr *did* know what had happened to Flip, was there?'

Julia's head jerked up. 'What? No! No, she . . . *of course* she didn't know. What are you suggesting?'

'What time did Starr arrive here?'

'Er . . . Saturday lunch time.'

'And that was when?'

'I . . . one, one thirty.' The sudden change in Connie's approach had thrown her. 'I wasn't expecting her. I told you that. She had the kids' clothes and food with her; said she needed a couple of nights here to organize everything before going home to her mum. I didn't know what to say. They were all there on the doorstep, waiting to come in.'

'And your husband was fortuitously away for the weekend.'

'Yes. I thought . . . well, Bernard came to the door and,

next minute, Prince was indoors with him. I thought she'd
be on her way to the UK before Friedhelm arrived home,
and there was no way I could refuse to help her, was there?'

'What were those things she had to organize before going
home? Did she tell you?'

'No, but . . . I mean they were splitting up for good,
weren't they? She would have to book flights, draw out
enough cash. Things like that, of course.'

'You had no impression that it had all been planned ahead?'

'They'd had a terrible *row*. You don't plan *that* ahead,
do you?' she cried showing some aggression.

Connie continued to push now annoyance had driven
sentiment to the background. 'You agreed to look after the
children overnight, in the belief that Starr would return this
morning. What did she have to organize that would take
that long? Did she tell you, Julia?'

'Of course. She was going to meet one of her brothers.
They're both long distance lorry drivers on the European
run. Chas had a two-night stopover before the return run,
and Starr wanted his advice and help. They've always been
close, meeting up when either of them travels near enough
to the base. I understood that she wanted some support from
him in her situation, but I thought he might take it into his
head to sort it by taking Flip apart piece . . . by piece,' she
finished slowly. Her hand went to her mouth. 'Dear God,
you don't think . . .'

Max's intention had been to interview the Veterinary Officer
who looked after the horses, the police dogs and any other
animals owned by military personnel, but he instead drove
past the office block housing this man and out through the
main gate. His determination to immerse himself in the
mystery of Keane's death was being undermined by something he needed to get out of his system without delay.

In his apartment he exchanged his white shirt, sober tie,
dark grey jacket and trousers for a navy T-shirt and track-
suit, carelessly flinging the discarded garments down as the
need for physical release grew ever more demanding.

Returning to his car, trainers, water bottle and sweat towel

in his hands, he was soon heading for the quiet solitude of
his regular running circuit. It was fortunate there was no
German police patrol in that area, because he exceeded all
speed limits in his urgency to reach his destination and
punish his body by pushing it to its limits, and beyond.

For the first half hour he ran fast, vaulting stiles and
leaping narrow streams in the drive to keep going. When
his heartbeat became thunderous and the pressure in his
skull mounted, he slowed to his normal pace and took regular
swigs of the glucose drink in the bottle swinging from a
cord around his neck.

When he reached the end of his usual circuit the anger,
the sense of inadequacy, the revived pain of Susan's and
the unborn Alexander's death beside another man had not
been banished, so he ignored his car and started round again.
Halfway along the way he had to acknowledge to himself
that it was impossible to run away from this second act of
betrayal because he would always return to where he had
started.

He sat for a long time behind the wheel, staring into a
darkness scattered with brilliant stars, totally drained of
energy and emotion, until there was no alternative but to
go back. That was it. His plans for a wife, a family and a
real home, at last, had been so much moonshine. He would
never see or speak to her again; never hear her call him
Steve in that husky, intimate tone. It had been unreal.
Goodbye, Livya!

Entering his apartment Max saw, with vague dismay, his
smart working clothes scattered over the bed and floor. By
nature and by his regimented upbringing he was a tidy
person who loathed living in a mess. But his priority was
a long, hot shower. He stood beneath the fierce, pummelling
water until his aching legs threatened to buckle under him,
then he towelled off and donned his bathrobe before padding
barefoot to the kitchen for a can of beer. That should put
the finishing touch to his physical exhaustion and knock
him out cold when his head hit the pillow.

Taking a can from the fridge he became aware of music.
A piano was being played in the connecting room, yet he

knew there was no piano there. Was he imagining things?
Can in hand he took the key from the table where Clare
had left it, and unlocked the door. The large room was
bathed in subdued lighting from wall sconces, and Clare
was sitting at a handsome upright piano playing a haunting,
cascading piece Max did not recognize. She became aware
of him and swung round on the stool.

'Sorry. I thought you were out.' Then she got to her feet
and walked across to him. 'You look terrible.'

In his mentally befuddled state he waved the can in the
direction of the piano. 'Where did *that* come from?'

'I should have asked you before I installed it, but . . .'
Taking the can from his hand she drew him to the long
sofa. 'It's a lengthy story, and I owe you a glass or two of
wine while I tell it.' Pushing him down on to the pale
leather, she fetched a glass from the cabinet and collected
a half-empty one from on top of the piano before bringing
them to the low table where a bottle stood. From it she
filled a glass to give him, and topped up her own.

'As a good neighbour I should have asked your permission before bringing anything into this shared room,'
she said, sinking beside him, 'but I had to make a snap
decision. Drink up!'

He did as he was told because he had no strength to
argue. The wine was chilled, sharp and slid down his throat
very satisfyingly. He drank it all, and watched, bemused
and utterly weary, as she refilled the glass.

'The Chelsea apartment is owned by my husband's stink-
ingly rich family. The furniture, ornaments, paintings, the
lot! Apart from my clothes and personal things the only
item in it that belonged to me was my piano. James always
scoffed because it wasn't a baby grand, but it's valuable
and prized by me for its history.'

'Oh?' he murmured, wondering what she was hinting at
and attacking the second glass of wine in the same way as
the first.

'My grandparents in Liverpool put their valuables in
store at the outbreak of war, but their home remained intact
and the store was hit by a bomb dropped by an aircraft

damaged en route to the target. Amazingly, the dear old piano stood untouched amid the wreckage. My mother inherited it and taught me to play the classics while Dad was away on racing circuits all over the world. It means a lot to me, so my parents gave it to us as a wedding present.'

'Oh,' Max said again, because he thought she expected some kind of comment and what else could he say? Wedding presents were not his scene.

'My in-laws were loftily amused. Amongst the silver, the porcelain and the objets d'art such a gift had to be put in a distant alcove well away from the glittering array on view for the guests. *They* gave us a Merc and a yacht. For James, of course.'

'Of *course*,' echoed Max, starting on his third glass of wine, finding her matter-of-fact tones undemanding.

'When we split up, the piano had to stay put because I was in mess accommodation. Coming to this apartment gives me the first opportunity to move it from Chelsea. James has been entertaining his popsies and other dissolute friends there, and I had fears of cigarettes being stubbed out on my precious instrument, and rings from wet glasses marring its lovingly preserved gloss. That would be a disaster.'

'*Absolutely*,' he agreed solemnly, attempting to nod his head.

'As I said, I would naturally have discussed it with you first, but my divorce should be finalized in a week or so and James emailed me on Friday notifying me that he'd arranged for Pickfords to collect the piano the following morning, and asking for the address it should be delivered to. You were in the UK, so I took a chance on your approval. It turned up just an hour ago.' Topping up their glasses again, Clare said softly, 'I'll only play when I know you're out, so it won't disturb you.'

'S'alright, won't disturb me,' he muttered. 'Like it. The tinkly thing you were playing. Liked it.'

'You mean this?'

She left his side and crossed to the gleaming piano. The cascading notes were very soothing. So was the wine.

Max awoke to find himself on the sofa, a pillow beneath

his head and his own duvet covering him. The sun was just rising.

Tuesday morning and it was unusually quiet in the Black house. Much as he loved his children Tom welcomed this second day of the school week, because the girls had been picked up early by the wife of one of the Corps' dog handlers and driven to the base to check on a litter of puppies before attending school. This was the third week this had happened and their parents knew why and braced themselves for the inevitable plea.

One of the sniffer dogs had become mysteriously pregnant and produced five pups. Her handler swore she had never broken loose from the compound to spend a night on the tiles. His mates caustically reminded him that it took two minutes, not an entire night, so where had he been while the rape was carried out? The fact that the bitch was also recorded as having been spayed added further speculation about the arrival of three bitches and two dog pups during a night a month ago.

Nora voiced her suspicions as she sat with Tom, who was enjoying a rare leisurely breakfast. 'D'you think they'll ask us tonight or wait until the creatures are old enough to leave their mother?'

'Beth will air her passionate knowledge of animals and advise waiting until they're weaned, but Gina won't be able to stand the suspense any longer. Have your answer ready.'

She gave him a sharp look across the breakfast bar. 'Is that your way of passing the buck, chum?'

He raised his hands in an innocent gesture. 'Me? Would I do such a thing?'

'Yes, you've been doing it since the night Maggie was born.'

Buttering another piece of toast, Tom said in oh-so-reasonable tones, '*You're* the one who'll have to clean it up when it poohs in the corner and wees over your slippers. *You'll* have to train it to obey commands. SIT! STAY! COME! *Walkies*,' he ended on a feminine trill before biting into the toast.

'Oh, very amusing! And who'll be hopping mad because

it chews your boots, sheds hairs all over your best suit or refuses to allow you to enter the house when you roll up in the middle of the night, as you're so fond of doing? A dog needs a *master*. If you're not prepared to show it you're the boss, it'll regard you as a threat to me and the girls if you even attempt to touch us.'

He sighed. 'Have a heart. I'm up to my eyes in a case . . .'

'You always are.'

'OK, so we tell them no.'

'*You* tell them no, and *you* win the unpopularity vote of the year.'

He grabbed the cafètiere, saw it was almost empty, then put it down again. 'Look, they haven't asked to have one yet.'

'That's right, slither out of making a decision concerning them.'

It took him by surprise. 'Are you spoiling for a fight? If so, let's go back upstairs and have a good old wrestling match.'

'That's always your answer, isn't it?'

After a moment's thoughtful silence, Tom said, 'Not always, no. The demands of my job and of three lively girls more often than not prevent close encounters of the sexual kind between us.' When she said nothing, he asked, 'Is there something wrong? Something not linked to the adoption of a dog?'

She avoided his eyes. 'I'm just pointing out that a dog will be one more responsibility. After the excitement's worn off it'll be me who remembers to feed it, brush its coat, get it registered and vaccinated, take it for walks, teach it road sense. I don't have much of a life of my own as it is. Taking on a dog . . .'

'We're *not* taking on a dog,' Tom said firmly, 'and *I* will tell them why.' Reaching for her hand across the pseudo-marble, he apologized. 'I was only joshing you just now. I do appreciate how much you do for us all, and how little time you have for the dressmaking sideline you love doing. The last couple of days have been heavy going over the Keane case, but the kids are safe and Max is back, so we

should soon be making headway. Once things quieten down
I'll . . .'

'Has he finally seen sense over that woman?' she asked,
pulling her hand free and getting up to switch on the kettle.

'I'm not sure *sense* is the right word.' He decided to go
along with her abrupt change of subject. 'He looks bloody
tense; jaw working, hands never still. He's certainly seen
something, and it's knocked him for six. I'm fairly sure the
affair is irrevocably over. Don't know how much that'll
affect his input. So far he's been convinced Keane was
murdered by someone he double-crossed over a shady deal,
then he changed that to some kind of kinky sex act that
went wrong. The latest is suspicion of a military cover-up
of an incident in Iraq.'

'What's his theory on the jellyfish?' she asked, tipping
dregs from the cafètiere and rinsing the container.

'Oh, that's the kinky sex that went wrong.'

'Hmm, never heard of that one. Isn't it usually plastic
bags over the head?'

'Maybe jellyfish are the new plastic bags.'

She turned and smiled broadly. '*Co-ool*, as our daughters would say.'

He smiled back. 'Forgiven?'

She nodded. 'More toast?'

'Wasn't there a doughnut left over from yesterday?'

'The forgiveness doesn't stretch that far. I can't have you
developing a paunch.'

'Just the usual stale crust then,' he said in plaintive tones,
knowing the curious little spat was over.

Any reflections on it were banished when he arrived at
Headquarters. Everyone save Max was there and raring to
go. Connie Bush and Olly Simpson had been very busy
following their visit to Rathausstrasse. After outlining the
information given by Julia Reiter, they gave the results of
their follow-up investigations.

'The woman in the apartment above confirmed that Starr
and the children had arrived there around thirteen thirty;
it was the loud voice and babies crying that caused her to
look from her window,' said Connie. 'I suspect she has a

chair permanently beside it. A widow living alone who's smitten with arthritis, what's going on out in the street is her major means of entertainment.'

'Her evidence makes Starr a likely candidate for her husband's murder,' Olly pointed out. 'It would take her half an hour to drive there from the base after she'd got the kids' clothes and food packed ready, so if Keane was killed some time around midday she could have done it just before she quit the house.'

'Yet there was apparently nothing in her manner that suggested to Julia that she'd done anything more than sneak away from the husband she no longer wanted,' said Connie.

'And Starr certainly didn't move the body later that night, because she was with the Reiter woman,' Olly reasoned. 'Incidentally, she had no idea her friend was a user. She was genuinely appalled when we told her.'

'I had a great deal of sympathy for Julia,' Connie admitted. 'Starr dumped herself and her kids uninvited on her, commandeered the landline phone whining to her mother and brothers for the rest of the day, then tootled off to meet the one named Chas the following morning leaving her two-year-old boy and an eight-month baby with someone they hardly knew. Julia was then told this so-called friend was killed in a road accident while she was doped-up to the nines, by two strange women with authorization to take away the children, then we arrived to investigate the murder of Starr's husband. It must have been a nightmare. Pity her husband was away on business.' She studied her notes. 'I checked out Friedhelm Reiter. He buys and sells antique books, first editions, rare copies. I'd say we can disregard him as Starr's supplier. He's fifty-eight, a widower who probably married Julia to gain a mother for the boy he had late in life.'

'Starr's supplier is on-base,' said Piercey expansively.

'You know something we don't?' Connie challenged.

'It's obvious. We know there's some kind of syndicate in operation here. We've been trying to crack it for several weeks. Of course it's on-base.'

'I've checked out Chas Walpole,' offered Olly swiftly.

'In fact, both the brothers drive for the same firm which trades with various companies here and in France. The truckies deliver export goods, then load up with the imported stuff. That way the vehicles never run empty. You've got to be tough for that job. Tough, and very sharp,' he added. 'I ran their pictures past Customs and Immigration on both sides of the Channel. Those lads are well known.'

'Because they're so frequently back and forth?' suggested Heather.

'That, and because they've three times started up serious brawls when the French truckies blocked the roads to ports. The other brother, known fondly as Beefy, was once suspected of bringing illegals into the UK, but when police were alerted and stopped him two hours from Dover, there was no sign of them.' He grinned. 'They're both marked men now and are invariably searched from bonnet to rear doors each time they leave or return.'

Tom interrupted him at that point. 'George Maddox was given to understand that Mrs Walpole and both her sons were on their way, yet one is already here.'

Olly nodded. 'He'll know why his sister didn't meet him by now, and I guess he'll wait for the rest of the family to arrive. One interesting point is that Julia Reiter had the notion that Chas could have done for Keane, but my check showed he was crossing France on Saturday afternoon, so he's off the hook. I toyed with the possibility that the brothers were Starr's supplier, but their vehicles have been taken apart too often by Customs for that to be viable.'

'One last point,' said Connie when she believed her colleague had ended his report. 'Starr told Julia she would return to her house when she knew Flip would be away, because she'd left some things there that she needed to collect on her way home. Home being the UK. Her exact words were, "I've got some posh frocks and stuff that I refuse to let the bugger give to one of his tarts." If she really meant what she said, it's unlikely she'd go to the house if she'd killed him there on Saturday.'

'*My* last point,' stated Olly, with a sideways glance at her, 'is that I checked out Julia's ex, Harry Fortnum. He and

Keane apparently fell out big time over the marriage to Starr, which indirectly led to Fortnum's own marriage ending on the rocks. There was a possible motive there.'

'And?' prompted Tom.

'He was wounded in Afghanistan and shipped home. He's presently at Headley Court learning to use a prosthetic hand.' He grinned again. 'Great aid to strangulation. Pity he was too far away to have done the deed. The Boss could have followed one of his WGs on that.'

'So I could,' said Max, who had entered very quietly.

Tom turned to him. 'Morning, sir. I'll bring you up to speed later. Plenty of interesting info, but no breakthrough yet.'

Max merely nodded and sat astride a chair, leaning on the back of it ready to listen. Tom thought he looked pale and hungover. Drowning his sorrows? With luck, they were ten fathoms deep and unlikely to resurface.

He nodded at Connie and Olly. 'Good work! So we have a situation where timewise Starr could have killed her husband before heading for the friend's place, but would have been unable to dump the body in the tank that night. There's no physical evidence to support a charge of murder, and she can't now be interrogated.'

Piercey glanced up. 'The claim that she'd return to pick up some stuff from her house rings true enough. I saw a few glad rags in the wardrobe that she's unlikely to have abandoned, and there was that row of beauty aids still in the bathroom. Knowing how much that stuff costs she'd have taken it with her to the UK.'

'Right, so we strike her from the list of suspects,' Tom decided.

'Do we *have* a list?' challenged Piercey.

Caught wrong-footed, Tom hastily compiled one. 'The mystery knight . . . and the other truckie brother. Where was he?'

'In Swindon, loading up,' said Olly. 'I checked.'

'And I'm sure the knight was Mel Dunstan,' added Heather swiftly. 'I spent yesterday afternoon checking out her alibi. We know she was at the stables with Staff Fuller on Saturday night, leaving there around twenty-two thirty.

She admits that, and claims she went directly to the Mess where she took a bath, called friends and read a book before sleeping. I've not found one person who had seen her, heard her, or could offer any evidence that she was there at the relevant time. Three women took a bath that night, so Mel's supposed long, luxurious bath must have been well after midnight. When she returned from her ride around the base wearing armour she'd hidden for that purpose,' she concluded darkly.

'She was going for nookie on the quiet,' said Piercey.

'No!' Heather flashed back. 'From my questioning I learned from several people that her fiancé had died in an accident a year or so back. She took her loss badly and hasn't even looked at a man since then.'

'So she was going for nookie with Staff Fuller,' Piercey returned provocatively. 'You said she'd referred to the sisterhood.'

'But she'd been with Fuller in the stables just an hour earlier,' Heather snapped.

'Maybe rolling in the hay isn't their scene.'

'Stop this nursery school squabbling and act like criminal investigators,' roared Tom in true sergeant majors' style. 'They should have put you two on horses, with long poles to jab at each other. I'll suggest it next time.'

Into the ensuing silence, Max said, 'So we have a woman who had access to armour and a horse, whose whereabouts at the time a knight was seen riding around the base is in doubt.'

'And she was alone in her room during the time the actual murder took place, according to her,' Heather added eagerly.

'So we put her at the top of the list.'

Tom felt a twinge of resentment. He had been handling this case from the start; Max had been part-timing throughout whilst officially on leave. Now his woman had ditched him, he aimed to take command having heard only half the evidence. This I Corps woman was going to be his next wild goose, that was clear. Heather, and probably one other member of the team, would be sent in pursuit of it when they should be following up on solid fact.

'We've already established that Lieutenant Dunstan has never before served with Keane. She came here five months ago – after the RCR had departed for Afghanistan – and Keane had been back only six days before he was murdered. She might have had the opportunity to choke the man to death, but what would have been her motive, sir?'

'If the nursery school squabblers start acting like criminal investigators we might find out, Sar'nt Major.'

EIGHT

Phil Piercey was disgruntled and expressed his feelings to his friend and colleague at a mid-morning break in the NAAFI.

'I've been given all the duff jobs on this case, Derek.'

'I've been right there beside you, mate,' said Beeny who, on joining 26 Section, had ruled that he would never answer to Beano or Heinz . . . or to *any* name other than his own. Amazingly, he had got away with it.

'Yes . . . well,' grunted Piercey. 'Connie and Simpson have been working their arses off over those truckies and a Jerry bookseller when it's obvious the dealer must be on the base. The Keane woman's just one user. There's a dozen more among the squaddies, you bet, so why all that time and effort checking out Starr's UK family? Eh? Tell me why.'

Beeny, the more placid of the pair, began on his apple turnover. 'They were just being thorough.'

'Huh! Busy earning Brownie points, you mean. "Good work", smarms Blackie with a smile. Then Squat Johnson gets the Boss all excited over some I Corps sub who owns a horse and speaks with a plum in her mouth.'

'You're wrong there, Phil,' he returned through a mixture of apple and pastry. 'Heather told me she comes from your part of the world and speaks the way you do – like a Cornish farmhand. Ooh-ah, they be turnips, they be,' he parodied outrageously. 'And don't let Heather hear you call her Squat.'

'So she is. Short and fat, and that beige hair makes her look like a walking mushroom when she wears those pale trousers.'

'She's clever.'

'Too bloody clever. Like now. What d'you bet the Dunstan woman is a real looker, which is really behind her theory she killed Keane and later took the corpse on her horse to the water tank? Maddox said Keane was a hefty guy. How did the woman manage to sling his dead body over a horse, for starters? And, saying she does get him to the tank, how did she manage to dump him in it? With a block and tackle? Nah, it's a load of crap! Dunstan's never had any contact with Keane. Where's the motive?'

'We criminal investigators are meant to find out,' quoted Beeny, pushing things further in his impatience with Piercey. They had worked together throughout this case and he was also bored with knocking on doors to ask questions that had so far brought no useful answers. He agreed that the Dunstan theory was feeble, and he shared Piercey's dread that it had become one of their boss's wild geese. However, he knew from past cases that theories were all very well, but it was the painstaking accumulation of facts that was needed to prove them. That was the task they had been given today. *Again*. It had prompted one of Piercey's frequent gripes, but it had not put him off his food. He had taken two apple turnovers, the second of which he was now wolfing down.

'Phil, you're certain the supplier is on-base, right?'

Piercey nodded, chasing pastry clinging to his chin. 'Has to be.'

'So we've been given the direction that'll lead us to the guy. We know there's a definite link with Starr, but apparently not with Keane himself, so we continue to push any contacts of hers. Female contacts who're getting supplies through a husband or boyfriend.' He slurped some tea from his mug. 'What gets me is these women have kids. They're raising a generation of new junkies.'

Piercey's eyes narrowed. 'I'll get the bugger, and put him in the glasshouse for a very, *very* long time.'

'Let's get started, then. Can you move after eating all that gunge?'

It was another unusually warm October day, which was holding at bay the first frosts that normally heralded a quite severe winter. The two young detectives were oblivious to the aesthetic delights of brilliantly coloured autumn leaves

against a clear, vivid sky, and the birds who had emerged
with joyous song and immaculate plumage after the summer
moult. They were not that type of men. Their minds were
set on tougher things, yet they looked innocent enough in
neat suits, plain ties and spotless shirts. They had once been
mistaken for Jehovah's Witnesses on a householder's
doorstep, so clean-cut and pleasant had they looked.

Yesterday they had managed to track down three of Starr
Keane's bosom pals, but they had not detected signs of drug
use either in their houses or in the behaviour of the women.
They had then moved on to a few members of B Company,
the Royal Cumberland Rifles, in the hope of finding some
link with Keane after all. No luck there, either, hence they
approached this second day of probing with the determination to uncover some reward for their diligence.

They began with those men of the RCR they had not
managed to question yesterday. The big disadvantage was
that so many were away on post Afghanistan leave. That
fact touched every aspect of the case. There was just one
lonely soul lying on his bed looking at girlie magazines;
so lonely that he actually appeared to welcome a visit from
the Redcaps. Unheard of!

Piercey then suggested to Beeny that they returned to the
married quarters to call on those wives they had not yet
talked to. Beeny was agreeable, so they split up and took
a road each. They were ostensibly investigating a murder,
so their questions camouflaged the true reason for their call.

There was no response to Piercey's knock on the first
two front doors, but the third was standing ajar. He knocked
on it and called the woman's name, but it was a small boy
who peered round the door a few moments later.

'Hallo, who are you?' asked Piercey briskly.

'Who are *you*?'

He was not experienced with children; never knew what
to say to them. 'I'm a man who wants to talk to your
mummy. Can I come in?'

'*No!*'

He pushed past the child, calling the woman's name
again. The place was clean but a total shambles. Toys, a

basket of clothes for ironing, newspapers and magazines littered the floor. An ironing board bearing an iron stood amidst the clutter, and a low coffee table held a large pink padded bag filled with numerous bottles of nail varnish and jars of hand cream. This was surrounded by Pooh Bear mugs, small plates containing crumbs, and a larger one on which lay a slice of very gooey cake over which a somnolent bee crawled.

'Mrs Marshall,' he called yet again, a flutter of adrenalin heralding the possibility of finding her hurt, ill . . . or dead.

'Yes, who is it?' came a faint voice from the upper floor, dispelling these notions.

'Sar'nt Piercey, SIB. Come down here, please.'

'I won't be long. I'm not dressed.' A short pause. 'There's a piece of cake left, I think. Make yourself some coffee.'

The boy was beside the ironing board, staring at him. Piercey vowed to have a word with his mother about the danger of leaving the front door open with her child free to run off, and any person free to walk in. Moments passed and he grew suspicious. The items on the table suggested a make-up party with friends, so why was she having to dress up there? Could there be some kind of sexual activity going on?

On the point of climbing the stairs he saw her at the top in a knee-length T-shirt, and start down. Great legs, he thought. The tits aren't bad, either. She's very definitely a man's woman, not a dyke. So what was she doing up there dressed in next to nothing?

'Hallo,' she said brightly. Too brightly. 'Oh, you haven't got coffee. Must have a coffee. And some *cake*. Big tough guy like you needs plenty to keep you going.' She giggled as she closed with him and squeezed his bicep. 'Oooh, *muscles*.'

That was when he was certain she was high and had no notion who he was, apart from a male visitor to provide some excitement. A rush of satisfaction went through him. This woman displayed the unmistakable signs he was looking for. Had she just had a fix upstairs, or was the nail varnish a cover for a communal session?

Grabbing her wandering hands he deposited her none too gently on the squashy sofa, then squatted on his haunches to question her. It was useless. She was on another planet, erotically charged-up and only interested in bonding with him. When she put her bare foot up between his bent knees and wiggled her toes against his crotch, he straightened up and took out his mobile. Corporal Meacher answered his call to the RMP post on the base, and Piercey swiftly outlined the situation.

'She's high and quite incapable, Ray. There's a boy of about three years old here with her. The door was open to the street when I arrived. She was upstairs. There's an ironing board set up with an iron plugged in. If she should switch it on and forgets about it the kid will be in further danger. I'll stay on site until one of you gets here with a woman from Welfare. Make it snappy. I've things to do.'

Closing the phone he unplugged the iron and took it through to the kitchen before collapsing the board that could easily fall on the child if he brushed against it. The boy watched him warily throughout, clutching a one-eared teddy bear for comfort. Piercey smiled to reassure him, but anger was not far away. Corporal Marshall had just gone to Afghanistan with the West Wiltshire Regiment. Surely he must have known what she was doing while he was living here with her, unless she had become a user after he departed two weeks ago and was overdosing herself for comfort. He would have to be made aware of the danger to his son. Another source of stress for the poor bastard.

Looking again at the mugs, cake and nail varnish Piercey surmised that the habit had started at some kind of girlie get together; just for recreational purposes while their men were away, something to give their spirits a lift, no worse than a few G and Ts. But it was. G and Ts produced a head ache, cocaine produced a craving that could never be satisfied. Also, it put children in danger. Piercey might not know how to handle them, but he was their fierce protector.

As soon as the two uniformed Redcaps arrived, one of them a woman, Piercey left them to it and went upstairs two at a time. The first place he looked was the bedroom. Again, it was clean but impossibly untidy. Clothes were strewn everywhere, shoes all over the floor, handbags piled on a chair. What he was looking for was not there. He searched in all the likely places without success. A glance in the boy's room encountered the usual lack of order but, unlikely though he knew it to be, he searched there. That just left the bathroom, but there was no sign of the evidence. Frustrated, he had to conclude that one of the women at the coffee gathering must have brought the stuff.

He left the Redcaps arranging a child minder for the boy and a visit by Clare Goodey before she took afternoon surgery. He knew Mrs Marshall would be unfit for questioning for some time, but it was essential to get from her the names of the women who had been present in her house that morning. It might be worth visiting all the West Wilts wives for evidence of other users. He would have some lunch before going to Headquarters for the list of their names and addresses. Those apple turnovers were not enough to sustain a big tough guy, as the Marshall woman had described him. Mmm, great legs . . . and she could do very interesting things with her toes!

Piercey was halfway through ham, eggs and chips when his ever busy mind produced an image that caused him to pause his enthusiastic transference of food to mouth. He finished his meal more slowly as possibility mounted to certainty, and all thoughts of a pudding were abandoned.

He drove to the RMP post and collected the keys to the Keanes' married quarter. Entering, he took the stairs at a run. There they were, all in a row like they had been in the Marshalls' bathroom. Donning gloves he unscrewed the lids of the pots that purported to contain homeopathic beauty aids, and laid them aside. He then spread a towel over the floor and began scooping out the various creams, tipping alongside them two collections of brightly coloured tablets. When he had done that he sat back on his heels and gave a triumphant smile. The depth of each pot was at least an inch higher than the outside base.

'*Yes!*' he breathed. 'I've cracked it!'

Max made himself black coffee while the team departed
on their separate tasks. He needed further caffeine stimulus
to get to grips with the plethora of facts on the Keane case.
Having made a late start on it he wanted to spend the
morning analysing the information presently available in
the hope of finding a thread of continuity he could follow
to a logical conclusion. Nothing would shake his belief
that the jellyfish was the killer's signature. Extending the
premise that there was a sexual issue behind the murder,
he was certain it was a case of *cherchez la femme*.

Tom came up beside him to make his own coffee, glancing
at the very dark liquid in Max's mug. 'Heavy night?'

'Overslept. No time for breakfast.' He turned to lean back
against the counter, sipping the hot, strong coffee. 'So you
discovered a bit more about the mysterious Brenda
yesterday.'

'Could be her. As I told the team just now, Brenda
Nicholson, aged twenty-eight, Staff Nurse at Cranfield War
Memorial Hospital, volunteered for service in Iraq in 2007.
She returned there the following year for a further stint,
then was discharged from the TA in the September. The TA
sergeant I spoke to had no info on her from that date, and
Cranfield told me she left to take an exchange appointment
in Europe for three years. The almoner was new to the job;
couldn't tell me where in Europe.' He poured milk and
added sugar. 'I tried Immigration last night, but they were
either asleep or in the boozer.'

'Both, probably.'

Tom grunted. 'I haven't had much time at home since
this began, so I left it at that in favour of a hot dinner with
my family. There's not the urgency to find her as there was
to finding the Starr kids, although Brenda needs to be told
hers no longer has a father.'

'If it exists.'

Tom glanced up sharply. 'The woman went into labour
on the day Keane flew back.'

'Mmm, I find the whole story of Brenda somewhat shaky.

In Iraq she's everything to Keane, but he marries the mother of the boy he sired the minute he gets home. A woman spurned is a vengeful creature, Tom. Right now, *she's* the top of the list of suspects, rather than the female knight with a horse named Jetset.'

'But a short time ago you backed Heather's theory on Mel Dunstan!'

Max shrugged. 'She had means and opportunity, but until we find some connection between her and Keane she's only an outsider. Brenda, on the other hand, has a strong motive and, on the Open Day, would have had plenty of opportunity.'

'She'd just given birth,' Tom protested.

'Had she? The evidence we have on that is pure hearsay. Ryan Moore was *told* about the text by Keane. Did he actually see it written? Come to that, everything about the reunion with this nurse is hearsay. Moore doesn't know her full name or where she lives at present. Connie found no trace of a woman named Brenda giving birth during the past few days, although that's not necessarily conclusive. Keane *told* Moore he had made her pregnant and planned to divorce Starr on his return from Afghanistan so they could marry.'

Tom looked pugnacious. 'Why would he invent all that?'

'To boost his credo at a time when it was all round the base that Starr was dumping dirty nappies on his gear to force him to leave the Army. For Brenda to tell him she was in the club before he left for the warzone, he had to have been seeing her on the quiet for at least two months. How is it his best mate had no hint of what he was up to until Keane told him when they were on stand-by to fly out? Moore had known Brenda in Iraq. Wouldn't a man confide in his closest friend the great excitement of his reunion with the woman he had been smitten with out there? Of course he would.'

'He did confide it to Moore.'

'Only on the brink of returning to active service, Tom. We've learned from several sources that the men hadn't complete faith in Keane; worried that he might wimp out

under fire after Iraq. He knew that. He also knew Starr was
spreading it around that he had agreed to leave the Army
after his return from deployment. Suggesting that the woman
he'd done the dirty on after Iraq was pregnant with his child
would sound like a thumb of the nose to Starr and, with
the curious logic some men have, prove he was man enough
for anything.'

Looking really aggrieved by now, Tom said, 'You're
suggesting Keane fabricated the whole business with
Brenda?'

'Possibly. Revenge can simmer for a long time, then
come to the boil when the opportunity arises. I've no doubt
she's here in Germany and we need to *find* her, Tom.'

'Isn't that what I've been doing, sir?'

Max gave him a steady look. 'No need to get on your
high horse. No criticism intended. I know I'm taking over
a case you've been handling perfectly well, but a fresh eye
often sees a new angle. Brenda's been hovering in Keane's
life for a long time and I'm anxious to meet her, aren't
you?'

Still straight-faced, Tom said, 'I can't see any way she
could kill him at noon then hang around unnoticed so that
she could dump him in the tank at midnight, whatever the
truth about her proves to be.'

'Oh, Tom, *Tom*! You've been in the business long enough
to know the impossible becomes possible once we have all
the facts and evidence.' Seeing his friend's lips clamp on
any further comment, he added, 'A man was strangled, his
corpse was displayed ten to twelve hours later in a manner
that was indicative of why he was killed. Fact. We have no
lead as yet on who did it. Fact. Let's pursue the elusive
Brenda meanwhile. If she did indeed produce Keane's baby
a week ago, he would have taken every opportunity to see
them both. If nothing else, Brenda will give us evidence of
his movements. What puzzles me is why, in the circumstances we've been led to believe, Keane would have been
on-base on Saturday. He was on leave, for God's sake. Free
to spend as much time as he wanted with the woman he
loved and his new son or daughter. Only explanation I can

come up with is that *she* was coming to see *him*. See what
I'm getting at?'

Tom gave a brief nod, then changed the subject abruptly.
'How did it go with the Veterinary Officer?'

'How did what go?'

'You were going to question him about the ownership of
horses re the wandering knight.'

Max had forgotten that task, and rather than bluster
through a pack of lies, said, 'Didn't have time.'

'Right. I'll go now.' Tom tossed back the remainder of
his coffee and walked to collect his car keys.

Max knew him well enough to accept that he was annoyed.
Fair enough. He had expected to be in command of 26 Section
for two weeks, but because his boss's love life had suffered
he had had that responsibility taken from him halfway through
a demanding, serious case. He was professional enough to
handle it, but Max sensed there was something else on Tom's
mind as well. Trouble at home?

There was certainly something additional on his own
mind. It was probably one of what his team called his WGs,
but he needed to pursue it to its roost. In his office he
switched on his computer and accessed SIB records to reassure himself he had not been mistaken. No, he had not
been. He then accessed the personnel file and saw a name
he knew well. Steven Cartwright, present location Catterick
Camp. A few minutes later he was talking to the man.

'Hi, Steve, how are things up in Yorkshire?'

Steven laughed. 'Business is thriving. Three reported
sightings on the premises of the large cat that reputedly
roams the moors. A corporal's wife saw it crossing her
backyard. Massive black thing with enormous yellow eyes!
A squaddie met it along the perimeter road late at night
and scared it off by waving his arms and shouting, and a
female medical orderly saw it on the roof of her accommodation and called the RMP post.' He laughed again. 'They
turned out in force, but it had gone.'

'Heard the Redcaps were coming. We're as unpopular
with overgrown cats as we are with everyone. Ah, well!'

'So what have I got that you want, Max? I take it this

isn't purely a social call after . . . how long? Three years?'

'Probably longer. We have a case concerning a guy who was in Iraq when you were OC in the area covered by the Cumberland Rifles. Seems he was involved in an incident when he shot and killed a man while on night patrol. The apparent hostiles immediately flashed the day's identification signal and the patrol was called in. Lance Corporal Keane was hauled off by your guys and kept incommunicado on suspicion of killing one of our own. The subaltern and the members of the patrol were held for the rest of that night and most of the following morning, until they were told an Iraqi who worked for the UN had provided details of the secret identifying signals for that week. The casualty *was* a hostile. Remember the case, Steve?'

After a moment's silence Cartwright said, 'What's all this about?'

'It's about a full corporal called Philip Keane, who was murdered here on Saturday. There's a probable link with a TA nurse who was out there at the time and helped him recover from the experience. Thing is, your report on the incident doesn't appear in our records.'

'Then there couldn't have been an incident.'

Max let that hang in the air for some seconds before saying, 'Fighting men don't imagine something as dramatic as that. Why is there no record of it, Steve?'

'Because it never happened. That's the usual reason.'

'No, the usual reason is because there's something havey-cavey or bloody embarrassing about the action that has to be kept quiet.'

'What has that fairy tale to do with this man's murder?'

'That's what I want you to enlighten me on.'

'Ah, stuck for clues and suspects?' He laughed heartily. 'Can't help you with that. Concentrate on what's going on in your neck of the woods and you'll eventually crack it. Got to go, Max. Just caught sight of a massive black cat with enormous yellow eyes. Cheers!' The line went dead.

After thirty minutes Max located Major Quail who had been in charge of Ops on the night in question and had aborted the patrol. He was now a lieutenant colonel at

Sandhurst, so Max called him and was answered by Captain
Morse, the 2IC.

'Good morning. Captain Max Rydal, SIB here. I wish to
speak to Colonel Quail on a rather urgent matter.'

The crisp voice replied, 'The Colonel is somewhat busy
at the moment. Try again later.'

'Perhaps you didn't hear me correctly,' Max said equally
crisply. 'I'm with the Special Investigation Branch in
Germany, so this is a priority call. Kindly put me through
to the Colonel.'

Within seconds Max heard a soft Scottish brogue in his
ear. 'Yes, Captain Rydal, what can I do for you?'

'Good morning, sir. I'm investigating the murder in rather
unusual circumstances of an RCR corporal. During the course
of my enquiries I've been told both by his company
commander and the sar'nt major that Keane was involved
in a disturbing incident in Iraq two years ago. It concerned
the killing while on night patrol of an apparent hostile, whose
companions subsequently flashed the UN recognition signal
for that twenty-four hour period. You were OC Ops at the
time and called in the patrol to hold all the men incommunicado while the corporal was questioned by Steven
Cartwright of SIB. By mid-morning of the following day it
had been confirmed that the casualty was, indeed, a hostile.'

There was silence from Quail, so Max continued. 'I'm
sure you recall the incident. It's unlikely that you would
forget something like that, sir.'

Still silence. 'There were various repercussions for the
corporal, which we think have some bearing on the motive
for his murder. I've scanned through the action reports for
that week in June 2007 and yours on that incident appears
to have gone astray. What I require quite urgently is a
written account of the patrol leader's radio contact with you
regarding the unforeseen secret identification signal from
men dressed as Arabs, your order to abort the patrol, and
details of the subsequent police probe which cleared Keane
of causing by reason of lack of information the death of a
UN soldier.'

This time Max let the silence run on. The man would

have to say something eventually, but he had a pretty good idea of what that would be. He proved to be not far wrong.

'You say I'd be unlikely to forget something like that, Captain Rydal. Of course I would not. I'm afraid you've been badly misinformed. There was certainly no incident of that nature during my six-month deployment in Iraq, so I regret I'm unable to help with your investigation. Sorry about that.'

The line went dead, and Max was then certain this was no wild goose he was chasing. Before he could ponder deeply on this there was a call from the Incident Room.

'Sir, I've traced Brenda. She lives a stone's throw from Mr Black.'

Max walked through to where Sergeant Jakes sat before his computer. He glanced up with a triumphant smile. 'So simple it didn't occur to me until just now. She became Brenda Keane so her kid would have its father's name on the birth certificate.'

Reading what was on the screen, with a small inset map of where to find her, Max gripped the man's shoulder. 'Gold star, Roy. Does Ingrid know she's marrying a genius?'

Jakes laughed. 'I still haven't sorted the seating plan to her satisfaction. I'll be a genius if I achieve *that*.'

Now fully alert after several cups of black coffee, Max felt certain they would be able to advance this case. In an upbeat mood he took up his mobile. Tom deserved to participate in this breakthrough, even if it proved that he, himself, was completely wrong about this woman who had featured strongly in the murdered man's life.

NINE

It was a second floor flat in a small dingy block whose stucco needed attention, but the steps giving access to four freshly painted doors suggested the landlord was in the process of smartening his property. Max rang the bell on the door numbered 33.

'This'll either be the breakthrough we need, or a big let down,' he said to his companion.

Tom merely raised his eyebrows. He had said little during the drive apart from revealing that the Veterinary Officer had not been in his office, yet Max sensed his quiet mood might have no connection with this case. Those girls of his were all of an age when rebellion and experimentation sets in and, despite the earlier onset of maturity these days, girls were more vulnerable than ever before. As they waited to discover if there was yet another child of Philip Keane's who was now fatherless, Max wondered if he was better off single without parental responsibilities.

The door opened halfway. He was unprepared for the reality of the woman who had been hard to track down. Even without make-up, and wearing a baggy grey T-shirt and jog pants, Brenda Nicholson Keane was a stunner. Blonde, with violet-blue eyes, she looked too slender to have given birth just days ago. How had Keane ever forsaken this beauty to marry the overlarge, overbearing Starr, even under pressure from her family? Had he actually been the wimp Starr's friends had called him?

Seeing the two tall men, she said swiftly that she was too busy to discuss religion with them. Before she could close the door Max showed her his identity.

'Captain Rydal and Sar'nt Major Black, Special Investigation Branch. We need to talk to you about Corporal Philip Keane. May we come in?'

She grew pale. '*Special Investigation Branch?* Oh, my

God, something's happened to him! Is it that wife's ghastly family?'

'It would be better to talk inside,' Max said quietly, knowing instinctively that she had no idea what they were about to tell her. This was no vengeful woman such as he had described to Tom.

'He didn't come back on Saturday; didn't call to tell me why,' she said, wide-eyed and still not moving. 'I've been trying to contact him, but he's not answering my emails and his mobile's on voice mail. What's happened?'

Tom took command by stepping in to the small hall and gently turning her to lead the way to an L-shaped room where a baby slept in a wooden rocking-cradle of old Germanic design. As Max followed he correctly interpreted the I-told-you-so glance over Tom's shoulder. Apart from the usual needs of an infant, the room revealed the occupant's taste. It was unlikely that the landlord had supplied the Wedgwood ornaments and two beautiful tiffany lamps.

Brenda crossed to the cradle and clutched the side of it as if to protect her child from harm. 'Something's happened to him; something bad.'

'We've been told you were in a relationship with Corporal Keane. Is that correct?' asked Max, knowing he was about to deal this woman a terrible blow.

'Yes.' It was little more than a whisper.

'Was he the father of this child?'

Tears began to slide down her cheeks as she then guessed why they were there. '*Was* he! You've come to tell me he's dead?'

'I'm sorry.' He indicated the sofa. 'Perhaps you'd like to sit down.'

Her grip on the cradle tightened. 'I read about that pile-up on the autobahn. Was it that?'

Max crossed to her. 'It really will be better if you sit down, Ms Keane. We have some questions for you. Perhaps Mr Black could make you a cup of tea.'

She gave a ghastly smile through the sliding tears. 'The number of times I've said that to bereaved relatives. How stupid! As if a cup of tea could possibly deaden the loss of a loved one.' Walking unsteadily to the large amber sofa, she sat and stared at a desert sunset picture on the opposite wall. 'He bought that for me when he left Iraq; said he never wanted to see another desert but he knew it had got under my skin.'

Max occupied the chair facing her while Tom sought the kitchen. Tea would not deaden the loss of her lover, but it was a source of comfort if only by giving her something to do with her hands.

'When did you last see Philip?' Max asked.

'*Flip!* He was known as Flip from childhood.' It seemed she had not fully registered the question until she eventually said, 'He arrived early on Saturday morning full of excitement. He'd told Starr there was no question of leaving the Army, and she'd flown into a rage and demanded a divorce. She threatened to ensure that he never saw the children. Not *ever*. If he tried to, her brothers would break both his legs. Thugs, the pair of them!'

'Didn't that bother him? Not seeing his children?'

'Of course, although he said a court would give him access. He loves those kids, but he now has little Micky.' The tears streaking her cheeks now ran down her throat as she added, 'When he first saw me with him he *cried*. It's very moving to see a man you love cry.'

'So Flip came here early on Saturday? What time did he leave?' She gazed silently at the desert picture. 'Ms Keane!'

'Oh . . . about eleven thirty, I suppose. But he never returned.'

'He had planned to do so?'

'Yes. Starr was to have the car. He had agreed to that because she was going home to the UK. With Prince and Melody, plus all their stuff, she needed it more than Flip. After giving her time to pack enough for a couple of days with a friend, Flip went back to collect his own gear. He was on leave so he was going to stay with me until he had to report back, by which time she would have cleared the place of her things and left for good.' She frowned. 'Flip took a taxi back. What was it doing on the autobahn?'

'It wasn't. He arrived back at the base. Ms Keane, at

around noon on Saturday Flip was murdered. It was Starr who died in the autobahn pile-up.'

She seemed unable or unwilling to take in these facts, staring at Max, at the desert picture, then back at him. He said, 'The children weren't in the car. They're safe and being cared for.'

Tom came with a large mug, and she took it automatically, warming her hands around it as she gazed at the tea. Max exchanged a look with Tom which showed that he was unsure whether Brenda had actually registered the truth about her lover's death, and he nodded an indication that Tom should take over. He did so after a moment or two, abandoning formality.

'Tell us about Flip, Brenda. How did you meet?'

She spoke to the contents of the mug. 'I was in Iraq with the TA at a time when things were pretty grim. They needed additional nurses in the field hospitals. Flip was brought in with a raging fever and by the time he left we had become close. We met up whenever we could. It was obvious to me that he loved his job and was very skilled at it.' Her faint smile crept over the rim of the mug to reach Tom. 'Strange to say they were such happy days; people were being killed and injured, kids being orphaned. But we were in love, you see.'

'Did he tell you about Starr?'

She sipped the tea pensively. 'His pal Ryan hinted that there was a string of lovelorn women back in the UK, but that's typical lads' joshing. I knew it was the real thing between us. We planned to marry when I got home later in the year. Such happy days! Then it happened and everything changed.'

The short silence was broken by the faint whimper of the baby who was moving restlessly and setting the cradle rocking, but he settled again.

'He was a different person afterwards. I could see the problem and worked hard to alleviate it. The confident, laughing and, I have to admit, *cocksure* Flip was on the verge of losing his nerve. It wasn't difficult to get the full story from him.'

'And that was?' prompted Max.

'Flip had been on a night patrol.'

Max felt a surge of excitement as this woman repeated facts given to him by Ben Steele, and to Tom by Frank Priest. 'Go on.'

'Of course, people who've never walked stealthily through the purple darkness of a desert night, knowing that at any moment something deadly could whistle through the air and put an end to your existence can't imagine the stress this puts on the human mind and body. Doing it just once would daunt most people, but soldiers do it time after time. It takes enormous resolution, particularly towards the end of a tour that involves living in basic accommodation, eating basic food, being absent from loved ones, hearing constant bombardment and knowing the dread that your next step on the sand might result in being blown apart. These men are tired, edgy and under continual mental and physical strain.

'Being charged with shooting dead one of our own troops shattered Flip. The worst twenty-four hours of his life, he told me. Even when it turned out that the casualty had really been a hostile, Flip couldn't get his mind around it. I was able to confirm that no casualties had been brought in that night, but the sense of guilt and remorse stayed with him and our relationship became that of patient and nurse. For a time I was afraid he'd never recover his confidence and courage, but he very gradually put the experience behind him.

'Unfortunately, he still saw me as some kind of saviour and persuaded himself he wasn't a good enough husband for me. Wrote from the UK to break off our unofficial engagement.' She frowned. 'That's when the Walpoles moved in on him. Between that mob and his strict, religious parents he didn't stand a chance.' She looked up swiftly. 'Did the Walpoles kill him?'

Taken unawares by this sudden proof that she had, indeed, registered all he had said, Max shook his head. 'We have no evidence of that.'

'Then who did?'

'As yet we have no definite lead,' said Tom. 'We hope you might clear up some points to aid our investigation. When did you meet up with Flip again?'

'Last autumn. I'd done another stint in Iraq which had revived my sadness at losing him, so I resigned from the TA and accepted a three-year exchange to Germany with the intention of starting a new life. When I got here I discovered that the RCR were actually stationed just down the road. I saw it as fate, and contacted Flip right away. He was desperately unhappy with Starr, and I was desperately unhappy without him, so the affair started again. We were so discreet no one knew we were meeting. My pregnancy sealed our happiness, and we made plans for a future together. He was so caring, so concerned about my welfare but it took me a while to recognize there was an underlying cause for the flood of calls and emails when he first went to Afghanistan. He was apprehensive about going into action again; feared he'd be unable to fire his rifle lest he shoot one of his comrades. He needed my reassurances, my steadying confidence in his ability. Once he'd successfully brought out his men from a Taliban ambush he reverted to the man I'd first met in Iraq. The perfect soldier.

'When he got back to base and came to see Micky and me, he *cried*. It's very moving to see the man you love cry,' she repeated as if to herself, as she fastened her gaze on the desert picture again. Then, seconds later, she doubled up and began to sob uncontrollably as the devastating truths of this afternoon could no longer be held at bay.

Tom was surprised when Max made a slight diversion and brought his car to a halt outside the house he presently rented for himself and his family.

'Lunch?' he asked, thinking Max expected an invitation.

'Thanks, but no thanks,' he returned with a smile. 'So I was completely up the creek about that nice woman, wasn't I? It comes of muscling in on a case that's already under way. What will she do with her life now, I wonder?'

Tom gazed thoughtfully through the windscreen. 'She has a choice of staying here and making the new start she had planned before meeting Keane again, or returning to the UK and befriending Keane's people who are the baby's legit grandparents. They're unlikely to gain any rights over Prince and Melody, who'll probably be fostered by a family which'll take them both, so Brenda could set up a secure background for Micky with her lover's mother and father, providing they offered the kind of doting affection they would surely feel for their only son's child.'

'Mmm, would strictly religious elderly folk – we've been told they had Keane late in life – accept what they would possibly regard as a bastard child?'

Tom sighed. 'We'll never know. Part of the downside of this job is that we only get "the story so far" and never read the concluding chapters.'

'We got further insight to Keane, however,' Max continued, causing Tom to wonder why he chose to sit here having this conversation. 'How could a man of a type to inspire such forgiving devotion in a woman like Brenda surrender her so easily, to throw in his lot with a loud-mouthed harridan?'

'We never met Starr, so you're making that comparison on hearsay,' Tom pointed out.

'Most of which indicated that the dead woman – a cocaine user, don't forget – would have been the devil to live with.'

'So Keane was a wimp, as defined by Starr's friends. A couple of painful armlocks by the truckie brothers and he agreed to their demands.'

Max gave him a quizzical look. 'Hearsay, Tom.'

'OK, so Keane was a sucker for kids. One sight of baby Prince being waved under his nose gave him the over-whelming urge to make more like him with the large, cuddly woman conveniently on the spot. Which he did, hence Melody. Maybe he got his sexual kicks from being dominated.'

'He was a full-blooded soldier, for Christ's sake!'

'He had to be reassured long-term by Brenda; in her own words he saw her as a saviour. In any case, if you took a peek in the bedrooms on this base at night you'd find all manner of strange things going on with full-blooded soldiers.

We've just heard about a guy dressing as a clown and kissing his wife like crazy in front of party guests just because she was obsessed with horoscopes, and . . .'

'Another riding around wearing armour at midnight. Yes, point taken, but I lean to the view that Keane changed dramatically during his time in Iraq, as Brenda just told us. Ryan Moore said much the same, as did Ben Steele. The curious thing is that the incident that caused the change officially never happened, and *that* makes me think Keane's death might somehow be linked to it.'

He nodded at the house. 'Take the rest of the day off. Brenda didn't create the breakthrough I hoped for, and when it does come you'll be putting in a lot of overtime. Take Nora out for a drive in the country, have a meal in a rural beer garden. Make the most of this wonderful unseasonal weather. When it ends, raw winter will be right here with us.'

Tom made no demur – he could do with some time at home before the school bus deposited the girls at the end of this road – but he sensed that Max was up to something. Chasing a new wild goose? He climbed from the car.

'I'll get Nora to drive me in in the morning.'

Max raised his hand in farewell. 'Enjoy yourselves, but watch out for bees.' He drove off.

Tom found Nora in the kitchen, ironing. He grinned. 'Glad to see you're making yourself useful, not having it off with the neighbour when I arrive home unexpectedly.'

He knew he had said the wrong thing when she failed to rise to his teasing. 'I suppose you want a swift bowl of soup and a pile of sandwiches before you dash off again.'

'Believe it or not, I've finished for the day.' He kissed her cheek because her lips were not offered. 'Forget the swift soup. I'm going to take you out for an al fresco meal beside the river. Pack that away and doll yourself up, we leave in ten.'

She grew still and gazed at him. 'You've no idea, have you? Because you have nothing to do, for once, you swan in and expect me to drop everything and amuse you. The girls need fresh blouses in the morning, you need a clean starched shirt and a spare in case you mess it up, and that's without T-shirts and shorts that manage to get covered in marmalade, gravy, glue, nail varnish, paint, tea, custard . . .'

'Hey, hey!' he said in concern. 'It can be left until this evening. I'll do my shirts and the girls can iron their own things, like they often do. Why're you making such an issue of it, love?'

Nora burst into tears. She was not a woman who cried easily, so he was dismayed and worried by this outburst. Having just left Brenda sobbing over a murdered lover, Tom's imagination plunged to the depths as he switched off the iron at the socket and attempted to comfort her.

'What's wrong? What's happened? Tell me, love. We're in this together. Always have been.'

She remained stiff in his embrace, which worried him even more and prompted wild, unwelcome fantasies. No, it could not be that. Their marriage was on a rock-solid foundation. Dear God, had she been told something shattering by Clare Goodey?

He held her closer, stroking her hair with an unsteady hand. 'Aren't you feeling well? Is that it?'

'I'm tired, that's all,' she muttered thickly, drawing away.

'No, it's not. There's something more. Something you're not telling me.'

She sat at the breakfast counter and absently dried her eyes on a T-shirt lying on the ironing board. 'The girls phoned during their lunch break about the puppy. I told them no, and they all chorused, *pleeese, pleeese*. You know how they do. They kept on and on.' She frowned. 'I . . . I told them they were selfish, ungrateful, demanding people and hung up on them.' She took a deep breath and exhaled slowly. 'It's only a puppy they want. They haven't had a pet since Fluffy died, and a dog's more involving than a hamster. It's good for kids to have an animal of some sort. Why did I treat them that way?'

Tom sat beside her and took her hand. 'Because you're tired, love, and don't want any more responsibility. You said as much this morning, and I'm fully in agreement. I'll sort it with them tonight, explain that a puppy's almost as time-consuming as a new baby. It has to be house-trained, given the correct weaning food at regular times, needs comforting when it's frightened by something and has to be prevented from wandering away and getting lost. We'd have to put a fence around the house to keep him in.'

He squeezed the hand lying limply in his. 'I'll make us both some soup and sandwiches which we'll have in the garden. After that you'll take a warm shower, put on your robe and spend an hour or so on the bed while I get rid of this ironing. Then I'll call Captain Goodey and ask her to come in and see you on her way home tonight.'

'*No*, Tom! I'm just tired. I wouldn't dream of fetching her here when she has genuine patients to visit. You're not to contact her.'

Her vehemence was due to exhaustion, he guessed, so he compromised by extracting an assurance that she would attend the surgery the next morning.

'I'll be cadging a lift to the base, anyway. Max dropped me off on the way back from visiting the woman who's just had a baby fathered by the guy murdered on Saturday.' He began to butter bread and grate cheese. 'He had some wild notion that the kid was an invention, and she had killed Keane herself. You know how he flies off at a tangent sometimes.' He glanced up swiftly. 'What are you doing?'

'Getting the tins of soup from the cupboard.'

'*I'm* OC this meal, ma'am. If you must get something from the cupboard make it a bottle of wine, and pour some in two glasses. Wine is a restorative, gives you energy. My dad taught me that piece of wisdom.'

Her lack of comment to that, which should have brought forth her views on men who come up with inventive excuses for having a drink, revived his concern. She certainly looked and acted like a woman who needed a long rest, so he would ensure she saw Clare Goodey tomorrow if he had to march her in the consulting room himself.

They ate their garden picnic and, although a bee investigated a late-flowering shrub, it did not approach them. Nora made heavy work of the cheese and tomato sandwiches; showed more interest in the wine. For once she made no attempt to question him about the case, in spite of his reference to the visit to Brenda, so Tom talked about the various general plans for Hallowe'en.

'I'll appropriate pumpkins for the girls, and we'll *hire* costumes. I'm not having a repetition of last year, when you were striving to make three witches' outfits in the middle of an order for a wedding gown and four bridesmaids' dresses.'

'No need for that. Gina can wear Maggie's and Beth can have Gina's from last year. They'll moan, but go off happily enough when the time comes.'

'How about Maggie? If she has something new it'll increase the moans twofold.'

'She's been invited to a swish party with Hans and his family. Very decorous. No witches or demons. She's going to wear the dress we bought her for her birthday.'

Tom frowned. 'When was this agreed?'

'On Sunday. You were involved in the murder in the water tank. Maggie was eager to go, and the Graumanns are fond of her. We know she's in safe hands when she's with them, so I said yes.'

He chewed a sandwich almost aggressively and finally had to voice his thoughts. 'That friendship's getting too particular for my liking. She's thirteen, he's sixteen. That puts him on the threshold of manhood. I know what lads of sixteen are like, and Maggie looks at least that age when she dolls herself up.'

Nora said wearily, 'Go on, finish the hackneyed speech. *And he's German!* Tom, I'm sick of hearing it. Maggie and Hans have an adolescent friendship. They're discovering feelings that are normal for kids of their age. That's all it is. He's a very nice lad with responsible, friendly parents. Stop behaving like a Victorian father, for Christ's sake!'

Tom was shaken. Although Nora had several times accused him of overreacting on the subject of their eldest daughter's long-standing friendship with the boy who lived across the road, she had never let fly at him like that. It revived his fear that she was holding back some alarming news regarding her health, that she was trying to handle on her own. He determined to get the facts from Clare Goodey in the morning. Meanwhile, he would ignore her strange mood.

'If they're all going to parties on that evening, it'll give us a chance to do something ourselves,' he said, forcing a smile. 'Dinner at the Golden Calf, perhaps?' Without waiting for a response, he added, 'Now, how about that shower and short nap?'

She gazed across the garden. 'If you're determined to take over the ironing, I'll stay here while you do it. We won't get many more days like this. I'll sit here and enjoy it. I haven't yet reached the age when I need an afternoon *nap*, Tom, although I might look it.'

He had been married long enough to know it was best to stay silent after comments like that. Whatever he said would be wrong. With careful tact he agreed it was too nice a day to spend indoors.

'Soon as I've finished with the iron I'll make some tea and join you.'

Thirty minutes later, while he was collapsing the ironing board, his mobile rang. Tempted to ignore it, he saw the caller was George Maddox and felt obliged to answer.

'Yes, George.'

'I'm here at the padre's, with him and Cap'n Steele, sir. Mrs Walpole and her sons have just arrived from the mortuary where they arranged for Starr's body to be flown home. Now they want to collect the children and remove all their belongings from the house. We've done our best to impress upon them that they can visit the boy and the baby, but can't take them back to the UK. They're kicking up merry hell about it, and the fact that I told them the house is a suspected crime scene and out of bounds to them. The brothers are pitching up ugly, so I've called Meacher and Stubble to stand guard at the place. I tried to contact Cap'n Rydal but he's not answering. You need to get down here or I might have to arrest them all. At gunpoint, sir!' he added significantly.

'On way,' Tom said heavily, certain Max had switched

off so that he could pursue something sensitive enough to demand just one pair of feet treading very lightly on the path to the truth. Well, he had access to people who could probably assist him, but Brigadier Andrew Rydal was on honeymoon at a secret location, and Livya Cordwell was the last person a jilted lover would want to apply to for help.

Nora was awake on the lounger when he took her a cup of tea and some cake from the well-stocked tin. He explained the problem and promised to return soon. 'Ban all talk of the puppy until I get here, and start *them* cooking the supper. Tell them I said you are to have a day off from that chore. Rest there in the sun. It'll do you good.' He kissed her swiftly. 'I'll have to take your car. See you!'

He wished he had asked Max to drive him to the base to collect his car, but it might be a good thing to leave Nora without transport. If any of the girls wanted to be driven somewhere she would have the perfect excuse to deny them. He *must* get to the bottom of what was wrong. He could not let it continue. Maybe he could take her away for a short break when this case was wrapped up. That would probably solve everything. He resolutely pushed away thoughts of a debilitating illness because they were too hard to contemplate.

Paul Finch and his Scottish wife, Mairie, were a popular clerical pair. He had been a sergeant in the Royal Artillery when he had 'got the call', so he understood soldiers well, and she had the gift of being able to find rapport with almost anyone. If they, plus George Maddox and Captain Steele could not cope with the Walpoles, they must be formidable in the extreme.

Maddox, looking formidable himself in uniform and armed, met Tom in the padre's garden. 'They're getting real nasty in there. Putting aside the fact that they've just viewed their dead sister, the two men are spoiling for a fight with anyone who'll take them on. The mother just wants the kids, but the truckies are bent on collecting everything from the house.' He turned and pushed open the door. 'None of them seems concerned about the murder of Keane.'

'Hmm,' grunted Tom. 'If Starr had survived, they'd have been concerned to the extent of how much she could claim as his widow.'

The square room seemed full to overflowing when they entered. Everyone was standing and voices were raised. A low table held a tray with a teapot, cups and saucers and a plate of biscuits. The cups were full of tea, the biscuits appeared to have been similarly ignored. So much for Mairie Finch's rapport with the Walpoles!

The woman and her two sons seemed to dwarf everyone else. Gloria Walpole was much as Tom expected from all he had heard of her. Obese with bleached hair dark at the roots, she wore white stretch trousers and a clinging blue top that outlined every roll of fat. Large gilt hoops dangled from her ears and each of her pudgy fingers bore a flashy ring. Yet, despite the starkly yellow hair and several wobbly chins, she had a pretty face dominated by large sparkling eyes. Right now they were sparkling with anger.

The brothers could have been twins. As tall as Tom, their girth put his in the shade. Beer bellies stretched to the fullest extent their T-shirts bearing a company logo, and three-inch wide leather belts supported their trousers below the swelling paunches. In their teens they had probably been nice-looking lads, but the years and their aggressive personalities had coarsened any inherited attraction to leave no doubt of their present brutishness.

One of these giants caught sight of the new arrival and sneered. 'Bringing in reinforcements? You can bring the whole effing lot but we know our rights.' He advanced on Tom menacingly. 'I don't know who you are and I don't effing care. Another bible-thumper, as you're not in uniform and toting a gun.' His sneer grew. 'We've just seen our girl lying there covered with a sheet. She's no concern of yours now. Nor are her kids. We're here to collect them and all their stuff from the house. As Starr's next of kin it's all ours by law. Pray to the Lord as much as you like, mate, it won't change anything.' He turned to his brother. 'C'mon, Chas, we ain't in the Army; they can't dictate to us.'

George Maddox stood in front of the door, wearing an

uncompromising expression and looking solid enough to prevent even this pair from moving him. Tom identified himself, adding that he was investigating the murder of Corporal Keane.

'SIB also liaised with the German police regarding your sister's death in a road accident; we traced the children and arranged for them to be cared for by responsible people.'

All this had been imparted in a neutral tone, but Tom put more authority into his next words. 'Let's get a few facts straight. You are presently on an army base where the responsibility for safety and public order is with the Military Police. In this instance, myself and Sar'nt Maddox. We are empowered to order you to leave if you become aggressive, abusive or truculent to an unacceptable degree. If necessary, we can arrange for you to be escorted through the gate by an armed guard. We can even have you put under arrest.'

He resumed the neutral tone. 'Now you're aware of the score I suggest you and your mother sit down and calm down. You're the guests of the Padre and his wife, so moderate your language and attitude if you want to remain here while we discuss your requests.'

'They're not *requests*, mate, they're lawful demands,' one of the brothers said forcefully.

'Yes, we want what's ours,' cried Gloria tearfully, pushing between her sons to confront Tom. 'I want my grandchildren. The Army has no claim on them. They're no more than *babies*. I'm not leaving without them. You can put me outside the gate, but I'll sit there – we all will – until you stop playing soldiers and hand them over. Look big, don't you, with guns in your belt, but you don't frighten us. We can splash this all over the tabloids, you know. We can mount a demonstration outside Parliament. My boys know people who can get a protest march going *any time they want*. You won't look so bloody clever then, will you? *Will you?*' she ranted, looking behind her at the uniformed captain and the Finches.

Ben Steele stepped forward, exchanging significant looks with Tom. 'Mrs Walpole, we've *tried* to explain to you that the situation regarding Corporal and Mrs Keane's children is dictated by *civil* law. Prince and Melody are *wards of court*, so it will be the duty of a *judge* to decide their future. It's *not* a military decision. We have no say in the matter.'

'But *you've* got them,' she yelled at him.

'*No*, Mrs Walpole, they're presently in a care home run by civilians.' He looked exasperated. 'The Padre, Sar'nt Maddox and I have all assured you of that, and we've said that we'll take you to visit them to see for yourself that they're being well looked after. We can't do any more than that. The matter is out of our hands.'

Suddenly, and distressingly, the defiant, bombastic woman subsided to the floor, sobbing uncontrollably. Her sons just stared at her, so Mairie Finch went across, took her hands and sat on the floor beside her.

'Best to let it come out,' she soothed.

Gloria gazed at her through the sliding tears. 'They're all I have left of my lovely . . . *lovely* girl. She'd want her mum to have them, see them grow up, *love* them,' she moaned through her spasm of grief. 'She'd *want* that. I can't let her down.'

Tom signalled Ben to join him and George Maddox by the door. 'Useless to reason further with them. She'll possibly calm down after this, so I suggest we forget the formalities and rid ourselves of them pronto. George, get someone to take her and one of the sons to see the kids then return them to wherever they're staying in town. I'll take the other guy to the house and oversee the collection of clothes and any personal items that obviously connect with Starr and the kids. Everything else will have to be left until ownership can be proved. Keane's people are sure to lay claim to some of the stuff.'

'Are they also likely to lay claim to the children?' asked Ben heavily.

Tom shook his head. 'Doubtful, I'd say. Seems they're quite a bit older. Probably wouldn't want the responsibility, and it's unlikely they'd behave like this lot if they did.'

'I hope you're right,' muttered Ben. 'What a tragedy this

is! Dying within a day of each other. Have you any leads on who killed Flip Keane?'

'We're following several,' Tom lied, glancing past the young officer. 'She's quieter now. Let's get them all moving out and on their way.'

Gloria Walpole's loss of composure had created the hiatus that facilitated fresh command of the situation. The bully boys meekly followed their mother from the house without a backward glance, leaving Ben to issue thanks and apologies to the Finches. A phone call from George brought a military police vehicle driven by a man as large and uncompromising as the Walpoles. Beside him sat a woman similarly uniformed and armed, to provide support for a bereaved woman's visit to her grandchildren. While the passengers climbed in, George had a swift word with the corporal, who nodded her understanding before they prepared to drive away.

'The keys to the Keanes' house,' Tom reminded her sharply.

'You already have them, sir. Phil Piercey collected them earlier.'

Her smile did nothing to soften his irritation over this evidence that Piercey was out on a limb again, which meant he could not shake off Chas Walpole until he had contacted the maverick sergeant for the key. He called Piercey's mobile, irritation mounting.

'Yes, sir?' said the familiar Cornish voice.

'Where are you?' Tom snapped.

'Connaught Road. Corporal Roger Marshall's quarter. Found his boy unprotected with the front door open to the street. Mother had just had a fix. She's right out of it, at present. I got Ray Meacher to call Welfare to organize someone to keep an eye on the kid.'

'So why are you still there?'

'Checking, sir. Just checking.'

'Bloody well check yourself into the Keane house to which I'm informed you collected the key. *On the double*, Piercey. I'll be there in five and the door had better be unlocked.'

Snapping the phone shut, he avoided George's gleaming eye and opened the door of Nora's car for Walpole. The man still exuded belligerence. Make that two of us, chum, Tom thought as he slid behind the wheel cursing Piercey for complicating this distasteful duty. What the hell was he up to?

When they arrived, Piercey's car was parked outside and the man himself stood at the open door as if he was a host welcoming guests, which darkened Tom's mood further. The bastard was even smiling. The smile faded as Walpole charged up the drive and pushed past him. Piercey frowned a question at Tom, who was close on his heels. Who he? it asked.

'One of the brothers after Starr's personal items,' he announced as he closed with his sergeant. 'Give a hand. I want him off the base asap.'

The two detectives joined Walpole upstairs, where he was banging cupboard doors and muttering. He rounded on them. 'So who's been in here helping himself, eh?'

'Nothing's been taken away,' Tom said firmly. 'As you've been made aware, this is a possible crime scene. Please disturb it as little as possible.' He began taking Starr's clothes from hangers in the broken wardrobe, folding them and putting them on the bed. He turned to Piercey. 'Collect some bin liners from the kitchen for Mr Walpole to pack Mrs Keane's and the children's clothes in.'

Walpole stood over Tom. 'Someone *has* been in here and taken stuff. Where is it?'

'Are you so familiar with your sister's every possession that you're so certain something is missing,' countered Tom. 'Have you ever visited her here?'

'Them creams and lotions of hers, where are they?'

As he had not searched the house Tom had no idea what he was talking about, although he did recall Max had made some comment about the dead woman he had seen being too attractive to need so many homeopathic remedies so maybe Keane had used them.

'If they're not here, she must have taken them with her when she left on Saturday. The German police report states that any personal identification and belongings would have been destroyed by the fire. You *were* given full details of the crash, weren't you?'

'She didn't take them. She told me they were still in the house, but she was going back in a day or two to collect everything else before heading home to Mum.' There was the first indication of grief on his face as he said, 'I was over here with a load. We was going to meet up like we did whenever one of us was near here. She was on her way to me when it happened, poor little bitch!'

Tom studied him silently for a moment or two. 'Were you aware she was using coke?'

'*No*. Would I have let her? What d'you take me for?' he demanded with renewed aggression. 'It was that bugger she married. He did for her every way he could, and I reckon he got what was due to him. Ruined her life. Dragged her away from her family to live in this dump. He promised to leave the Army when he got back from playing soldiers for real, then told her he never said so. Broke her up, that did. That so-called friend she went to must've given it to her to cheer her up. Instead, she *killed* Starr!'

Piercey arrived with the bin liners in time to hear that last statement. 'Your sister died in a road accident, Mr Walpole. Can we help you pack the things, or would you prefer to do it alone? Perhaps I could put together the kids' things, although most of them seem to have gone already. They'll be at the care home, along with everything else left at the friend's house.'

Walpole switched his verbal attack to Piercey. 'You were already in here when we arrived. Where've you put all those pots of stuff Starr had?'

Tom was surprised by the flare of interest on Piercey's face, but his tone was normal when he asked Walpole to describe them.

'Ah, when we first checked the house we found pieces of a pot like that. It appeared to have been thrown at the wall.' He indicated a yellow stain. 'Stuff with rather a strong smell, here and on the carpet. The broken pieces were removed as a hazard. There were no other containers in here,' he added, waving an arm at the complete bedroom. 'If they held beauty preparations surely your sister would have taken them with her.'

Highly incensed, Walpole said, 'I've just told this bozo *she left them here!* Said so when she called to arrange our meeting. One of you guys has had them. That's theft, that is. I want them handed over before I leave this house.' He turned on Tom. 'I can make things difficult. *Very* difficult. Me and Beefy's got friends in the right places.'

'Don't issue threats to me,' warned Tom. 'We're making a concession in allowing you on these premises. The usual practice is for us to bag up personal effects and send them to next of kin. You seem to have forgotten that your sister's husband was murdered just a few days ago. His family will want the things *he* left in this house. Collect those items you came for, then Sar'nt Piercey will drive you to where you're lodging. If the cosmetics turn up they'll be forwarded to your mother.'

Tom felt some satisfaction in giving Piercey the task of chauffeuring this obnoxious character who, after searching every cupboard and drawer on both floors, grabbed the bin liners Piercey had filled with clothes and toys and left without showing any interest in claiming such items as DVDs, ornaments or framed photographs of the children at various stages of growth. Several showed Starr with them; happy, smiling groups.

Tom drove home pondering Walpole's interest in a few pots of cosmetics against photographs his mother would surely prize. It had been quite a day, one way or another. Giving Brenda such shocking facts about a man she had sincerely loved and supported, then the selfish reactions to death from the Walpole family. Not the mother, perhaps, but those brothers were dyed-in-the-wool thugs.

Dealing with the grief of two very different women in very different circumstances highlighted his own concern over Nora's uncharacteristic behaviour. How would he cope with losing her to some dread illness? How could he ever be father *and* mother to three vulnerable girls? It was too terrible to contemplate.

He drove fast in his sudden anxiety to reach Nora and hold her close. Leaving the vehicle on the driveway, he let himself in the house and headed through to the garden, led there by the sound of excited voices. His daughters were playing with a puppy on the lawn, while Nora looked on with a fond smile. Oh, dear God, he thought, is this dog her parting gift to them?

TEN

Heather Johnson decided against questioning Staff Sergeant Fuller about Mel Dunstan. Those two were too close for the frank appraisal of the female knight's private life she sought, yet only someone who knew Mel reasonably well could provide the more intimate details that would justify her own suspicions of the I Corps subaltern. So, after gently encouraging a dozy bee from her windscreen, Heather drove across the base to the gymnasium.

Second Lieutenant Joanna Carstairs, known by the obligatory pseudo-masculine Jo, was one of the PT Instructors who had dressed as a clown to give comedy displays on the trampoline during the Open Day. Heather had opted to interview her because she lived in the same Mess as Mel, and because she would have spent a lot of time with her during planning meetings prior to the day of their public performances. Jo would surely be able to shed light on Mel's behaviour during the run-up to Keane's murder.

At the back of Heather's mind was the truth that she was acting on the slender facts that Mel had been taking a break from the jousting during the time that Keane actually died, and that she could have been the knight seen at midnight. For what reason? asked an inner voice. Witnesses had not seen a body slung over the saddle. Even Piercey's wild theory of a dead man sitting upright with a pole supporting his back would have needed another rider to lead the horse. She sighed. Was she being rational over this hunch?

The first sight of Jo Carstairs caused Heather to sigh again. Tall and ash blonde, she had a wonderfully toned, beautifully proportioned body. All that daily exercise, of course. Yet Heather knew she would never acquire that gorgeous image. She took plenty of exercise, but her bone

structure and 'hippy' shape prevented her from being
anything other than short and dumpy.

She watched the class performing energetically on the
mass of equipment, until Jo called them together and set
them doing one hundred press-ups before crossing to the
smartly dressed intruder.

'Can I help? Are you lost?'

Heather showed her identification. 'My colleague, Sar'nt
Piercey, interviewed you concerning the murder of Corporal
Keane RCR on the Open Day. A witness had seen a clown
roaming the base after dark.'

Jo smiled broadly. 'That was Ronnie Phelps. His wife
still hasn't seen the joke. I thought it was a real hoot.'

'Perhaps his wife's sense of humour doesn't run in that
direction.'

'She doesn't have a sense of humour.'

'Then he's either a brave or a stupid man to have done
it,' concluded Heather. 'We also have a witness who saw
a mounted knight crossing the Sports Ground.'

'Oh, that was me.'

'*You!* I thought you were one of the clowns.'

After a swift glance at the puffing, panting troops nowhere
near the end of their press-ups, Jo smiled again. She was
a very smiley person, which was particularly annoying after
blighting Heather's hopes of evidence to support her case
against Mel Dunstan.

'I was honour bound to support my own Corps by
performing on the trampoline, but I'm also a member of
the Court and could have participated in the Jousting. It
was the same with Pete Saunders, the Veterinary Officer.
He was on duty on Saturday and moaned on and on about
not having the chance to show what he can do with a lance.'
Another broad smile. 'He and I have a love-hate relationship. He's rather cocky, but I fancy him; he's flattered and
plays up to me. Whenever we ride together he shows off.
His horse is far superior to mine, which dupes him into
believing he's a better rider.'

Her eyes brightened with amusement. 'For fun I sent him
an anonymous challenge to a midnight joust, which he

accepted because he can never resist the chance to prove how marvellous he is at all things equestrian. I had switched on the floodlights at the Sports Ground; the lists were still in place and I admit it was very romantic when we rode in with visors down and lances held high. Two mystery knights ready to prove their worth.'

By this time Heather began to wonder if she had wandered into Barbara Cartland territory, yet she could not help asking the outcome.

'Norval, that's Pete's horse, was unsettled by the bright lights and played up when he saw me charging towards him. In truth, I think the light reflecting off my shield dazzled him. On the third run I hit Pete's shield almost dead centre just as Norval shied. Pete was unseated and fell.' She gave a gurgling laugh. 'I pinned him on the ground with my lance as a signal of his defeat, then I rode off. He has no idea who his opponent was because I didn't ride my mare. I keep trying to lead him into telling me about it, but he won't. He's not so full of himself, however. Terrific fun!'

Tom Black was right, thought the bemused Heather. The base holds an Open Day; military discipline goes to hell and the garrison runs amok. She forced her mind back to why she was there and halted Jo when she looked set to return to her class.

'Give them a break,' she said crisply. 'I need some answers from you now I know you were out and about at midnight on Saturday. Did you encounter anyone else wandering around? See anything unusual or curious?'

'I didn't go near the water tank.'

'Forget the tank. Did you see anything at all that seemed odd?' She almost added, *odder than two idiots jousting at midnight*, but decided to let that slide.

Jo pursed her mouth. 'Only the stragglers heading for bed. Nobody acting suspiciously. Tell the truth, I didn't have great vision through the visor.'

'Why didn't you take the helmet off?'

'I didn't want someone to identify me and tell Pete.' Her amusement faded as she put two and two together. 'You don't think it was because *I* was involved in that murder.

Check with Pete Saunders. He'll confirm the jousting on the Sports Ground.'

'I'm sure he will,' said Heather, smiling over what she was going to say next. 'But he doesn't know who his opponent was, does he? You made certain of that.'

Ignoring the men and women who were now chatting to one another as they sat on the floor recovering from the press-ups, Jo began another sentence then stopped as she realized she could not provide an unbreakable alibi. Now visibly flustered, she said, 'Look, Mel Dunstan saw me take Drew Meredith's gelding from his stall. She was with Staff Fuller at the other end of the stables. She *must* have seen me. We were the only people there at that hour.'

'Still doesn't prove what you did on leaving the stables.' Heather seized on this lead to what she had really come for. 'I've already interviewed Mel Dunstan. She told me she was not aware of any horse missing when she was discussing the forthcoming races with Sheila Fuller.'

'But she must have heard . . . I mean, you can't *sneak* a horse from his stall. There's a lot of snorting and clattering. Why would she say that?'

'You tell me,' returned Heather. 'How well do you know her?'

By now looking rather worried, Jo said, 'Let me dismiss this platoon, then we'll talk in the office. I can sort this.'

As Heather watched her give an encouraging word to soldiers delighted to be spared the final ten minutes of physical demands on their bodies, she wondered if she had got it all wrong with the Dunstan woman. This unexpected development provided food for a great deal of thought. Had she stumbled on a breakthrough from a surprising source? Jo Carstairs had unwittingly put herself in the hot seat by admitting that she had deliberately hidden her identity while riding through the base, even when returning to the stables. Was she as lighthearted as she made out, or very canny? It would be wise to seek every bit of information about this athlete on returning to Headquarters. If there was even the slightest link between her and Flip Keane, Heather would find it.

They went into the small office used by all the PT Instructors, and Jo closed the door before flopping in the swivel chair with a groan.

'It seemed a delicious joke at the time. Still did, until you came along. Of course, I know about the corporal being drowned in the water tank. Or strangled. There's so many yarns going around about it. I never expected to be *connected* with it. It's just too way out. I didn't *know* the guy, never met him or his family. I have little to do with the regiments. I work with Headquarter Company. Have done the whole time I've been here. Believe me, it was pure coincidence that I was riding through the base around the time he was murdered,' she protested. Then she had an idea. 'The witness who saw a knight; it could have been Pete. He was wearing the full jousting gear too.'

'You think *he* could have killed Keane?'

'No! You're putting meaning to my words that isn't there.' She leaned forward with sudden urgency. 'Here's something interesting, though. Pete had already taken Norval when I reached the stables, which means *two* animals would have been led out while Mel was chatting to Staff Fuller about the races. How could she have failed to notice *that*?'

Heather sat on an upright chair facing her. 'I've not seen the stables, so I can't answer that. I'll repeat my earlier question. How well do you know her?'

'As well as I know most people I pass in the Mess, or occasionally sit next to for meals. She's with I Corps.' She gave a twisted smile. 'Everyone knows brain rarely mixes with brawn.'

'She's snooty?' probed Heather.

'No, not that. She's just not really one of the girls.'

'One of the boys?'

'Even less so, I'd say. They call her the Ice Maiden.'

'She's a loner?'

'Not exactly. She mixes well enough, but doesn't cultivate close friends. She's on easy terms with Sheila Fuller because of their mutual passion for horses, and there's apparently some kind of distant relative in the REs, but apart from them she keeps her own company. The story goes that seven days before her wedding her fiancé died. She took it hard and has never recovered from the loss. I heard she was hopelessly smitten, which makes nonsense of the Ice Maiden tag, doesn't it?'

'How long ago was this?'

'A couple of years, according to camp gossip.'

'I didn't get the impression she was suffering from long-term grief, but perhaps she's the sort who can hide their feelings and concentrate on their work. Although you normally have little contact with her you probably saw more of her in the run-up to the Open Day. Planning discussions, rehearsals. How did she strike you at those meetings?'

'Strike me?' Jo seemed puzzled by the question. 'God, I don't know. I perhaps got the impression that her heart wasn't really in it. She'd been co-opted by Fuller, who's highly competitive against the men, but Mel's no feminist.'

'You sensed that she was reluctant to compete?'

Jo shook her head, frowning. 'Now I come to think more deeply about it, I'd say she was abstracted. Certainly not entering into the spirit of the occasion like the rest of us.' She glanced across at Heather. 'Maybe she *is* suffering from long-term grief, which comes to the fore when she's not working.'

Leaving the gymnasium in a dissatisfied mood Heather knew she had been given information she had not wanted to hear. So certain was she that Mel Dunstan had been the midnight knight, she was now faced with evidence that the rider had been one of two people who must now be regarded with more suspicion than the I Corps officer.

Before returning to Headquarters and her computer, she drove to the dog compounds near the surgery of the Veterinary Officer. On meeting this blond, upper-crust man for the first time, she fully appreciated Jo's description of him as a cocky individual. Captain Peter Saunders made the difference in their ranks very clear by addressing Heather by hers throughout, and said with a hint of arrogance that he had been very well aware of the identity of his opponent when he received the anonymous challenge.

'It's just the sort of thing she would do,' he explained. 'Has her head in the clouds much of the time. Reads romantic slush set in the Middle Ages,' he added, with a smile designed to indicate that what he read was far more erudite.

'But you nevertheless turned up at the Sports Ground to meet her challenge . . . at midnight,' responded Heather with faint emphasis on *midnight* to suggest surprise. 'Wasn't that also somewhat fanciful?'

His smile vanished. 'What is the point of your visit, Sergeant? I'm a very busy man. My only assistant is off sick.'

'The point of my visit, sir, is to check on your movements just before and after falling from your horse during the joust. We're investigating the murder of Corporal Keane, RCR, whose body was discovered in the water tank just after midnight on Saturday. You happen to be one of several people moving around the base at that hour.'

'Mmm, I heard you were totally stymied on that,' he said with a touch of condescension. 'I can't oblige, I'm afraid. Before I took part in that ridiculous business I was fetching Norval from the stables and fitting myself out in style. As I rode off I did spot Lieutenant Dunstan's car drawing up outside the stables. She would have seen my Range Rover parked there. Ask her. She'll confirm it.'

Something else Mel Dunstan had apparently not seen, or felt was not important enough to offer as evidence, thought Heather. 'And after you'd been defeated in the joust, sir?'

He looked daggers at her. 'Norval was startled and unseated me, that was all. He's highly bred and nervous. He reared in fright when he saw Captain Meredith's gelding charging towards him bearing a rider wearing strange gear. If you have any knowledge of horses you'll understand that, Sergeant.'

'I prefer dogs, sir. When you rode back to the stables, presumably not alongside Second Lieutenant Carstairs, was your visor up or down?'

'Up, naturally. How else would I have seen where I was going? Sergeant Johnson, I did *not* drop a body in the water tank in passing. Neither, I can say with certainty, did Second Lieutenant Carstairs. She rode ahead of me all the way, and I saw her dismount and take Pennycuik to his stall. I then continued to this surgery where I tethered Norval, removed the hauberk and tabard, drank two cups of tea before returning to the stables. They were deserted by then. It was one thirty.

Feeling happier because she believed what this rather shallow man had told her, Heather then asked if he had seen anyone else moving around the base during that period.'

'Only Lieutenant Dunstan parking her car outside the Mess.'

'At one thirty' she asked eagerly.

'Earlier. When I was riding here to the surgery to change my clothes. Presumably she was returning from her visit to the stables that I spotted an hour or so before.' He added in the manner of an adult to an over-eager child, 'Don't read anything into that. She frequently goes there before turning in, to check on Jetset. A horse is a greater responsibility than a dog, Sergeant. Now I must shoo you away. I have two small operations listed for this afternoon.'

After Piercey gladly offloaded the pugnacious Walpole at a small guesthouse in town, he drove back to Headquarters. The sole occupant of the Incident Room was Reg Prentiss, whose wife had given birth to an eleven-pound boy after a difficult labour. His parents-in-law had arrived to take charge, so Reg was seeking refuge by voluntarily manning the SIB emergency line. He looked half asleep, so Piercey made coffee and took him some.

'Anything?' he asked the new father.

'Just Captain Goodey wanting the Boss. Said he's not picking up his mobile, and she needs to make contact.'

Piercey glanced at the clock. 'In another hour they'll both go home, then she can walk next door and talk to him live.' He grinned. 'Unless he's taken leave after all, because his popsie said sorry and gave him the come-on.'

'Oh? Have I missed out on a bit of scandal?'

Piercey walked to his own desk, laughing gaily. 'You've

missed out on something far bigger than that, Reg, believe me. While you've been changing nappies and crooning lullabies, I've cracked a big one single-handed.'

'This jellyfish murder?' asked Prentiss in amazement.

'Keep those ears flapping, Daddy-o, and you'll hear all about it tomorrow.' He booted-up his computer and was soon so engrossed he did not hear his colleague's snoring. As he worked his smile grew broader and broader.

After dropping off Tom, Max had gone to a small inn not far from the base with the intention of having a decent lunch, but after looking at the menu he realized he wanted nothing more than a bowl of soup. The meeting with Brenda had eliminated someone who he had considered to be a strong suspect in the Keane case. It was frustrating and left the investigation wide open. The Dunstan woman was Heather's long shot, that was all. They had no evidence against her.

He had not been with the case from the moment of discovery of the body, but he was desperate to solve it. Success in that direction would soften the sense of personal failure that was dogging him. He needed to be seen as a man in control of his life; professionally on the ball and one step ahead of the team he commanded. He had told Tom to take the afternoon off because he needed to be alone for a spell.

After finishing the soup, he took a walk along a path that wound through sparse woodland, bludgeoning his brain to make sense of all the data the team had accumulated. Odd facts added up, but none made an illuminating total. There was either a missing factor that would make immediate sense of it all, or the killing could be logged as momentary madness by someone recently returned from the warzone who had imagined Keane to be the enemy. If that was the case, the investigation could continue for weeks and might never be successfully solved.

With that thought adding further frustration, Max walked back to his car with the intention of pursuing the one aspect of the case he was determined to probe. It would not bring a solution, but rooting out the truth would bring partial balm to his bruised pride.

Returning to base, Max managed to track down Ben Steele doing a number of lengths in the swimming pool. He was very happy to abandon the exercise and talk. Draping a towel around his shoulders, he confessed that swimming was not his favourite pastime.

'I finally completed the paperwork following our return, so I'm off to the UK tomorrow,' he said with a grin. 'My mother's laid on a couple of family parties, and so has my girlfriend's aunt. Add some general celebrating with friends, and it seemed wise to shed a few pounds before the heavy intake over the next few weeks. Have you news for me regarding Flip Keane's death?'

Max shook his head. 'Sorry, no. I just want to check some facts with you. Can we go where our voices don't echo and there's no smell of chlorine? We can't talk against the noise of these swimmers. It's a confidential matter.'

'Can it wait for me to shower and dress?'

'Yes, if you're happy to pack in the swimming, Ben. I'll sit in my car. Join me when you're ready.'

Max felt a pang of envy when Ben emerged and crossed to where he was waiting. Young and fit, with an engaging manner, Ben was going home to a waiting girlfriend and a series of parties. Lucky man!

'You're welcome to tea and choc digestives in my room,' he said bending to the window. 'That's what I usually have after a swim.'

'Hop in,' said Max. 'I won't keep you long away from them.'

When Ben was seated beside him, he said, 'I'd like you to tell me about that night patrol in Iraq, when Keane believed he had shot one of ours and you were all held incommunicado. In detail, please, and I'd like the names of every member of that patrol.'

Ben looked anxious. 'It hasn't resurfaced, has it? I understood we'd been cleared of blame.'

'You have. It's been mentioned several times in relation

to Keane's recent state of mind, that's all. Just remind me of the facts.'

It was clear that Ben was now unhappy about repeating what he had willingly told Max earlier, and even more unhappy about giving the names of his men who had shared the experience. As the leader of the patrol he could have been branded irresponsible, unable to control those under his command. Max vowed to reassure him when he finished speaking, but before he could do so Ben's mobile rang. The young captain listened with a deepening frown, then said he would be there shortly.

'Sorry about the interruption, but you'll probably want to know about this, too. That was the padre to tell me Starr Keane's family have arrived there from the mortuary. He thinks I should talk to them as Flip's Company Commander, because they're demanding the children and won't accept that he has the authority to deny them. I'll have to get him off the hook.'

As he scrambled from the car Max thought Ben looked as though he felt he had also been let off the hook. After a few minutes of reflection, he drove to Frank Priest's quarter in the hope of finding him at home. He was lucky, but only just. He was packing his car with cases and bags for a trip to Spain, starting in an hour. The sergeant major took Max to a small room at the back of the house and seemed disturbed when he learned the reason for the visit.

'I wasn't on the patrol, sir, so I can't give you any info other than what I knew was going on when they were all locked away for questioning.'

'Just tell me what you know about the affair,' said Max, who then once more heard about something that officially never happened. The facts were just as Ben had related fifteen minutes ago.

Leaving the Priests to get under way, Max sat in his car for a further spell of reflection. Ben Steele, Frank Priest, Ryan Moore, Brenda; all these people had spoken of an aborted night patrol that had badly undermined Keane's confidence as a fighting man. Ben, Priest and Ryan Moore *could* have got together to invent that patrol, but not Brenda.

She had been well out of their orbit for two years, so there was some military or political aspect of the affair that had to be hushed up. Had Keane been killed because he had managed to uncover the truth? Brushing aside his earlier conviction that the murder had a sexual motive, Max now grew convinced of this new slant and set about following it up.

Deciding not to use his office at Headquarters, where he could very well be disturbed by members of the team wanting to speak to him, Max headed for home. Once there, he made a thermos jug of black coffee and settled, with it and a mug beside him, at his computer.

For two hours he trawled through every possible site that might shed light on the patrol that never was. Nothing. They had been very thorough; wiped it from every operational report.

The participants had thankfully accepted the fiction that had been fed to them, and had no way of discovering, as SIB had, that it *was* fiction. Keane's murder had resurrected it. His calls to Steven Cartwright at Catterick and Lieutenant Colonel Quail at Sandhurst must have caused a few ripples of concern. He was about to make a few more.

Three telephone calls later he was none the wiser. Each man had either laughingly told him he was being led by the ear by men who enjoyed putting one over on the Redcaps, or that he had got the facts wrong and should check dates and units. Finally, Max contacted the Provost Marshal's office and was told very sharply to stop making waves. When he explained that the information he needed formed one aspect of a murder investigation, the answer was that he should concentrate on more pertinent aspects.

'Drop it! That's a direct order, Captain Rydal.'

Having drunk all the coffee, Max went to the kitchen and poured himself a brandy and ginger ale in deeply thoughtful mood. Then, because he found his apartment too reminiscent of Livya, he took his drink through to the central room and sat in one of the large chairs near the window. The interlude with Clare here last night was well to the back of his mind.

What had occurred on that patrol was extremely sensitive, that was certain, but no way would he leave it in the air. He could not officially pursue it without incurring action that would damage his career, so he would have to call in some favours, or ruthlessly exploit friendships. The simplest solution would be to get the information from his father, but Andrew Rydal was on his honeymoon at a secret destination. His ADC had just confessed from Max's bed that she had used him as a substitute for her boss, so that source of information was taboo.

While he was racking his brain for the best person to lean on heavily for the facts he needed to know, he was startled by the arrival from the other apartment of Clare Goodey.

'Knew you were here. Saw your car outside,' she said, crossing to him with some papers in her hand. 'I've been trying to get you for the past couple of hours. Your people had no idea where you were, and you'd switched off your mobile.'

He got to his feet. 'I didn't want to be interrupted. Was it important?'

'It depends on how you view it, Max.'

By then noticing her expression, he asked, 'Is there a problem?'

'I have here the result of the post-mortem on Corporal Keane. The hyoid bone was not fractured, so death was not due to strangulation. The bruises on his throat were caused by Keane's own hands as he fought for breath during an anaphylactic shock resulting from a bee sting. They found the insect in his trachea when they opened him up. Their findings are that it was an accidental death. There was no murder, Max.'

ELEVEN

Tom waited in Nora's car while she talked to Clare Goodey. Waited with apprehension. He had challenged her solo decision to allow their girls to bring home the puppy. However, it had not been a final adoption of the appealing small animal. Strudel (yes, she had already been given a name by them) was there on a three-hour try-out. She was returned to her mother and siblings at homework time, which was when Tom had questioned Nora's U-turn as they sat in the garden with glasses of wine to watch the rising moon replace the setting sun.

She continued to study the gold and silver sky. 'When you went off to sort that poor woman who's being denied her grandchildren, I started thinking how awful it would be if anything happened to *us* and our girls were taken away by social workers who refused to allow our parents to raise and love them. What heartbreak!'

Tom's concern increased. Why was she having such thoughts? 'That case is different. The Keane children are still infants. Gloria Walpole's husband walked out ten years ago, and she has no more than basic income from her job in the local supermarket. Keane's parents are in their seventies. The children will have a better life with foster parents who can give them all we give ours. The boy will soon adapt; the girl is just eight months old. For six of them her father was in Afghanistan, so she'll have hardly formed a bond with him yet.' He had put his arm along her shoulders. 'Nothing's going to happen to us, love. Whatever made you so maudlin?'

'My outburst over the phone when they begged to have Strudel. They're good girls, Tom. They don't badger us for everything under the sun the way some kids demand from their parents.'

'That's because we've always been firm about not

spoiling them. They get enough to rate with their friends, but value their things more.'

'They really want this puppy; all three want her equally. Strudel isn't just the latest gadget or footwear which'll be uncool within a few months. She'll give them delight and unreserved love for *years*. I suddenly felt they should have her canine companionship.'

That had alarmed Tom further. To replace hers? 'You were adamant this morning that you didn't want the extra responsibility. Are you sure about this?'

She had smiled up at him, rather sadly, he thought. 'Yes, love. When she's fully weaned, Strudel will be joining the Blackies.'

So now he was waiting outside the Medical Centre, fearful and sweating. What would she tell him when she emerged? Her expression was not encouraging as she slid on the passenger seat beside him, but he tried to sound unconcerned as he asked what the verdict was.

'I'm slightly anaemic, which is causing the tiredness,' she said in heavy tones. 'She's given me some iron pills. Should be an improvement in a few weeks.'

'That's it?' he demanded, certain he was not hearing the full truth of what had been said in the surgery.

'That's it,' she repeated. 'When the pills start to work there'll be no holding me. Come on, get to work so that I can have my car back.'

Still worried, Tom put the car in gear and drove across the base to Headquarters. Nora gave him a brief kiss as she rounded the bonnet to take his place at the wheel, then drove off without her usual small wave in farewell. Something was badly wrong, he knew it. Why was she keeping it from him?

He walked through to his office to find the whole team gathered to hear Max make an astonishing announcement.

'We no longer have a murder to investigate. The postmortem report has come in. It concludes that Philip Keane suffered a fatal anaphylactic shock after being stung by a bee he had swallowed.'

'There was an old lady who swallowed a fly
I don't know why she swallowed a fly
Perhaps she'll die'

Piercey quoted softly. 'Substitute bee, and there you have
it.'

'But he was strangled,' protested Heather.

'Captain Goodey said an anaphylactic fit produces the
same desperate fight for breath, same irregular heartbeat,
same sense of terror. The bruises on his throat had been
caused by his own hands attempting to ease the pain.'

As Tom walked over to him, Max nodded a greeting,
then continued. 'The pathologist found the bee in Keane's
trachea. There's no doubt it was an accidental death. I'm
sure the news comes as something of a let-down after the
in-depth work you've all done, but I suppose the upside is
that a first-rate soldier who had everything going for him
wasn't deliberately robbed of his future by a human hand.

'We've all been pestered by the plague of bees during
these weeks of abnormal autumn warmth, and Captain
Goodey has treated a number of patients with bee stings.
She told me some people are actually allergic to the sting,
which induces an anaphylactic shock whichever part of the
body is targeted. They need very prompt medical help. In
Keane's case, the swelling produced by the sting closed his
airway and he effectively choked to death.'

Into the silence Tom said, 'So we're left with the task
of tracking down whoever found Keane's body and decided
to dump it in the water tank with the jellyfish around its
neck.' He glanced at Max. 'That was definitely done by a
human hand.'

Max gave a twisted smile. 'Can't pin that on the bee. So
we now look at the case differently. I came in on it late,
so I suggest you recap the initial findings then gather input.'

With half his mind on Nora – she would not be acting
so strangely due to simple anaemia – Tom began to review
the facts gleaned over the past few days. The issue no longer
seemed so vital. The unwelcome possibility of murder by
a colleague no longer existed; those people who were close

to Philip Keane could find some comfort from that. Perpetrating a bizarre act with his body was a much lesser crime. Still unwelcome, but his parents and Brenda need not be told of that distressing act.

'The most likely supposition is that Keane took a drink without noticing a bee in the vessel. Easy thing to happen if he was in a hurry with his mind on the acrimonious split with Starr, which we know occurred on Saturday. Brenda claims he arrived at her flat early that morning with the news of the planned divorce. He stayed there long enough to allow Starr to pack enough for a short stay with Julia Reiter, then left at around eleven thirty to fetch his own gear from the house before his intended return to spend the rest of his leave with her and his new son.

'Keane's body wore only underpants, which makes it more than likely that he was at home when he died. Taking into account the time Keane and Starr would each have taken to travel their respective distances, the margin is so slender there is a possibility that they overlapped and Starr witnessed her husband's death. However, Julia Reiter was certain her friend was unaware of her widowhood, so I'm suggesting that they passed each other on the road. We'll never know if Starr watched him die and simply walked away.'

'But she intended to go back to the house after organizing her trip to the UK, to collect the rest of her stuff,' Connie pointed out. 'Was she callous enough to leave his body lying there for two days before calmly packing-up her remaining things with him still sprawled on the floor?'

'Unlikely,' ruled Tom. 'Despite all we've been told about her aggressive attitude towards Keane, she's reported to have been a marvellous mother and a fun-loving friend. However upset she might have been over the final split in the marriage – and there's no evidence to suggest she knew about Brenda – I believe she died unaware of what had happened to Keane.'

'The timing is about right,' Beeny observed. 'They say death occurred between midday and fourteen hundred. So, if we accept the premise that the underpants indicate he was

at home packing his gear when he took the fatal drink, it means someone discovered the body and took it from the house at some time between noon and midnight. I'd guess it was taken soon after death, because the body-snatcher had no way of knowing Starr wouldn't return at any moment.'

'Or the BS could have discovered it late on Saturday evening in the deserted house,' said Connie. 'I don't think we should assume it was removed earlier.'

'One thing we can safely assume is that the person who removed the body didn't happen upon it by chance,' said Max suddenly. 'It was Open Day. Personnel were mostly engaged in or watching the events taking place, so why would anyone casually call at his house expecting him to be there? I'd say whoever carried out the removal and desecration of the body went to the quarter for a specific purpose.'

'I can give the answer to that,' said Piercey, who had been silent since his murmured rhyme. 'He went to collect the cocaine in the bottom of those pots of herbal remedies.' Visibly pleased to have delivered a bolt from the blue, Piercey elaborated. 'Starr Keane had been distributing the drug by that method. We all thought she must have been some kind of hag to need so many aids to her appearance, yet the Boss said she was a nice-looking woman and pictures of her with her kids bore that out.

'I didn't connect the two until I visited Corporal Marshall's quarter and found his wife had clearly just had a fix. There were similar pots in *her* bathroom, and there was evidence that she had had a girls' get-together tha morning. I went back to the Keanes' house and emptie the pots. Each had a false bottom. There was coke three of them. The rest must have already been distr uted.'

Tom was furious. 'Why didn't you call this info in'

Piercey was unperturbed. 'I would have, sir, bu' called me in to supervise the removal of Starr's belor by the brother, then told me to drive him to his l As it happened,' he added swiftly before Tom coul again, 'he ranted on about the absence of those much I suspected that he and his sibling might be

them over in their trucks. He seemed scared witless that someone had taken them.

'One thing, sir. He was genuinely and deeply distressed that his sister had indulged. Kept saying someone must have given her the drug; she'd never have touched it because of the kids. Seems likely to me that she was so upset over the split with Keane, she recklessly had a snort to perk herself up and had no notion how to use the stuff.'

'That's all supposition,' snapped Tom, trying not to over-react to this man who could not resist going alone on a case.

Piercey had his answer ready. 'I checked out the herbal company named on the labels. It went to the wall three years ago, so I contacted a pal in the Met. He came back with the info that the bankrupt stock had been bought by one Roddy Jensen . . . who happens to be a director of the import-export company the Walpoles are employed by,' he added with quiet triumph.

Max broke the ensuing silence by congratulating the maverick sergeant on some very sharp investigating, adding, 'So your conclusion is that whoever visited the Keanes' quarter on Saturday was after those pots?'

'Exactly, sir.'

'So why leave them there and instead take the body he'd unexpectedly found and put him in the water with a synthetic jellyfish round his neck?'

Piercey was unusually lost for words, but he had had his moment in exposing an international operation for Interpol to pursue, and he had also effectively checked a drug problem on the base. Brownie points galore!

Olly Simpson suddenly entered the lists. 'Is it possible to force a person to swallow a bee?'

Nobody appeared enthusiastic about this input. After their concentrated work attempting to trace a murderer there was a general sense of anti-climax. The more exhilarating task of working out the connection between the killing and the subsequent treatment of the body had had them all on their toes. Piercey's investigative triumph added a sense of having had the flesh of the case stripped away leaving them with just a few bones to gnaw.

'Yes,' Beeny said eventually. 'If someone had held Keane's nose and made him drink. Has anyone ever used a bee as a murder weapon?'

Tom frowned. 'We're entering very deep waters, but there have been cases where victims were forced by that method to drink poison, acid, aviation fuel, anything obnoxious, with the purpose of killing or seriously disabling. In those cases the perpetrators had the substance with them, but who would have a convenient bee?'

Heather then offered her findings, such as they were. At the end of her statement that the midnight knight had probably been either Jo Carstairs or Peter Saunders, Tom said, 'So there's no evidence to support your suspicions of Mel Dunstan?'

'No, sir,' she agreed heavily.

'Any to tie either of the other two to the business at the water tank?'

'I haven't found any.'

Max got to his feet and looked at them all. 'Pointless to invent suspects. In view of the present state of play, I suggest we take a well-deserved day off and come back tomorrow for a fresh look at the facts we have now. Thanks, everyone.'

After Max had handed the baton to him at the start of the meeting, Tom felt it had been snatched back with the granting of a day off for the team without reference to him first. Because of that he walked in silence to collect the keys to his own car that were in his office.

Max was in the doorway as he took them from the hook and turned to leave. 'Everything all right?'

'Fine.'

'I didn't want to spoil your evening by giving you the p.m. findings right away.'

That added to his resentment. 'You knew last night?'

'The Doc gave it to me when she arrived home.'

'I hope it didn't spoil *your* evening,' he said, then regretted it. Max was trying to deal with a broken relationship instead of enjoying two romantic weeks with a woman he had been hoping to marry. The ties of friendship overrode irritation. 'Let's have coffee and decide where the case stands.'

Max nodded; said as they walked to where the kettle stood, 'It's a different case entirely now. In fact, if whoever found Keane had immediately alerted George Maddox, there'd be no case at all, but he went to that house for a definite purpose, which I'm pretty certain was to do Keane some harm. We could possibly have "intent to murder".'

'Difficult to prove.' Tom filled and switched on the kettle, then put sugar in two mugs.

'Ever since Clare Goodey gave me that report I've been wondering if the intention all along was to strangle him at the water tank. Deprived of the satisfaction of doing that, a mock-up of the murder had to substitute for the planned crime. Yet, why not use rope, a chain, a belt?'

He's worrying at that symbolic notion again, thought Tom with irritation returning. He needed to go home to Nora. 'He wanted the body found first thing on Sunday. The water tank was set to be emptied that morning, so that's where it was dumped. The jellyfish was handy, that's all.'

'Who knew the water tank wouldn't be drained until Sunday morning?' asked Max significantly.

'The REs.'

'On the orders of Lieutenant Sears, who was in Afghanistan for a period at the same time as the Cumberland Rifles.'

This wild goose was well and truly tamed. Tom sighed. 'We checked him out twice.'

'I know. I checked him out last night. He was also in Iraq at the time of that night patrol that never was, Tom.'

That did get his full attention. 'Serving in the same area as the Cumberland Rifles?'

'That very same area.'

The kettle boiled and switched itself off while they stood developing the significance of that, unaware of steam issuing from the spout.

'I spent yesterday p.m. very fruitfully. Ben Steele confirmed details of that aborted patrol and was in the process of giving me the names of all its members when George called him to help with the Walpoles. I then contacted everyone

I knew, to no avail. When I eventually went right to the top I was ordered to leave well alone.'

'So that's the end of that!'

'Tom, there were others on that patrol led by our friend Ben Steele. If, as I suspect, the business with the water tank is indicative of a real desire to harm Keane, we might not have seen the last of chummy with the jellyfish. All but three soldiers on that patrol are presently off-base on leave. I suggest that trio should be watched as unobtrusively as poss. while the rest of the team follows up Piercey's discovery of those pots containing coke. There'll be other pots around and, if it's an all-girls syndicate, kids will be at risk.'

He looked at his watch. 'I'm getting a flight to the UK in two hours. An old friend has agreed to meet me at Heathrow. I'll endeavour to return on the late plane and I'll want an early meeting with you tomorrow. Keep your schedule clear.'

Max gripped his shoulder, then went out to his car and drove away leaving Tom frowning beside the empty mugs. Was he now suggesting there was a plan to take out every member of that patrol two years ago? Surely the wildest of geese. If he had been ordered by the Provost Marshal's office to drop it, Max was surely risking his career by ignoring that absolute command. Was he so damaged by Livya Cordwell's departure he was recklessly prepared to destroy his future with SIB?

Leaving the boiled water and the prepared mugs where they stood, Tom drove home deeply concerned on several counts.

The Lufthansa flight arrived on schedule, but was directed to circle for twenty-five minutes because of storm conditions over Heathrow. Max was never a happy flier. Racing across the sky in a tubular vehicle packed with people strapped in their seats was not his favourite means of travel. This additional period in the air, during which passengers grew restive and several babies began to scream from the atmospheric pressure on their tiny eardrums, made Max more than usually keen to land. Jim Collingwood had been extremely reluctant to have this meeting and too much delay might lead him to think better of it and cry off.

He was there beside the Information Desk, however. They shook hands solemnly and walked through to the Departures Hall, where they headed for one of the restaurants. Once settled with their respective meals, Max studied his friend from university days who had pursued a very different course in the Army. Jim's close-cropped hair had silver threads already, and his fresh undergrad features were now scarred and weatherbeaten. Those devil-may-care eyes that had been many a maiden's downfall had become hard and confrontational. Those years in the SAS had added twice as many to Jim's life experience.

'Thanks for coming,' Max said at last.

'As you said, I owe you one.'

'From a long way back, Jim. I'm only calling it in now because there's no other way I can get the info.'

Jim's eyes narrowed. 'What happened to the Brig?'

'He's on his honeymoon.'

'Game old dog! What about you, married again?'

'No.' Max did not add that his failure in that area made success in another so essential. 'You?'

Jim shook his head. 'Cindy left me because of the job. Now I'm out of it I'm working as a night security guard. What woman would want to take on a husband then sleep alone?'

'Couldn't you work days?'

'Huh! Wander around the local shopping centre chasing pre-teen hoodies who snatch old dears' handbags? There's more action going down during the hours of darkness on an industrial estate.'

'What made you leave?' Max asked with genuine interest.

His companion slurped some beer, then wiped his mouth with the back of his hand. 'You get to the stage when you've had enough, no longer see the point of it all. That's the time to go. If you're not firing on all cylinders you're of no use to your mates, so you pack it in. That's when you realize it's the only thing you know. Authorized thuggery.'

'You could become another Andy McNab.'

Jim's expression told Max his opinion of that option.
'I'm considering moving on. Spain, Cyprus, Oz. Sunshine
and a free and easy lifestyle. Open a bar, a club, a fitness
centre.'

'Contact me when you've set it up. I might then be ready
to take up a partnership,' Max said with a grin.

'Bring a wad of dosh and you'll be in, no questions
asked.'

After a short silence as they enjoyed their food, Max
broached the reason for their meeting. 'Did you manage to
track down what I wanted?'

'Didn't have to. I knew already. The Regiment's a small,
close-knit unit. When any of our guys are killed we know
the full details. When it's through friendly fire, we get very
angry.'

Max then knew his suspicions had been spot on. Ben
Steele's night patrol had crossed the path of an SAS mission.
It was known throughout the Army that Special Forces acted
with the utmost secrecy. To that end, they were notified of
any units active in the same area and avoided them. Death
or injury due to friendly fire meant someone along the chain
of communication had slipped up. Badly.

Jim gave Max a look so penetrating he could have been
interrogating a prisoner for information. 'When you called
you said you wanted this to help with a murder investigation.
Was the victim named Keane?'

Max was not too surprised. The SAS had access to everything. 'So it *was* one of yours he killed!'

'Scudo. A Portuguese guy who'd been with us a long
time and was one of the best. We all rated him; never put
a foot wrong. Officially posted as killed in action, but the
truth is known throughout the Regiment. As I said, it caused
a deal of anger.'

After digesting this information Max decided against
revealing that there was not, after all, an actual murder
involved in his bid for the truth. 'I believe someone linked
to that tragic accident decided it was time Keane paid for
what he'd done, albeit in ignorance, but I've been stymied
by the total cover-up of the incident. Even our own records

have been wiped. I've only known that to happen once before; during the Cold War. Before my time, but like your close-knit unit things like that are known in mine.'

'Did the truth ever emerge?'

Max drew in his breath. 'No, Jim.'

'Because it was too dangerous to be made public. Like this is, Max. I may be out of the game, but the rules still apply. No way can I tell you what was under way that night two years ago.'

'I didn't expect you to, but you've confirmed my belief that it was what the Americans call a blue on blue – an attack by Allied troops – thereby promoting grounds for reprisal.' He frowned. 'I suppose there's no way I can learn the identity of the other three on that oppo with Scudo.'

'No.'

'Fair enough. I accept the rules in force on that. Let's try another angle. How about next of kin?'

Jim leaned back and exhaled noisily. 'The same persistent guy I knew at Uni. And every time we've met since those days. Right, the NOK details are available to anyone who knows the poor bastard's real name, so I checked them out for you. English mother, Portuguese father. Both now living in retirement in Madeira. Eight kids. Five male. Two girls work in tourist hotels in the Lake District, one is a model for toothpaste ads.' He leered. 'Along with other modelling jobs, no doubt.'

Max waited patiently, allowing Jim his moment of revelation. He had given up his daytime sleep to come there. He deserved an appreciative audience.

'The eldest son was killed when a dockside crane collapsed on him; the youngest is a Downs kid still living with the parents.'

'And the other two lads?' asked Max, already sensing what the answer would be.

'They all joined the Army.'

Tom's concerns over what had transpired at the briefing did not abate as he covered the miles. What had begun as a high-profile investigation into a bizarre murder, and the

alarming disappearance of a woman and two children, had
evolved into a drug-induced fatal road accident and a death
from ingesting a bee. He could not forget Piercey's mocking
recitation about the old lady who swallowed a fly, nor the
fact that that same maverick sergeant had produced his
discovery of the source of the drug supply like a magician
pulling a rabbit from a hat.

Passing through the main gate, Tom headed for the house
he rented on the outskirts of the town telling himself he had
personally achieved damn-all on the Keane case. *Connie*
had coaxed Ryan Moore to reveal the re-emergence of
Brenda; *Jakes* had traced her with an intelligent guess that
she might have changed her name for the benefit of the
baby. The *Polizei* had found Starr. *Piercey* had investigated
those herbal remedies and fingered the Walpole heavies.
Clare Goodey was behind the truth about Keane's death.
Max was presently on a crusade to clear the mystery
surrounding a night patrol when Keane had or had not killed
an ally. Sergeant Major Black had been superfluous
throughout.

Turning on to the drive he cut the engine and sat deep
in thought. Was he losing his touch? Frank Priest had
mentioned that business in Iraq two years ago, but he
had neglected to follow up on it. Hearing about Starr's use
of cocaine, should he have ordered a comprehensive search
of the Keanes' house for her supply? Had he failed to co-
ordinate evidence with his usual acumen and allowed his
team members to take command? He had not yet even
worked out the significance of that bloody jellyfish. Olly
Simpson might get there just ahead of Max on that, when
that dumbo Tom Black would realize it had been staring
him in the face all along.

Raising his unseeing gaze from the steering wheel, he
then focussed on Nora's car neatly parked in the open
garage. The sight gave him little comfort. She had made
him ineffective at home, too. After shaming him into
accepting the task of ruling on the subject of owning a
puppy, she had then told the girls they could have it. It had
been making itself at home in the garden when he had

arrived home prepared to be firm with his refusal to them.

Rising resentment ebbed away as he recalled his fears over why Nora might have decided they should have the little dog's company. Taking a deep breath, he determined to take that situation by the horns and resolve it without delay. He had been presented with the perfect opportunity. Their daughters were at school and six hours lay before him without the possibility of interruption. He would switch off his mobile; put the bloody thing in a cupboard while he got to the nub of whatever Nora was witholding from him.

She was in the kitchen putting away the things she had bought on her way back from seeing Clare Goodey. She glanced up as if startled from absorbing thoughts by his entry.

'Whatever are you doing here at this time of day?'

'Case solved,' he informed her with feigned lightness of tone. 'The Doc discovered the identity of the perpetrator. We can't charge him and incarcerate him in the glasshouse because he died during the execution of his crime. Max has given us all a day off so we two are going to make the most of it.' He pulled her against him and kissed her before she suspected it. 'I'll finish putting this stuff away while you go up and put on your glad rags. I'm taking you for lunch at the riverside inn Max is so fond of, and I'll not accept any excuses about being too busy. I don't care what else you might have planned, we're going to have a care-free day out. Go on, look lively!'

Hesitating for barely a moment, Nora went without a word, leaving him to stack her shopping in the fridge and cupboards. Tom then joined her in the bedroom to change his formal suit for casual trousers and shirt. Nora was buttoning a cotton skirt she had had for longer than he could remember. With three growing girls to clothe she rarely bought anything new for herself, yet she spent hours making beautiful dresses for weddings and other joyful occasions. She loved the work, but it now struck Tom that it was always for other women.

'So tell me about the case. Who killed Corporal Keane?'

she asked, starting to brush her brown shoulder-length hair.

'A bee.'

'*What?*'

'I'll elaborate in the car,' he said, knowing he must clear that subject from the agenda before tackling the vital one.

Having done just that by the time they arrived at the inn, Tom suggested they walk beside the river until they grew hungry enough to tackle the large lunch he planned to order at one of the tables in the gardens running down to the water's edge. Nora agreed with what Tom thought was a suggestion of resignation, which worried him anew. Now he had set the scene he was anxious about how to broach what he was afraid to hear.

As they walked, Nora suddenly slipped her hand around his and gripped it tightly. 'This is like old times. When we were young.'

Rubbing his thumb caressingly over the back of her hand, he said, 'We're not exactly on our way out yet, love.' The minute he had made the light-hearted comment he read something fearful into it, and further words stuck in his throat.

'Remember that day in Lyme Regis, when we tramped to the highest viewpoint with four heavy bags because I was determined to have an old-fashioned picnic? No Tupperware boxes of cheese sandwiches and jam tarts for me. *I* was going to spread a tablecloth on a tartan rug, use regular cutlery and china plates, boil water to make tea in a china pot with *leaves* not the despicable teabags. I took bridge rolls, paté, smoked salmon, chicken patties, petits fours and a charlotte russe.' She gave a faint chuckle. 'In a cut-glass bowl!'

Tom gazed reflectively at the shadow patterns on water running deep along this stretch of river where Max hired his skiff on Sunday mornings. 'I was then convinced you'd never take on an ordinary bloke like me, who *always* had cheese sandwiches and jam tarts, with teabags in chunky mugs on picnics. I was scared stiff I'd get my finger stuck in the handle of one of those fancy bone china cups you'd brought.'

Nora glanced up at him. 'That's the first time you've admitted that.'

He met her eyes. 'Forgotten beneath the major events of that day.'

They walked in silence as they recalled the violent storm that had broken soon after Nora had set everything out on her starched tablecloth; a cloud burst that had made the cliff edge dangerously unstable.

'I wasn't really sure you were the one I wanted until you went down after that stupid lad who ignored your warning,' she said quietly. 'You could have taken the easy option and waited for the Yellow Hats to arrive.'

He shook his head. 'You know that wasn't an option, love. He was dangling from a ledge over a forty-foot drop and would've crashed on the rocks before the rescue helo had time to get there.'

'You could've crashed on the rocks with him.'

He grinned at her. 'The dilemma about whether I was the one you wanted would have been settled very decisively, in that case. Wonder where he is now, and what kind of man he's become. One thing's certain, he ruined your posh picnic.'

'And Mum's best cups and saucers were scattered by the rotor's downdraught. Wonder where those two missing cups ended up.'

'I told you; in some startled chough's territory.'

She smiled up at him. 'I had no idea what a chough was. I thought it had something to do with the Army.'

'That's the first time *you've* admitted *that,*' he returned slyly.

Nora stopped walking and gazed across the sparkling river to the meadows beyond. 'It's been such a beautiful autumn. You don't know how often I've longed for us to have time to try and recapture that heady period before Maggie came along.' Her voice grew slightly unsteady. 'The years are rolling past so fast, Tom. I've forgotten what it was like to be a carefree girl flirting with a good-looking young soldier. Weather like we're having now, glorious sunshine that lights the vivid colours of the leaves, has set me yearning for that girl who wanted a posh picnic to impress or daunt the persistent Tom Black. The yearning is there, but that girl has gone forever.'

'No!' cried Tom, reading something terrible into her words and seizing her arms. 'You'll always be that girl to me. *Always!*' Spotting a wooden bench a few yards ahead, he led her to it and induced her to sit there with him. Now the moment had come he grew surprisingly calm.

'We're not moving from here until you tell me what you've been keeping to yourself all this week. What did Clare Goodey say to you this morning? The whole truth, love.'

She gave a heavy sigh. 'I *am* anaemic . . . but I'm also pregnant. Our fourth child should arrive in early June.'

He stared at her in emotional hiatus. 'You *can't* be pregnant.'

'I am, Tom.'

'Did you stop taking the Pill?'

'Of course not! I didn't want this. It's one of those freak conceptions.'

'Oh God!' Hearing the dismay in his voice, he was reminded that he had believed she had a terminal illness and should be rejoicing. Trying to come to terms with the thought of broken nights, dirty nappies, teething grizzles and laboured feeding sessions once more after a gap of seven years, he asked, 'She couldn't have made a mistake, could she?'

Nora's slow shake of the head dashed that hope. 'I did a positive test before I saw her, and I've missed two months. Morning sickness will arrive shortly.'

It suddenly dawned on Tom what this meant for *her.* Before the return of all he had regarded with dismay *she* had first to endure the trials and tribulations of pregnancy again. Morning sickness, swollen ankles, swollen stomach, tiredness, aches and pains and the actual birth. All that in addition to what she already did for three lively girls aged nine, eleven and thirteen.

Reaching for her he held her close and stroked her hair.

'The Keane case is virtually over. I'll invite Mum and Dad
for a couple of weeks, then you and I'll do what Max had
planned; drive off and stop wherever we fancy. You can be
a carefree girl flirting with a soldier again. We'll even have
a posh picnic.' As an afterthought, he murmured, 'With luck
we'll manage it before the morning sickness starts.'

They sat in silent reflection, now sharing the impact of
this unforeseen complication to their lives. Through the
cloud of dismay Tom's kaleidoscope of thoughts eventually settled on a picture of two children who had just been
orphaned and taken off by strangers while more strangers
decided who should give them the home and love they
deserved. In the centre of this picture was a large brassy
woman in deep distress, crying, 'They're all I have left of
my lovely girl. She'd want her mum to have them, see them
grow up, *love* them. She'd *want* that. I can't let her down.'
He frowned. How could he regard this Blackie embryo as
unwelcome? Every child should be loved unreservedly, and
this one would become one of a close happy family.

His spirits began to lift. Maybe it was a boy this time.
Soon, Tom was imagining all the father–son pleasures ahead;
things he had so often wished for when the overwhelming
feminine activities at home excluded him. Maybe he would
follow his father into the Army.

TWELVE

Returning on the late flight, Max had then driven through rain and a chilly, gusting wind which showered the road with those leaves that had presented such a colourful spectacle when he had travelled that way earlier in the day. The Indian summer had come to a stormy end.

On reaching his apartment he had been too engrossed in seeking the facts he needed to prepare for the morning for thoughts of Livya to bother him. When he eventually went to bed he set a favourite CD of Paraguayan harps on the bedside player, but he fell asleep after just two tracks still thinking about that jellyfish.

It was with faint surprise that Max sensed his call to Tom at seven thirty from his office the next morning had woken him. How often had he been told Tom hastened to the kitchen for his breakfast while the female majority created chaos on the upper floor? From the background sounds he appeared to be in the midst of it right now.

'Late night, Tom?' he asked dryly.

'Apologies,' came the unabashed reply. 'I didn't realize there was any longer an element of urgency. Be with you in thirty.'

Max laughed. 'No reason to miss breakfast. HQ at nine will be soon enough. I'm having two people brought in for questioning. You'll find it interesting, I promise.'

His next call half an hour later was answered by John Sears just as Max made to hang up. He sounded breathless and, on being told who was calling, said testily, 'Kicking off right on the dot, aren't you? Is it that urgent?'

'Yes,' Max snapped, with the impatience of a man who had been up and active for two and a half hours expecting everyone else to be as keen. 'And I'm afraid you're not going to like what I have to say.'

He was right. Sears reacted vigorously, and gave out the information with a bad grace. It was expected that a commander should defend his men – Max did not blame him for that – he just took exception to the man's attitude. After disconnecting he wondered if it was because he was still feeling bruised, and had overreacted to the kind of resistance the Redcaps encountered on a regular basis. However, his third call brought the delighted response he had expected from Heather Johnson.

Tom arrived ten minutes before nine, by which time Max had sent out the team to search for further samples of cocaine ostensibly distributed by the Walpole brothers. Over mugs of coffee in his office, Max related the gist of his meeting with Jim Collingwood which had led him to what he believed would clear up the remaining aspects of the Keane case.

'I chased an entire flock of WGs this time, Tom. I admit I let my imagination run riot when I should have listened to my guts which were telling me that the jellyfish was the key.'

Tom frowned. 'Surely the *bee* was at the centre of this case. I still don't see . . .'

The sound of someone arriving brought an end to their conversation, and they went out to conduct the sober-faced, muscular sergeant to an interview room. Once seated, Max asked if the man knew why he had been summoned.

'No, sir,' he replied crisply, although wariness in his eyes suggested the opposite.

'You're aware that we're investigating the death of Corporal Philip Keane?'

'Yes, sir, but it's all over the base that he got stung by a bee. He wasn't murdered.'

'That's correct. He died from an anaphylactic fit following that sting. You are here to tell us how his body got in the tank with the synthetic jellyfish you made tied tightly around his throat to simulate strangulation.'

Looking at Tom, he said, 'Like I told you the morning after, I didn't know Keane, Never heard of him till that happened.'

'We have evidence to the contrary,' said Max, switching on the tape recorder and giving the introductory details of who was present, the date and time. Then he began the questioning. 'Are you Sergeant Gabriel Cruz of the Royal Engineers?'

Cruz looked aggressive. 'What's this about? I don't know anything.'

'Just answer the question,' ruled Max in fully official mode.

After a moment of resistance, Cruz said, 'Yes.'

Max nodded. 'Are you of Portuguese descent?'

Again long hesitation before the affirmative was given.

'Are you related to Sergeant Fabio Cruz, who was killed in action in June 2007?'

It now began to dawn on him where this was leading, and he nodded sullenly.

'Speak for the tape,' ordered Tom.

'He was my brother,' he admitted almost in a whisper.

'The brother serving with 23 Regiment, Special Air Services?'

'Yes.'

'Are you aware of the manner of your brother's death?'

'No.'

'We have evidence to the contrary, Sergeant.'

Cruz tried to brazen it out. 'What they do is top secret. Everyone knows that.'

Tom introduced a new angle. 'Was your brother to have been married seven days after he was killed?'

'Um . . . yes. Yes, he was.'

'Married to whom?'

Cruz was openly worried. 'I don't actually know. We . . . we weren't all that close.'

'You hadn't been invited to the wedding?'

'They wanted a quiet affair. Because of his job,' he added inventively.

'According to your father the entire family had been invited to a full-scale celebration in Cornwall, where the prospective bride's parents run a large market garden,' said Max, who had phoned Cruz senior in Madeira from

Heathrow. Max then asked if Cruz still claimed he did not know the name of his brother's fiancée.

'I just said, we weren't close.'

'Really? At the time of his death your Section was also in Iraq. Lieutenant Sears told me an hour ago that you met up with Fabio and another of your brothers whose regiment was in the same area of operations.'

'Oh! Yes, I'd forgotten that.' He forced a smile. 'We talked about the job, like guys do. It's women who cackle on about weddings.'

'So the immediately imminent marriage wasn't mentioned? You and your brother didn't express regrets that you couldn't be there? You didn't wish him and his future bride well?'

'I . . . probably. Yes, I guess we did. It was two years ago, and we *were* in a warzone,' he reminded them in a buddies-in-arms tone.

Tom said, 'Do you know Lieutenant Dunstan of the Intelligence Corps?'

Momentarily thrown, Cruz stammered,' No. Well, I know she's on this base because our boss mentioned that he jousts with her, that's all.'

'So why d'you think he told us she often visits you?'

'Dunno. He's mistaken.'

'You never meet up with her on a one to one basis?'

'Never.'

'So Sergeant Figgis, Corporals Fane and Edwards are also mistaken in saying you're very friendly with her?'

Cruz was now seriously rattled. 'Look, what's this about, sir? Why am I getting the third degree?'

Max looked him sternly in the eyes. 'We have reason to believe you knew it was Philip Keane who fired the shot that killed your brother, so when you discovered his body at some time during the Open Day you decided to make a statement with it in the water tank.'

'Why would I do that?' he demanded wildly.

'You tell us.'

Silence.

'Where did you find Keane's body, Sergeant Cruz?'

Still silence.

'Bad enough to lose a brother to enemy fire, but to learn one of our own killed him would hit really hard. If you then came across that person lying dead, the opportunity to make some small gesture of revenge would be hard to resist, wouldn't it?' Maintaining his uncompromising eye contact, Max asked quietly, 'Where did you find Keane's body, Sergeant?'

Cruz's resistance collapsed dramatically. Shoulders sagging, he gazed at the scratched surface of the table and spoke as if to himself. 'When I heard about it I could have killed Keane with my bare hands, but the RCR had left Iraq by then. Things hotted up for us out there soon after. Two of our lads were blown up trying to diffuse land mines and I . . . I suppose something like that . . . well, I just wanted to kill the ragheads who'd killed my mates.'

He looked up at Max then. 'When I came across him lying there, it all came back. The desire for revenge. I wanted his death to be grotesque. I needed to *mark* him in some way; show the anger of my parents, three sisters and three brothers.'

Into the silence, Tom said, 'Initially you had wanted to kill Keane with your bare hands. Choke him to death. So you simulated strangulation in the tank.'

Cruz nodded. 'Yes.'

'How did you transport the body to the tank from where you found it?'

'Carried it.'

'So it was lying near the tank? Where, exactly?'

Cruz swallowed. 'Not *carried* it, as such. Lifted it into my car, then drove to the tank.'

'From where, Sergeant?'

'Over by the Armoury, sir.'

'The Armoury was fenced off during the Open Day.'

Cruz stared back, lost for words, and Tom added pressure by asking, 'How did you know the body was that of Philip Keane, know with such certainty as you happened to be driving past? It would have been dark. Lieutenant Sears revealed this morning that you didn't leave the vicinity of the water tank from the time the public came on the base until they left. Sergeant Figgis claimed you and he spent most of the evening together, and you confirmed that. If that's true, it must have been around twenty-three hundred when you found Keane. Why were you driving near the Armoury at that hour?'

Against the extended silence came the faint sound of people entering the premises, and Max silently congratulated Heather on her immaculate timing.

'I'm going to pause this interview, Sergeant Cruz. A member of my staff has just brought in Lieutenant Dunstan for questioning. We would like to hear her testimony before we go into your explanation of your movements last Saturday night.'

Cruz reacted energetically. 'Why're you questioning Mel? She had nothing to do with it.'

'So you do know Lieutenant Dunstan. Well enough to call her by her first name, apparently.'

'Leave her out of this, sir,' he begged Max. 'It's a *family* thing.'

'A family she was set to join two years ago,' he retorted, getting to his feet. 'Mr Black and I will return after hearing her account of what happened.'

Pausing as they walked to the other interview room, Max spoke quietly to Tom. 'He's lying to protect her. Witness statements prove he couldn't have found Keane, and I suspect we're now about to confront a very sharp lady.'

'Against whom we have no solid evidence.'

Max smiled. 'The scene of crime lads lifted fingerprints from the platform beside the water tank. If hers match an unidentified set she'll have to explain what she was doing there. Let's see if we can outwit her before resorting to that.'

The two women were sitting in silence when they entered. Heather was wearing a jacket with her plain navy skirt now autumn was showing its true face; Melanie Dunstan had added a khaki pullover bearing two pips to her uniform. Having been unsure what to expect of this young woman who liked to joust as a hobby and who must be highly intelligent, Max's first impression supported the belief that she was a very sharp lady. Neither glamorous nor butch, the large-boned subaltern had an attractive narrow face and large greenish eyes bright with awareness.

Max introduced himself and Tom, then thanked Heather who departed wearing a satisfied smile. Tom loaded the recorder and set it running to give the introductory details, while Max concentrated on the young woman sitting with evident composure and patience.

'Lieutenant Dunstan, you undoubtedly know that our investigation into the death of Corporal Philip Keane has proved it to have been the result of a fatal bee sting. We now have to establish why his body was subsequently put in the water tank with that jellyfish round its neck. We believe you can throw some light on this.'

Throughout this speech she sat relaxed, meeting Max's forthright gaze with a matching optical challenge. 'Why would you think that, Captain Rydal?'

'Were you engaged to Sergeant Fabio Cruz, 23 Regiment, Special Air Services, who was listed as killed in action in Iraq seven days before the planned wedding?'

To his surprise she smiled and softly clapped her hands. 'Bravo! I thought you'd give up long before tracing that connection. However did you do it?'

Rising to this provocation, Max said, 'We're investigators. We don't give up easily.'

Tom came in quickly with, 'Were you aware of the circumstances of your fiancé's death?'

'That it was a blue on blue? Yes, the info came in within a matter of hours. The task of finding *who* had murdered him took me much, much longer. I eventually narrowed the search down to a night patrol by men of the Cumberland Rifles.' She let out her breath slowly and a frown appeared between her eyes. 'Unfortunately, my endeavours to track down this killer were halted for six months. The burning desire for revenge, on top of my grief, caused a breakdown. I was out of action for half a year.'

'When you returned to duty did you resume your campaign to trace whoever was responsible for Fabio Cruz's death?' asked Max, taken unawares by this ready confession.

'Of course,' she said with a touch of contempt, 'but by then all official records had been wiped, including ours. I tried every available means, but the top secret sensitivity of the mission that night had created a solid wall that couldn't be penetrated.

Max knew that all too well and he guessed what she would say next. He had worked the same way.

'As always in these cases, although records can be wiped, the participants' memories can't. Men can be silenced by the Official Secrets Act, but men are human and have the usual weaknesses.' Her eyes narrowed. 'I set out to exploit that fact. I cultivated the friendship of an RCR captain attached to GCHQ earlier this year. As I guessed, the Cumberland Rifles believed the fable dished out to that patrol by your guys in Iraq. The bastard who shot Fabio was regarded as a hero for putting an end to a raghead.'

For the first time Max glimpsed the passion kept rigorously in check by this outwardly controlled woman. It flared in her eyes, it set her hands gripping each other tightly. As Tom was about to speak Max kicked his foot to prevent him. Amazingly, Melanie Dunstan looked set to offer a full account without any prompting.

'It only needed a little flattery to get all the details, including the name of the "hero". Keane by name, too keen by nature.' She gave a vicious smile. 'I'll remember that name as long as I live.'

Max made no attempt to interrupt, and she soon continued. 'I applied for a transfer out here but, by the time a vacancy had occurred, the RCR had departed for Afghanistan. Annoying, but I could wait another five months. My one dread was that Keane would return in a wooden box and deprive me of what I had to do for Fabio. Those five months at least gave me time to plan the many options available but, when I heard about the Open Day I knew that would give me the greatest freedom for the job.'

She leaned back in the chair and unclenched her hands, a return of calmness replacing the temporary tension.

'I'd encouraged brother Gabbi to grow very fond of me over the five months, and I'd also made a play for Pete Rogers of the Cumberland Rifles HQ Company. Men are so *gullible*,' she added with contempt. 'He never realized I was just using him to keep a tab on Keane's movements when he returned. Pete faithfully recited the bastard's address and marital status, along with the fact that his wife had spent the months while Keane was away with her mother in the UK. That told me Keane was unlikely to spend his R and R there, so I finalized my plan of attack.'

Tom was unable to stay silent at this. 'Your plan of attack?'

She had been concentrating solely on Max, and now faced Tom as though surprised by his presence. 'How I was going to kill Keane.'

'By choking the life out of him?' suggested Max.

Her gaze returned to hold his. 'Top marks! I was brought up in the country, Captain Rydal. You need strong hands to deal with animals, and mine were going to kill him slowly and painfully while I told him why.'

'You freely admit it was your intention to murder Philip Keane?'

'*Avenge*. There's a difference.'

'Go on,' he said grittily.

'I parked nearby where I could watch the house, but I thought I was out of luck when I saw a taxi pick Keane up soon after nine. I knocked and said I'd been sent to take her husband to HQ Company urgently. That gross woman said I could take him to the abattoir for all she cared.'

Mel smiled. 'I then heard a catalogue of his sins before learning that she was leaving him and going to a friend for the weekend. Then she said he would be back in a couple of hours after giving her time to pack. I was quite chuffed by the knowledge that he'd suffered long years with that harridan.'

'Just two,' said Tom harshly.

She flicked a glance at him. 'Pity!'

'So you returned during your lunchtime break in the

jousting, in the expectation of finding Keane there alone?' suggested Max.

'I saw a taxi bring him back just before thirteen hundred, gave it ten minutes, then knocked. He came to the door in a towelling robe and I gave out the same tale about reporting to HQ; waffled about not knowing why he'd been summoned. He looked irritated, but he accepted the lie and offered me a cold beer while I waited for him to dress. I declined, and he took up an open can he must have been drinking from when I arrived, and headed for the stairs.'

Max imagined the scene as she continued with a confession she clearly regarded as a triumph.

'I started to follow him, but he suddenly gave a queer kind of howl, dropped the can and staggered around clutching his throat.' She gave a reminiscent smile. 'It was quite a sight, believe me. Eyes bulging, tongue hanging out as he fought for breath, and a look of sheer terror on the bastard's face.' Her smile broadened. 'He gradually sank to the floor, gurgling and clawing at his throat. A wonderfully spectacular way to end his life, and I had a grandstand view.'

Returning from that memorable vision, Mel's shining eyes fixed on Max once again. 'Of course, I had no idea what had caused what I thought was some kind of epileptic fit and, when the pleasure of what I'd witnessed faded, I realized I'd been robbed of my need to avenge Fabio's murder.' She paused as if relishing the moment. 'It was then I saw that I could still make an unmistakable statement with Keane's body.'

'So you sought the aid of the man who might have become your brother-in-law,' said Max.

'Poor besotted Gabbi! I knew he'd do what I wanted, but I had to wait until midnight and I was due to take part in the next joust within twenty minutes. I removed Keane's robe and hung it on the bathroom door. Then I collected his loose change, wallet, keys and mobile, backed my car up to the empty garage and thrust him into the boot until I needed him again.'

Tom then challenged her, his voice and manner betraying

his anger at her callous description of a man's tragic death so immediately after fighting for his country.

'You're admitting that you deliberately coerced Sergeant Gabriel Cruz into being an accessory to your failure to report a death, and to further mistreat the dead body of a fellow soldier?'

Mel's eyes flashed. 'Keane had murdered Gabbi's *brother*, for God's sake.'

'You keep using the word *murder*, Lieutenant Dunstan, but the facts are that the SAS team was wearing Arab dress and lack of intelligence that others were operating in the same area led to a case of *death by misadventure*. Keane was not to blame for what happened.'

Her face suffused with vivid colour. '*Not to blame*! He robbed a vital, clever and wonderful man of the rest of his life, and he robbed me of the possibility of ever being happy again. I wanted, I *needed*, to take his life so that I could at least find some kind of peace with Fabio's spirit. Watching Keane die that way wasn't enough.'

Max thought it time to bring the interview back on track. 'So you simulated asphyxiation in the water tank with that synthetic creature Fabio's brother had made.'

Mel gave a malicious smile. 'Have you managed to work out why?'

Max had discovered the answer to that last night. 'Because that purple-hued jellyfish is commonly known as a Portuguese Man O' War.'

Tom was clearing outstanding paperwork before going off on leave when Max returned from his in-depth meeting with the Garrison Commander, Colonel Trelawney. He got to his feet and suggested coffee.

'Later,' said Max. 'I'm afraid it's much as we feared. Despite her admission of intent to kill, she was in no way responsible for Keane's death. There's no evidence for a theory that she forced him to swallow the beer in that can. All she can be charged with is failure to report a death, and for wasting police time by putting the body in the tank in an attitude that suggested murder. Her fingerprints prove she was on the platform.'

Tom was disgusted. 'An entire SIB Section working flat out on the case! Pity you didn't discover that about the jellyfish at the start, as you were so sure it should be telling us something.'

Max met that with a faint smile. 'It wouldn't have meant anything at that stage, Tom. The pity is that I didn't see that night patrol in Iraq as the key to the case earlier than I did. Without the info Jim Collingwood supplied we might never have discovered who had done what she did with the body.'

'Meanwhile, we were chasing up clowns and knights, and searching for the enigmatic Brenda,' he said heavily. 'So what's the verdict regarding Mel Dunstan?'

Max sat and leaned back in the swivel chair facing Tom. 'The GC has ruled that she remain suspended from duty and confined to her quarters pending an appearance before a medical board to determine whether she has fully recovered from her mental breakdown. Whatever the outcome of that, her career is irrevocably damaged.'

'She *hasn't* recovered,' declared Tom. 'Her attitude and behaviour during the interview was almost creepy. She's away in fairyland. Finding peace with Fabio's spirit!' he quoted dismissively. 'So her lover was killed in a warzone; so are hundreds of men. Their women have to cope with their loss. I've no time for beyond the grave stuff.'

Max regarded him with interest. 'You don't believe in an afterlife?'

'Sure I do. It's in the hearts and minds of all those who knew and remember you with affection. Any suggestion of getting through to the *other side* is dreamed up by manipulative charlatans.'

'Thousands wouldn't agree with you.'

'That's their choice but, in my opinion, they're very unhappy people. Like Mel Dunstan.' He changed direction. 'What's the decision on Gabriel Cruz?'

'He can be charged with wasting police time during an investigation into the death of a soldier on this base. Failure to report it is questionable in his case, because the body was placed prominently in that tank; no question of trying to hide it. In view of the fact that he was infatuated with the Dunstan woman, Trelawney thinks Cruz should just be disciplined and posted to another RE Section. It could be argued by a sharp defence that he had simply obeyed an order from an officer, and there's no argument against that.'

Tom sighed. 'So the case that began as a huge bubble has burst to leave no more than a somewhat slimy residue.'

'Cheer up. It taxed our ingenuity and kept us on our toes.'

'Yeah,' he replied sourly, 'and we learned a lot about the danger of bees in beer cans.'

'Keane's parents will find that easier to accept than his murder by a colleague. To me, the saddest aspect of the case is that two children were orphaned by a garden insect and an impulsive experiment with drugs.'

'Speaking of that,' said Tom, 'I'm just concluding my report on the findings of our pals in the Met. After consulting Customs and Excise, they ruled out the trafficking of drugs by the Walpole brothers during their regular cross-channel road journeys.'

'So we were wrong on that?'

Tom smiled. 'Oh, no. That pair of bully boys sent the stuff to Starr by post. Who would be suspicious of beauty preparations mailed to a sister unable to obtain them out here? They'll go down for a long time.'

Max wagged his head. 'Another nail in Gloria's coffin for any hope of adopting her grandchildren. You know, Tom, it's the loose ends left by cases we deal with that often bother me. That woman has lost her daughter, her daughter's children and both her sons in the space of two weeks.'

'Even her husband walked out on her.'

'Now there's a woman who would be justified in having a breakdown, but Gloria Walpole will soldier on because she's made of sterner stuff than Mel Dunstan.' Max paused thoughtfully. 'Do you appreciate how fortunate you are? Understanding wife and three loving daughters. Oh, and I gather there's soon to be another member of the family.'

Tom stared in disbelief. Nora would never have given him that news. How could he possibly know? There was only one other person, but surely she would not have been so unprofessional as to betray a patient's confidential details . . . unless it was pillow talk!

Max quizzed him on his reaction. 'Not a secret, is it? I saw the tiny mutt when I spoke to Corporal Timmins at the kennels just now. Taking little bitch. He said she's been given the name *Strudel*.'

Tom laughed at his own misunderstanding. 'You should get one. A companion for long, lonely evenings.' After a pause, he asked, 'Is the break with Captain Cordwell final?'

'Yes.' It was brief and invited no further discussion on the subject. 'As it happens, I've decided to get a companion far noisier but more exciting than a puppy. As you know, my favourite film in my collection of war stories is *The Great Escape*, with Steve McQueen's fabulous motorcycle chase. I'm going to get one and go cross-country scrambling. By the time you return from leave, I'll be up and running.'

'Sounds great. Let's drink to that.' Tom stood and headed for the kettle and coffee jar, telling himself Max would never find a new woman that way.

Max noticed there had been further improvements to the flats when he arrived around mid-morning. The landlord was continuing his efforts to smarten his property, after which he would doubtless increase the rents. Faint sounds of a baby crying told Max his call was not in vain. Sudden silence heralded a response to his knock. Brenda opened the door with Micky Keane held against her shoulder.

'Oh,' she said, clearly taken by surprise. 'I didn't expect it to be you.'

'If it's inconvenient I can come back later,' he offered, realizing how little he knew about babies' routines. 'I should have telephoned.'

'No. Come in. It's just that I didn't think there'd be any further contact with you.' She walked to the room where Philip Keane's desert picture hung on the wall, leaving Max to close the door and follow.

'I hope I'm not interrupting something vital with the baby.'

'No. I've just fed him and induced a hearty burp. He should settle for sleep now.' She lowered the contented infant into the old-fashioned rocking cradle and, watching her, Max found it impossible to superimpose the image of Livya. Why had he ever imagined she was this type of woman?

'Oh, please sit down,' said Brenda, straightening and turning to face him.

'This is just a brief visit to tell you something that I hope might make things a little easier for you to accept.'

'But you've time for a cup of coffee? I'm ready for one, and it would be nice to have company while drinking it.'

'Thank you. Coffee would be welcome.'

'How d'you like it?' she asked, walking through to her kitchen.

'Black, no sugar.' He crossed to the cradle where Micky was faintly whimpering, and began to rock it, feeling a shaft of sadness for the man who would never see his child grow.

'Are you a father?'

He turned in surprise at her re-entry. 'No, I'm a widower.'

'So we have something in common.' She put the tray on the table, then joined him beside the cradle where he told her about the true cause of her lover's death. When he had finished, she gazed thoughtfully at her son for a while before looking at Max with misty eyes.

'I've always believed our lives are mapped out for us at birth. When Flip wrote to tell me he had married Starr I should have accepted that our futures weren't meant to run alongside each other. I lied to you, Captain Rydal. I didn't accidentally discover the RCR were stationed nearby. I came here with the express purpose of stealing him from his wife. Fate, in the guise of a bee, made it certain we wouldn't have a life together.'

Max found her reasoning applicable to his own hopes of marriage with Livya. He had stubbornly refused to recognize the truth.

'You'll have a future with Micky,' he pointed out. Then,

before he knew it he added, 'When my wife was killed in a road accident she was pregnant with our son.'

Her hand rested on his arm in sympathy. 'A double blow!'

It was more than half an hour later that Max took his leave of this single mother who was a nurse, and had been a military medic. Brenda walked with him to the door.

'Thank you for coming in person to give me the comforting fact that poor Flip wasn't murdered. I appreciate the gesture, Max.'

He could not help asking, 'What will you do now?'

'I'll stay until my contract runs out. I've made friends here and it's better for Micky to have stability for the first year or so of his life.'

Max nodded and offered his hand. 'Well, goodbye, and good luck with your plans for the future.'

As he walked away she called softly, 'Micky and I enjoy having visitors, so any time you're passing . . .'

Max waved a hand in acknowledgement and began to descend the steps. The motorcycle he was now on his way to collect was principally for the thrills and spills of cross-country scrambling, but there was no reason why it should not take him along this road now and then.